THE GREEN BLADE

"*The Green Blade* is a beautiful, emotionally engaging tale of sacrifice and love. Mary Rose Kreger doesn't shy away from the darkness that her characters face, and the light they courageously bring is brighter for it. I ached for Will and Philia in their trials and rejoiced with them in their victories. **If you're in the mood for a heartfelt and profound fantasy adventure, look no further than *The Green Blade*.**"

–KATELIN CUMMINS, Book Coach and Editor

"This was an utterly amazing read! I absolutely loved it. It was an emotional rollercoaster the whole way through, and a masterfully written story of sacrifice, love, and finding strength in the darkest times… unique, inspiring, and touching. I'll be returning to read it again and again!"

–JULIA W., Teen Reader

"[The main characters] took what they were given with grace and faced it bravely. I loved both of them."

–TEEN READER

"It's been wonderful to get a chance to meet these characters and fight alongside them, both for the struggles in their world, and the ones in my own. The beautiful moments were shining reminders for me that, despite the suffering, there can still be a happy ending. So keep fighting."

–GRACE WOODS, Award-Winning Legend Fiction Author

"A fantasy adventure that shows what heroism looks like when strength fails you...*The Green Blade* isn't just about a stunning realm of enchantment, ancient history, and magical wars. It's about the cost of showing up when you're burnt out, when everyone's counting on you, and you don't know what else you have to give. When all is lost, and the only choice left will kill you but save everyone else.. .what will you do?"

–DOMINIC DE SOUZA, Fantasy Author
and Founder of Legend Fiction

The Green Blade

THE GREEN BLADE

MARY ROSE KREGER

Summary: *Princess Philia Pendragon and her loyal watchman, Will Owain, must battle dragons, usurpers, and other dangers as they journey across the Isle of Avalon, seeking a cure for Philia's Curse.*

Note to Parents: This book contains mature themes presented in a manner appropriate for teens 13 and older, including: intense action scenes, torture, and characters experiencing severe depressive symptoms and thoughts of death.

First edition 2025

*For my father, who gave me the gift of life; and
For Father A., who gave me the grace to survive.*

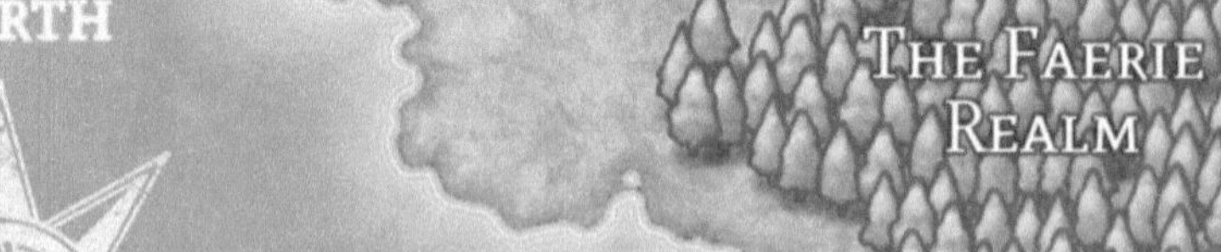
THE WESTERN ISLES
WATCH'S HEADQUARTERS
MYSTIC WAY
GWYNEDD CASTLE
FLAXEN GROVE
ASCENSION BAY
CAIR TINTAGEL
KING'S HEARTLAND
VALLEY OF FELDSPAR
NORTH
THE FAERIE REALM

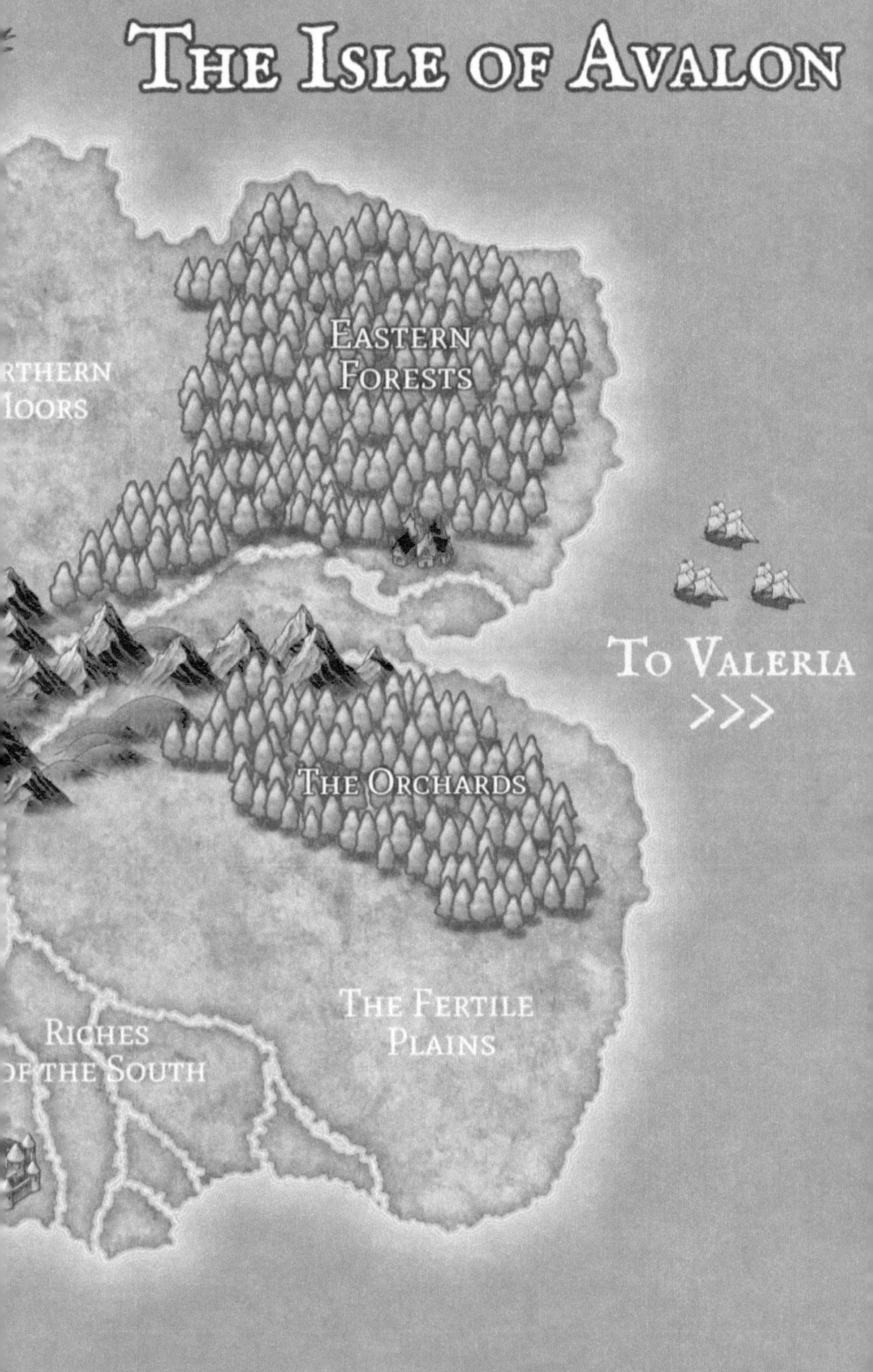

THE ISLE OF AVALON
NORTHERN MOORS
EASTERN FORESTS
THE ORCHARDS
TO VALERIA
>>>
THE FERTILE PLAINS
RICHES OF THE SOUTH

TABLE OF CONTENTS

Dramatis Personae

The Noble House of Pendragon

Princess Philia Pendragon – *heir to the kingdom of Avalon*

King Bran Pendragon – *ruler of Avalon, and Philia's father*

Queen Vivien Pendragon – *Bran's wife, and Philia's mother*

Lord Amaranth – *the King's half-brother and would-be usurper of the Avalon throne*

Ewan Pendragon – *Amaranth's son and heir, Fiona's son, and Will's half-brother*

The Loyal House of Owain

Sir William Owain (Will) – *Philia's watchman and son of an Avalon lord*

Lord Madoc Owain – *Will's father, Fiona's husband, and lord of Gwynedd, an Avalon province*

Lady Fiona Owain – *Will and Ewan's mother, Madoc's wife, and Amaranth's unwilling mistress*

PART ONE

The Wood

1

The Interrogation

AFTER A SHORT sleep and a hot meal in the Headquarters' mess hall, Will Owain asked for the site of his half-brother Ewan's holding block. Two of his fellow watchmen showed him the way and unlocked the cell for him.

"Wait outside, please," Will said. "I'll call if I need help."

The guards glared at Ewan. "We'll be right outside, son of Amaranth," one of them growled.

Ewan ignored them. His attention was focused on Will.

Will didn't mind. He had few qualms about intimidating the boy who had cursed the Princess.

He probably thinks I've come to give him a private beating session.

The holding block was simply furnished. A straw mattress on one side of the space, and a crude chair next to a small, barred window. Sunlight shone through the cracked windowpane, illuminating Ewan's tense figure.

They'd seen each other earlier that morning, during Ewan's interrogation with Master Raven and the King's Watch. Ewan had seemed sorry for hurting Princess Philia, but he'd also claimed she had a Curse that couldn't be undone. By anything or anyone.

No one had liked that answer very much. Particularly Will.

He crossed his arms and met Ewan's grey-green gaze. His half-brother's vivid red hair stood in shocking contrast to his milky skin. The longer Will studied him, the tighter Ewan's lips curled into a feral, wolf-like sneer.

"You look a lot like my mother." Will said. It galled him that this was so.

"And you act a lot like her," Ewan smirked. "Bet it drives you mad that you can't save her."

Will didn't know if Ewan meant his mother or Philia, but either way, it unnerved him how close his guess skirted to the truth.

"Shut up and tell me how I can save the Princess."

"I've already told you, it can't be done. Philia must pay the price for her curse."

"I refuse to accept that."

His half-brother pulled back his head and laughed: a horrible, bitter sound. "Of course you do. And it's not the only thing in your life you can't accept." Ewan picked at the metal cuffs chafing his wrists. "Amaranth has our mother for good. He'd kill her before he'd let anyone take her. He'd kill and torture you for trying. But deep down, you already know that. Don't you, William Madoc Owain?"

Will pressed his lips into a hard, determined line.

"But, as I said, you won't accept that. You'd rather die trying to save her." Ewan's gaze was razor-sharp. "And *that's* where you're like our mother. No wonder she let you take the ring from me."

"What are you talking about?" Will paced across the cell in ag-gravation, glaring daggers at Ewan.

"You have it with you right now," his half-brother nodded. "Stole it right out of my pocket last night. Mother told me that would be impossible." He shrugged with apparent nonchalance. "So I reckon since you could take it, Mother meant for you to have it all along."

A ring. What ring? Will searched his memories from the night before. *Oh!* Did Ewan mean the leather pouch he'd taken from him, right after they came through the Way? The pouch was in Will's pocket right now, although he wasn't fool enough to give Ewan any sign of its whereabouts.

Ewan sighed and rattled his chains. "Another reason for my father to beat me when he finds me again. What a shame."

"I imagine Amaranth will be mighty pleased at the mischief you've caused," Will retorted. "Cursing an innocent girl for daring to be born."

"Right you are, Owain. Cursing Philia wasn't fair. I wouldn't have done it, but I'm no hero. Father would have made me pay for my disobedience."

Will didn't want to feel any pity for the Princess's attempted assassin. Still, he guessed that Ewan was in some ways just as much a victim of circumstance as their mother.

"There has to be some way to save her," he insisted.

"If there is, I'm sure you'll be the one to find it. A bit *obsessed* when it comes to saving those you love, eh?"

Will stalked closer, his expression grim. His fingers glided smoothly over his sword *Llewgalon's* hilt. "I misjudged you, brother. You *do* know a thing or two about me, after all."

Ewan spat contemptuously at *Llewgalon*. "You won't learn anything from me *that* way. Mother and I get plenty of it at home." Ewan's chains rattled loudly as he raised his forearms and tugged down his sleeves. There, etched into his skin from wrists to elbows were dozens of half-healed scars. "Father always has so much to teach us," he whispered.

Will dropped his hand from *Llewgalon*, as if the hilt had burned him. Ewan's marks matched the scars he'd seen on his mother's arms, during his strange dream-vision in August. They were a disturbing reminder of Lord Amaranth's cruelty, even toward his own family. They also reminded him of where Ewan had come from, and the mission Will had yet to accomplish. *Come and find me, Will.* His mother's words haunted him, even now.

"Let me go free, and I'll take you to her." Ewan offered, reaching his arms out in supplication. "Maybe we can rescue Mother after all— her two loyal sons."

Will hesitated. He'd returned to Avalon. He was free now, to rescue his mother. Free also, perhaps, to choose how to do so…

Stop it, he berated himself. *Ewan is the last person you can trust. He's an enemy, not an ally.* Will picked at a loose thread on his cloak. *Still, if anyone knows how to get to her, it would be him….*

Ewan leaned closer, his smile growing. "Set me free, Owain, and we'll bring her home."

It was all Will had wanted for the past ten years. Everything he'd trained and fought for. He might never get another chance like this again.

Remember who you're speaking to, Will. Remember what he did to the Princess.

He thought of Philia, weeping silently in his arms, after Ewan first placed the Curse on her. They didn't know it at the time, what had happened to her, but Will would never forget it. Her first real experience of pain. She was like a wounded lamb.

Now, they all knew the truth about her Curse. Now, the pain was written clearly on Philia's face, with every movement and breath, no matter how she tried to hide it.

"Never, son of Amaranth," Will answered, disgusted by his moment of weakness. "I will not betray the Princess in order to pursue my own interests. And when I do bring Mother home, it shall be on my own terms."

He tapped the grate on the door, and the guards allowed him to exit.

Before the door had closed behind him, Ewan threw his parting shot. "Careful, Owain. Interfere with my father, and he'll make you pay. He *always* makes you pay."

Will suppressed a shudder as the door scraped shut. Ewan's words had touched on his greatest fear.

Will I have the strength to stand up to Lord Amaranth when the time comes? Or will I prove to be as weak and useless as this villain claims?

2

The Curse of the Way

PRINCESS PHILIA PENDRAGON was supposed to be resting, but how could she, with her father finally at her side? She had grieved for him during her ten years' exile in modern Wales. Yet now he sat beside her: Bran, King of Avalon, here in the flesh. Her father had accompanied her ever since they'd arrived at the Watch's medical wing for treatment. The stinging pain in Philia's left hand had only worsened in the hours since Ewan gave her the Curse.

Last night, Philia and her parents had journeyed through an ancient forest of oak, aspen, and pine to reach the fortified settlement and training grounds of the King's Watch. The Watch was Avalon's most elite intelligence force, as well as the guardians to the gateways between Avalon and the human world. Their headquarters was located deep in the Sacred Wood, only a short distance from the gateway that had transported Philia back home to Avalon.

After passing through layer upon layer of the Watch's tight security, Philia and her father were at last left alone in a private room in the medical wing.

While they waited for the healers, a few servants brought them breakfast—steaming bowls of oatmeal, dotted with berries and smothered with tangy cream; freshly scrambled eggs, and a honey-drizzled loaf of *gwemka* bread.

"Here Philia," her father said, hesitantly offering her the loaf. "Do you remember *gwemka* bread? It's all you wanted to eat as a child."

She accepted the bread with a smile. Its tantalizing cinnamon aroma made her mouth water. "Oh yes, Father. How could I forget?" Philia didn't remember many things from her first six years growing up on the Enchanted Isle, but she did remember *gwemka* bread.

"Try it," he urged. "I asked the servants to bake it especially for you."

"Oh!" Philia blushed, flustered by her father's kindness. "Thank you."

She closed her eyes and sank her teeth into the bread loaf. The hard, toasted crust gave way to a soft, flaky center, sprinkled with dried fruit and swirls of Avalian spices. It was rich, wholesome, heavenly. It tasted like safety, and home.

"May I see your hand, my dear?" her father inquired. His turquoise eyes waned melancholy.

She swallowed, then tentatively opened her left fist. A sideways "s" shape, the symbol of the Curse of the Way, was carved into her palm. She could still feel its potent magic gnawing into her hand. Last night, the Curse had taken the form of a miniature snake, wending its way beneath her skin as it marked Philia with a magical death sentence.

Her father cradled her hands in his own, then lifted them up into the morning light. She shifted nervously in his grasp. Could he see the burning pain of her Curse? Could he hear the desperate cries of the miserable crowd? She wanted to hide it from him. To experience the Curse's full weight once had nearly killed her. She didn't have the strength to watch it replay again now on her good father's face.

"My brave one," he whispered.

She paused, studying him.

"If only I'd been there…" King Bran murmured. "I failed to protect you. I'm so sorry."

Philia stared straight ahead, pretending to watch the morning sun pass through the room's high windows. Her tears blurred the rosy light and soft blue ceiling into a sea of purple.

"What could you have done?" she managed to say. "I was still lost in another world."

Only a day had passed since Philia had received the Curse of the Way from Ewan, while she was still in Scotland. In those scarce 24 hours, Philia had returned to Avalon and reunited with her father, the King.

Whatever father thinks, this is not his fault.

A tall woman entered the room, with long, wavy hair the shade of freshly tilled earth. Deep-set blue eyes examined Philia, before the woman dipped into an elegant curtsey. Her golden skin seemed to emanate a soft glow, like a beauty model on Instagram but far more real.

Philia knew she shouldn't, but she was staring. The woman's facial features—her nose, cheeks, and ears—were sharp and dramatically defined. Unique from any face she'd ever seen in the human world.

She gasped as she put these qualities together. Towering height, sharp features, glowing skin, incredible grace—this woman was a Faerie.

The Faerie turned toward the King and offered her respects. "Good morning, Your Majesty. I am Lady Agnes, the Healer Proficient you assigned to work on the antidote for the Curse."

"Welcome, Lady Agnes. You may rise."

Lady Agnes rose to full height, then stepped forward. "I'd like to give your daughter an examination, Your Majesty, if I may," she said. "Then together we can determine a course of action. The Curse's antidotes are still being tested. None of them can cure the Curse completely yet. But we do believe some of them can keep your daughter alive longer."

"Long enough to find a cure?" the King responded firmly. His grip on Philia's hand tightened.

Lady Agnes' gaze shifted to Philia. "Yes, Your Majesty. That is what we hope for."

The Faerie's words spun around Philia's head. *Keep your daughter alive longer…*

How much longer? Philia wanted to ask. *How much time do they need to find a cure?* Yet she remained silent in her father's presence. His love was a tangible, radiant force, but Philia also sensed his fragility. A fine-spun glass; a celestial palace carved of ice and snow. Her hot, eager questions might shatter him.

She took his hand. "Father, may I have a few moments with Lady Agnes alone?"

Her father startled, glanced between the Faerie and his daughter. For the span of one weary, labored breath, she wasn't sure whether her father would stay or go. Then he was up on his feet, kissing her forehead, and heading toward the door.

"Five minutes," he stated, to the room in general. "Then I shall return."

The door swung closed behind him in near silence. Philia knotted her fingers in her lap, peeking at the healer out of the corner of her eyes.

Lady Agnes in turn studied Philia. "How did it happen?" she asked.

Philia told her about Ewan's attack after the Masquerade, the crystal ball he cracked open over her hand to release the Curse, and how Ewan said the Curse actually began some three weeks before, in Scotland. She told the healer about the constant burning pain running up and down her arm, especially around the scar on her hand, and her overwhelming fatigue. While she spoke, Lady Agnes checked her pulse and examined the black scar on her palm.

"How long do I have, Lady Agnes?" Philia asked, mustering her courage. "Can the antidote really save me, or is it just a false hope?"

The Faerie frowned, drawing a finger along the length of the scar. Her touch was ice cold.

"This Curse is designed to be unbreakable," she answered shortly. "The King has commissioned me and my Order to construct a cure for it. For the past ten years, we've tested many variations of an antidote."

She paused. Philia heard running water in the adjoining garden; birdsong echoing from the rafters.

"We've made a tincture that can numb the Curse's pain," Lady Agnes explained. "And tonics that can extend the victim's life. But so far, the end results remain the same."

Philia shook her head, trying to read Lady Agnes' expression. To no avail. If the Faeries expressed their emotions visually, they did so differently.

"What do you mean, my lady? What—what were the end results?" Her voice came out small and scared.

Lady Agnes pulled in a tight breath. "The victims have all died."

This time, Philia saw Lady Agnes's crystal tears, glistening brighter than any human tears could have done. They slipped down either side of the healer's cheekbones and fell into Philia's lap. The tears held their shape like tiny gems, before soaking into her dress.

Philia was too stunned to ask her more. They sat in silence.

"Have you used a Faerie's cloth before?" Lady Agnes pointed at the slate grey curtain hanging neatly from a curved line in the ceiling, against the east wall. The long cloth extended across the chamber and all the way down to the wooden floors.

"What's it for?"

Lady Agnes rose, a movement too graceful to be human. Her long, wavy hair swayed with each silent step towards the curtain.

Without being asked, Philia followed Lady Agnes across the room. The morning sunlight faltered, dimming the space to a peaceful, muted grey.

The Faerie stopped at the cloth and laid her hand delicately on the drapery. At her touch, pure-white threads stitched themselves outwards from the Lady's fingers, creating intricate patterns across the cloth.

Lady Agnes cast a questioning glance at the Princess. "Can you see this?"

"Oh, yes." Philia studied the result like a new installment in an art museum. "It's like…a mountain valley filling with drifting snow. Or newborn lambs nestling into their mothers. Deep frost, melting, on the first day of spring." But there was more to it than a pretty scene, Philia guessed. "What does it mean?"

Lady Agnes turned back to her and smiled. "A Faerie cloth reveals a person's inner form. The part of us that we cannot see from the outside, Your Highness, but that is real—perhaps *more* real—than our passing, physical form." She dropped her hand from the cloth. Each pure-white thread receded and unraveled itself, until the cloth was once again a neutral color.

"Was—was that *your* inner form?" Philia asked, feeling a bit foolish.

"One aspect of it, yes."

Wow. Philia wondered what her mother's form might look like, or her good father's. Her best friend Laurie's cheerful heart, and Will's fierce one. What a gift it would be, to learn a little more about a person, or about oneself, with just one touch of a cloth!

"If we are to help you heal from the Curse, we must first examine the Curse's nature and how it is affecting you," Lady Agnes continued. "I believe that if you touch the cloth, we will learn more about your situation."

The curiosity bubbling up inside of Philia quickly morphed to apprehension. What could the cloth reveal to her about the Curse? Surely something quite different from Lady Agnes' pure, sweet scene. Something twisted, perhaps. Or even ugly.

"Will my parents see this?"

"You will see it; I will see it. That is all."

"What if it shows us 'I'm good as dead already', like Ewan said?" she blurted out.

"If that *is* true, wouldn't you prefer to die prepared?"

Philia sniffed and rubbed her eyes on her sleeve. "I'd prefer not to die at all." Then before she could change her mind, she pressed her scarred palm into the Faerie cloth.

No pleasant woodland scene for Philia; no sunlight filtering through colored glass. No windswept fields of wildflowers; no resonating violins, nor any other beautiful, *enchanted* thing that Philia could have hoped to be "revealed" by the Faerie cloth.

Instead, maroon stitches pooled like blood from Philia's trembling fingers. Her scar itched and burned, leaving a charred black outline around her hand, and the horrible stench of scorched flesh.

Philia recoiled, but her hand remained stuck to the fabric. "Help!" she cried.

Help us! A cacophony of voices retorted back in her head. *Save us, Philia Pendragon. Set us free!*

As the voices cried out, the threads flowing out from Philia's fingers took on a more definite shape. There, vividly embroidered in red, gold, and tangerine, were the childlike faces of the miserable crowd. *Arthur's children*, they had called themselves last night, and Philia was their *mother*. The longer she pressed her hand into the Faerie fabric, the more they poured from her Cursed fingers, until they filled up the entire cloth, from floor to ceiling, and wall to wall.

For a space between two breaths, she and Lady Agnes gazed at the cloth with horror.

Then the crowd turned as one towards Philia's contact point with the cloth.

"Who are you?" Philia whispered. Shivers of terror ran through her body. "What do you want?"

With a heart-wrenching cry, the crowd rushed toward her in a flurry of stitches and purls. *Save us!* They demanded. *Deliver us, now!*

Lines of gold thread stitched over her fingers, fixing them in place. Philia screamed, struggled, and finally wrenched herself loose. Her hand came away, the edges bloody and torn.

Lady Agnes pushed Philia aside, fully breaking her connection with the cloth.

"Elloway con gritha, phantome!" she declared in reprimand. She pressed both her hands into the cloth, her shoulders straining with effort. "Elloway con gritha!" she repeated.

The miserable crowd began to unthread themselves back into the Faerie cloth. All the while, each one of them kept their eyes fixed on Philia.

"L–lady Agnes." Philia stammered.

Once the crowd had vanished, Lady Agnes lifted her hands from the cloth and met Philia's gaze.

"Are you alright, lamb?"

No! Philia's heart screamed. *Everything is wrong. I am wrong!*

She had seen the miserable crowd before. They had appeared to her in a vision, immediately after she'd been cursed. If the Faerie cloth truly revealed a person's inner form…did that mean the crowd was now *inside* of her?

"Don't let my parents see this," she breathed out loud. Cold sweat beaded down her spine. "Please."

"I can keep what we saw today private. But it's my duty to tell them about your Curse, and how I will attempt to heal your malady."

Philia retreated from the Faerie cloth until she reached her bed. The sweet smell of lavender wafted up from the mattress.

Lady Agnes followed Philia, then whispered words of healing over Philia's torn hands. They mended so easily. If only her Curse could be fixed in the same way.

"I—I don't want to see my parents right now." She hugged herself and leaned forward. "Tell them I'm resting."

"Tell us yourself, dove," came a new voice. Low, deep, and feminine. The most familiar voice in Philia's world.

She hazarded a glance upwards. "Mum?"

"Oh *Philia*." Her mother, Queen Vivien, stood framed in the doorway, the King at her side. She held a question in her gentle brown eyes.

Philia rubbed her hands up and down her lap. The movement distracted her from the burning sensation in her Cursed palm, and the desperation leaking into her heart.

"Mum," she choked out. "I'm…*dying*."

The Queen sat beside her and tightly clasped her hands, while the King hastened to her other side.

"I'm dying, I'm dying." She spit the words out, so they couldn't dig their sharp talons into her aching heart.

"Is it true?" Mum asked Lady Agnes. Her mother's face appeared as placid as an Arthurian lake, but Philia could feel the desperate tremble in her hands.

"It's farther along than I expected," the Faerie admitted. "The antidotes we store here at Headquarters will do little but numb the pain. And only for a time." She turned towards the King. "We will have to send messengers to our other laboratory, for the latest antidote. But it will be experimental, Your Majesties."

Beside Philia, the King stirred. "Experimental?" he asked. "As in, *untested*?"

"Yes, Your Majesty," Lady Agnes answered, her voice less than a whisper.

An untested antidote? Philia lamented. The scar on her left palm pulsed and burned. *Is that my only defense against the miserable crowd?*

The King moaned like a wounded animal.

"By the Seven Founders, and the Starry Citadel, and the sacred rush of autumn's wheat," he cried, "is there no remedy for my child?

None, for my only one, born in blood, stolen from me in pain, returned to me with joy, only to be stolen yet again?" His boots stamped and scraped against the floorboards. "Ay, no father can bear this wound!"

His grief jolted Philia, and she moved to embrace him. With her cheek pressed against the soft velvet of his tunic, she could hear the drum-drum, drum-drum, of his heart. He still smelled of horses and leather. He was still strong and solid and just a wee bit wild.

And now he had become that tumultuous tempest on the Irish Sea—the one that Philia and her mother had risked their lives to cross. The storm that had left them shipwrecked, injured, and alone.

"Father," Philia pleaded, burrowing her face deeper into his chest, "I'm still here. Pr-present moment, remember?"

She had meant them as comfort, but her words seemed to break him.

"Why can't the filthy knave act like a true man, and settle his grievances with me?" the King growled. "Why must he go after our child, Vivien?"

"Because he knows it will hurt you more," Mum wept bitterly.

Just then, the door to Philia's chamber swung open with a very conspicuous bang. Philia peeked between her parents' arms to see her best friend Laurie standing in the doorway, arms crossed over her chest. Laurie was almost six feet tall, with a fine caramel complexion, long black hair, and the best sabre fencing skills in all of Scotland. Except for maybe Philia's cousin Dylan, who was perfect at pretty much everything.

"Haggises and hounds," Laurie shouted over the room's mournful din, "enough with all this blubbering, Your Majesties. Philia isn't *dead*."

All three of the Pendragons, plus Lady Agnes, turned and stared at the friendly intruder.

Laurie colored a little at their attention, then soldiered on. "I mean, we're in Avalon, aye? You know, the Enchanted Isle where people have gone for centuries to get *healed*? Where magic grows out of the very earth? If there's any place that can heal Philly, it's here." She stomped her glittery green sneaker for emphasis.

If nothing else, Laurie's timely interruption got everyone to stop crying. For which Philia was grateful. After all, she wasn't dead…yet.

"Thanks, Laurie," she said, smiling weakly.

"There now," Laurie answered, marching into the room. "Chin up, girl." She reached into the pocket of her blue jeans. "And also, a message for you, Your Majesties," she continued, offering a sealed envelope to the Queen.

The Queen took the envelope, opened it, and frowned. "I'm afraid your father and I must leave you, my dove," she said to Philia. She handed King Bran the letter over Philia's shoulder.

"And that is well and good, Your Majesties, for the Princess needs rest," Lady Agnes said. The Faerie stepped lightly to the elegant cabinets lining the north wall. A moment later she returned, carrying a vial of rose-colored liquid in both hands.

"Here, Your Highness," she said, presenting the vial to Philia. "The first antidote—for your pain." Her gaze swept to the Faerie cloth, then back to the Princess.

"Take, and drink."

Philia took a deep breath, then drank the whole vial in one swallow. The antidote had a pleasant cherry-hazelnut flavor, and filled her almost immediately with a soothing sense of well-being.

Lady Agnes took Philia's glass and then studied her patient. "This version of the antidote tends to make my patients drowsy. Which would be well, Your Highness, since you are much in need of rest."

Philia's eyelids were already getting heavy. "It's…not so bad," she yawned. She curled herself onto the infirmary bed and let the antidote lull her to sleep.

3

Dawn of the Dragon

SILVER BARS OF moonlight coaxed Philia from a deep, dreamless sleep. The healers had transferred Philia to the finest chamber in the Watch's medical wing: an oval-shaped room with vaulted ceilings, wooden cabinetry, and shining, oak-planked floors. Her sick bed, positioned near the room's center, was piled high with woven blankets and sprinkled with fragrant rose petals.

When Philia raised her eyes, she was startled to discover she was not alone.

A new Healer Proficient had entered the room. She was tall and Fae like Lady Agnes, but the similarities between them ended there. Midnight hair fell about the healer's attractive face like sharp daggers, each section drawn to a perfect point.

"Your Highness," she said sweetly, bowing low. "I hope you are resting well?"

Philia sat up in her sick bed and straightened her garments—a comfortable dress and leggings gifted by the infirmary staff.

"Yes, my lady," she answered politely.

The Faerie stood still, watching her. Philia wondered how she'd been allowed to enter her room. Her father had posted several guards outside for the night.

"May I have your name, my lady?" Philia asked, grabbing the sheathed dagger hidden under her sheets and pressing it to her thigh. She was glad her father had lent it to her when they arrived at Headquarters.

Across the room, the Faerie stared at Philia with unblinking eyes.

"They call me Lady Jade."

Her tone was pleasant and smooth. But the moonlight descending from the high windows seemed to slide around and away from Lady Jade. As if her very presence repelled its light.

The Princess shook her head. *You are so weird, Philia. It's probably just a trick of the light. Or a side effect from the Curse.*

Lady Jade advanced. Her outward appearance was nothing less than stunning, but Philia's instincts screamed, *Danger!*

"Mum?" she called, wondering when her mother had left the room. The last thing she remembered, Mum and Laurie had been playing cards at her bedside. "Father? Lady Agnes?"

The Faerie strode faster. "Your parents can't come for you tonight, little princess." Her attractive lips spread open, revealing a line of jagged teeth. "I've already seen to that."

Philia cried out in alarm and drew her hidden dagger from its sheath. Her bare feet slapped the hardwood floor as she swiped the knife before her, warding the Faerie away. She leaned against the bed to keep from falling over.

Lady Jade continued marching forward, never breaking eye contact with Philia. A round brooch on her burgundy cloak caught the Princess's attention. Its delicate enamel design depicted a sinuous black and gold serpent.

"Take your dagger," the Faerie demanded, "and spill your own blood."

The Faerie's words held a strange persuasion to them. Although the Lady's suggestion was both violent and shocking, Philia's body felt compelled to respond. The dagger in Philia's right hand trembled and turned to her left.

"Take it," Lady Jade repeated, her command emphatic. "Spill your own blood."

The Princess's dagger swung straight towards her other hand. The sharp edge nearly sliced her callused palm before Philia could jerk it away.

"Stop this at once!" Philia tried to set the blade safely aside, but her fingers refused to let go.

"Come now," Lady Jade said, creeping closer. "You said yourself that the Curse has made everything wrong." Her almond eyes crinkled with mirth. "That *you* are wrong."

"Who gives you the right to say such things?"

Philia was trying to put on a brave face, but doubt gnawed at her heart. Ever since her cousin Ewan had marked her with the Curse, Philia had felt…tainted. Contaminated by what had been forced upon her without her consent.

In the same way that Lady Jade now asserted her will over Philia's.

Philia gritted her teeth, determined to keep the dagger at bay.

I will not become this Faerie's weapon, to be used against my father and his kingdom.

For a few precious seconds, she succeeded. The knife remained more or less stationary in her grasp.

"Spill it, Your Highness," Lady Jade urged, with a ravenous smile. "Let the King's daughter provide the blood for the offering."

The dagger in Philia's right hand slipped, missing her left by a hair.

"That's it." Lady Jade clamped her hand around Philia's wrist. One nudge of the Faerie's hand, and a curving ribbon of blood coated Philia's palm. Thick, ruby drops oozed to the floor.

The Princess cried out and fought for release, but Lady Jade held her fast. She tore the serpent brooch off her cloak and pressed its enameled surface into Philia's fresh cut. Philia winced as the cold metal came in contact with the Curse-mark on her palm.

One touch to her scar, and the brooch's black and gold serpent began to wriggle and thrash against her palm. It quivered in ecstasy, like a child coming home to its mother. The Curse inside Philia welcomed the miniature serpent, expressing its deep affection with excruciating shockwaves of joy.

"Stop. Please *stop*..." Philia staggered and dropped to her knees.

Lady Jade pried the dagger from Philia's uninjured hand, then drove the weapon once, twice, thrice into the hardwood floor.

The violent pounding reverberated off the walls and rattled the window panes. The ground shook with each stroke.

"The Fortunate Isle produces all things of itself..." Lady Jade muttered, kneeling beside Philia. "The ground of its own accord produces everything..." The Faerie retrieved the serpent brooch from Philia's failing grasp. "In Avalon, all cultivation is lacking, except for what nature provides."

The Faerie dropped the brooch into the knife hole she'd gouged in the floor.

"No," Philia moaned. Whatever Lady Jade was doing, Philia had to stop her. She reached out to take her dagger back from the Faerie.

But Lady Jade's strange rituals had aroused the Curse. As the Curse fattened itself on the Faerie's sorcery, it also stole some of Philia's strength. Her body interpreted this weakening as *pain*.

Philia collapsed to the floor, curling up tight to hide her stricken face. She wanted no witnesses to the Curse growing deep inside of her. This, her only comfort: the Curse's agony belonged to her alone.

If Philia could not save herself from death, at least she could spare her loved ones all this *hurt*.

The anguish rose to a dizzying peak, and then lessened.

The Princess stirred and opened her eyes. She was still curled up on the floor, her arms folded over her head. The Curse's debilitating pain had faded to a manageable ache.

A couple of yards away, Lady Jade crouched beside the knife hole she had gouged into the floorboards. Philia's dagger lay on the ground between them.

Wake up, Philia, her heart whispered. *You are the Princess. And your kingdom needs you right now.*

Her arms wobbled and stung as she raised herself to a sitting position.

Something strange was happening where Lady Jade had dropped the brooch into the hole. The floorboards rumbled and shook, and a baking heat arose from the opening, which had quadrupled in size.

"For Avalon!" Philia groaned.

She staggered to her knees and took back her knife with both hands. The hilt tingled and sparked with energy. Delicious, soothing warmth rushed through the metal, a refreshing counter to the Curse's infection. The bleeding from Philia's left hand slowed, then stopped. Intentionally or not, some of her royal Pendragon blood had bonded with the ordinary dagger, now providing a welcome support before Philia's new enemy.

She clambered to her feet and pressed towards her attacker.

"Leave this place," she ordered Lady Jade.

Lady Jade's expression wavered with apparent uncertainty. She glanced between Philia and the hole in the floor, then shuffled backwards towards the opposite wall, by the courtyard windows. The Princess's sickbed now stood between them.

"Whoever assaults me, assaults my people and my kingdom," the Princess declared, walking around the bed's perimeter. "You must stand trial before my father and explain your actions to him."

Lady Jade shook her head in amusement. "Both you and the King will understand soon enough, little Princess." She thumped a fisted hand over her chest and bared her teeth. "With the coming of the Master…and his accompanying feast."

"The Master," Philia repeated. "What—?"

A wave of blistering heat struck Philia from behind. She half-turned towards it, shielding her face with her sleeve. Beneath her, the floor shifted and groaned.

"What is this?" Philia shouted over the sudden rush of wind.

In the room's center, the knife hole widened into the size of a human.

"Ah," Lady Jade exclaimed, "It is the most ancient magic of this Isle. Any seed planted here" –she gestured at the knife-hole— "bears abundant fruit."

Her razor-sharp eyes met Philia's.

"Brace yourself, little Princess." Lady Jade gestured intricately with both hands, turned once, and then she was gone.

Kaaaaa—BOOM!!!

The explosion lifted Philia off her feet and sent her careening into the opposite wall. Her head missed the chamber's large medicinal cabinet by inches. As she slumped against the wall, winded, something sticky and sweet slid down the side of her face. She licked her lips and tasted cherries.

The antidote, she thought, recognizing its sweet cherry-hazelnut flavor.

Glass jars rattled off the cabinet's shelves and shattered across the floor. Philia flinched as shards of glass and pungent salves fell across her lap. Bergamot and witch hazel, cinnamon and sage. Someone had needed each of these medicines, and now they were splattered about the room.

One final glass rolled off the heavy wooden cabinet. This time,

Philia had the presence of mind to hold out her long skirt to catch it. A half-filled jar of the antidote bounced onto the fabric. Philia snatched it up and clutched it to her chest. For all she knew, it was the only one left.

A horrible, shrieking cry arose from the room's center.

Out of a gaping seam in the floor, the one created by Lady Jade, crawled an immense serpent. Its ugly black and gold body expanded and contracted, allowing it to pump itself from the ground like a sandworm from *Dune*. On its horned head was a crown of glittering metallic spikes, each one longer than Philia's forearm and dripping with violet ooze.

She froze in place. Her face had gone white in terror.

The serpent corkscrewed out of its hole, piling itself in scaly, muscular layers, until its body moved only a yard away from where Philia crouched on the floor. By now, it looked more like a dragon than a snake. It also radiated heat. Sweat gathered on Philia's forehead from the creature's oppressive warmth.

The dragon's horned head slithered over its writhing body and fixed its sentient gaze on the Princess. Moonlight sparkled off its crown of needle-thin spikes, and steam curled from its nostrils. When it opened its mouth, Philia nearly fainted. A Dumpster filled with rotting meat carcasses would have smelled better. She gagged and covered her nose.

Philia wished she could say that she'd never seen a dragon like this before. But she had: enameled in black and gold, pinned to Lady Jade's cloak, and then dropped into a knife-hole in the floor.

This was the exact same dragon, only *alive*.

Any seed planted here, Lady Jade had said, bears abundant fruit.

Philia's heart pattered irregularly in her chest. *By the Founders, what is this kingdom that I have returned to? Where anything, both fair and foul, can emerge from the very earth?*

The last detail Philia noticed was the Faerie cloth, which Lady

Agnes had hung on the chamber's east wall. The dragon's movement had made the cloth drift upward, so that it draped over one long stretch of the serpent. It activated at the serpent's touch.

In finely embroidered lines, the cloth revealed a tall, grim male Faerie with wispy, white-blond hair. A soft smile curled his waxy lips, but his pale blue eyes looked dead. His black and gold armor bore the sign of the serpent.

Philia swallowed, ignoring the metallic taste in her mouth. She knew this Faerie. He was her father's greatest enemy, and the mastermind behind her Curse.

"Lord Amaranth," she said.

Amaranth leered at Philia, as if he were more than just an impression on a Faerie cloth.

But what is his image doing on the cloth? Isn't the cloth supposed to reveal a person's interior state?

The Faerie cloth had activated at the serpent's touch. Was there a link between the dragon and Lord Amaranth?

4

Carry Me

"GET AWAY FROM her!" A new voice cried. Then a spring green blade slashed through the Faerie cloth, slicing Amaranth's embroidered likeness in two. A young watchman clad in chain-mail stormed through the opening, brandishing his Valerian glass sword.

Philia's heart leapt at the young man's bravery—in order to slice through the cloth, the warrior had mounted himself onto the dragon's back.

Her face flushed. It was Will.

Will threw out both arms to steady himself on the serpent's writhing body, then lifted his sword *Llewgalon* to strike. The serpent, perhaps feeling Will's weight on its back, swiveled its head towards the warrior.

"Seek shelter, Your Highness!" Will shouted.

"No way, watchman!" she retorted back. Will's actions had renewed her courage. She tottered to her feet and brandished her dagger for battle.

Will lifted his sword with both hands and drove it deep into the serpent's flesh. "For Avalon!"

The dragon barely flinched. With surprising speed, it snatched Will into its massive jaws, enclosing him in an ivory cage.

Will cursed and clung to the dragon's huge left fang, then drove his blade into the beast's upper palette. Black dragon's blood poured from the wound, and the sour, metallic stench of torn snake-flesh filled the chamber. The creature roared and jerked its head, causing Will to lose his balance. Philia watched him slam against a crooked wall of dragon's teeth.

Awful screams reverberated about the chamber. Not just from the dragon, but also from Will. The dragon's sharp movements had crushed his upper body against the beast's inner jaw.

Will cried out as he tried to wrench himself free.

Philia hadn't been strong enough to fight Lady Jade, but she needed to be strong enough now to fight the dragon. Her watchman's life depended on it.

Founders of Avalon, hear me, she prayed. *Come to my aid!*

"I'm coming, Will!"

What could she use to make the dragon release him? Her foot bumped against a spilled jar of salve, and she realized: *the medicines*. In Wales, her mother would use cinnamon and clove to keep snakes away from their garden. Maybe gigantic snakes also didn't like certain smells?

Her eyes roved across the floor as she searched for potential ammunition. She spotted a pair of broken, half-emptied medicine jars only a few feet away.

Snatching both jars, she hurled the first one at the beast. It thudded against the serpent's side, then fell away. A strong, herbal scent sweetened the air.

The dragon went very still, flicking the air with its tongue like a snake, taking in the smell. It gave Will a chance to peel himself off the dragon's stake-like teeth.

Philia winced; three crimson ribbons ran down the back of his tunic. Will groaned and stumbled deeper inside the dragon's mouth before falling out of her sight.

"Will, can you hear me?" she cried.

He made no answer.

The dragon, however, turned its attention back to Philia. One great golden eye, the size of a Viking's shield, fastened on the Princess. She marveled at its intelligent gaze. It felt more like an encounter with a person than a beast.

She swung back her arm. "Let go of my watchman!" With all her remaining strength, she hurled the second medicine jar at the dragon's nose. It soared right up the creature's steaming nostril.

"Ooh, good shot, Philly!"

She jerked her head towards the sound.

"Laurie?" She caught sight of her friend and a growing number of the King's Watch, pouring into the edges of the sick chamber with weapons drawn.

The dragon snorted and made an odd wheezing noise.

Philia scurried back to the relative protection of the chamber wall. Across the room, the watchmen aimed their bows.

Then the dragon *sneezed*.

Well, technically it was a sneeze. But to all the human and Faerie-sized people in the room, it felt more like an explosion.

Philia, who was closest, got lifted up in the dragon's sudden intake of breath, then tossed across the room. She slammed into the hardwood floor, badly bruising her right shoulder and hip. She clenched her mouth closed to stifle a whimper.

Just great, she complained to herself. *As if you needed any other part of you to hurt right now.*

Black liquid spewed from the dragon's mouth, landing with a sizzle on everything it touched. Along with the burning liquid came the body of Will Owain. He landed with a jarring thud only a few yards from Philia. Black and crimson blood covered his clothing and part of his face.

Philia shuffled over to him on all fours. Out of the corner of her eye, she saw Laurie and several watchmen heading toward them, but the dragon's long, spiked tail blocked their path.

"Will, speak to me," she pleaded, touching her hand to his cheek. Her fingers stung where they touched the black ichor on his skin, but she didn't pull away.

His grey-green eyes fluttered open.

"Philia," he whispered.

She kissed his bloody forehead. "Oh God, I thought you were dead!"

A shadow of fear darkened his features. "Me, too," he panted. "Philia…the dragon—it's—" He went rigid, his face contorting in sudden pain.

Philia watched in alarm as fresh blood seeped out from beneath his garments.

Above them both, the dragon roared. The King's Watch had loosed a volley of arrows. Some of them penetrated its skin, but did no significant damage. They did annoy the serpent, however. It slithered forward and looped itself in a tightening circle around her and Will, trapping them within a fortress of shimmering snakeskin. The dragon's huge body also prevented the King's Watch from approaching them.

Again, Philia was struck by the creature's intelligence. It was after Philia and now Will. They had offended it, and now it sought revenge.

"Shut up, Philia," she muttered to herself. *You have no idea what this beast is thinking.*

A strange roaring sound filled her ears, almost like loud radio static. After a moment, the unsettling noise sharpened into words:

"Philia Pendragon. I would deal with you."

Philia glanced around, but there was only a semi-conscious Will and the dragon.

"Pendragon. Listen, you mite, or I will gladly grind your lover's hands to powder, then feed him limb by limb to my young, while he still lives."

She swallowed, horror flooding her gut. There was no question now who that strange feminine voice could be. She was speaking with the dragon.

With incredible speed, it snatched Will once again into its jaws and shook him like a rag doll.

"STOP!!!" Philia screamed, waving her useless little dagger at the beast. "I'm listening, please stop!"

The dragon stopped shaking Will, choosing instead to wrap its colossal forked tongue around his body. Its tongue licked up Will's fresh blood and left a strange, bluish residue on his skin.

"Hold on!" Philia half-sobbed. She drove her dagger into the nearest stretch of serpent-skin, but it bounced off its scales. Her dagger was made of steel, not Valerian glass, like Will's blade had been.

"Hey, dragon!!!" she shouted. "I'm listening! What do you want from me?"

The dragon's great golden eye focused on the Princess. As before, its lips did not move, but Philia could still hear its words in her mind.

"*Pendragon*," it hissed, "*give me two things, and I will not eat him. Your lover.*"

Despite the life-or-death situation, Philia felt herself blush. "Why do you keep calling him my lover?" she asked. "We've made no promises to each other."

The dragon's eyes narrowed into slits. "What would you prefer I call the young man devoted enough to die for you? For your *mistake*?"

Philia involuntarily took a step back. "Mistake" or not, she was the one who had summoned the dragon. Lady Jade had used her royal blood to make the dragon sprout from the ground. Philia was the reason Will was now trapped in its jaws, his face a flawless depiction of distress. The bluish-purple blisters forming on his arms and neck, where the dragon had licked him. His steadily weeping wounds. The silver cast to his skin.

All. Her. Fault.

"I am so sorry, Will," she cried. "The dragon is here because of me. This evil faerie formed it out of a brooch coated with my blood."

Will stared at her like she had two heads. "What faerie?" he rasped, but the dragon silenced him by bruising Will between her teeth. Her fangs pressed into his chain mail, holding him tightly but not puncturing his armor.

He didn't cry out or struggle, so at first Philia thought he had passed out. But then Will stirred. His eyes looked distant, almost as if he was listening to someone…

Is the dragon talking to him, too?

"Enough of this, Pendragon!" the dragon hissed. "Give me but one cup of your blood and the jar of antidote, and I will release him alive. Do this for me, and I will leave this place."

Philia's hand pressed against her waist, where she had strapped the jar of antidote inside of a makeshift belt.

"It's the antidote I want, not your people," the dragon continued, as if reading Philia's mind. "As tasty as some of them might be."

Its tongue lashed against Will's body, drawing out a sharp gasp from her watchman.

"Yes, I will do it!" she answered hastily.

In response, the dragon lowered its head towards Philia, until they were face-to-face. The stench of its rancid breath made her gag. Will lay gruesomely displayed between two rows of the dragon's incisors. He was so close, Philia could see his left arm dangling out of the dragon's mouth, palm up. Blood dripped off his fingers like fresh-squeezed juice.

She leapt forward and seized his hand, covering it with tender kisses. The coppery taste of his blood coated her lips.

"I'm going to get you out of here, Will," she told him. "I've made a deal with the dragon to make it go away."

Will stirred. "You can't trust her." His voice was a ragged, burnt-out husk. "Amaranth's sent her to destroy all the Curse's antidotes. She…told me."

"She? Wait—Will, you can talk to dragons, too?" A thrill of wonder passed through her.

"Apparently so." The faintest smile brightened his face.

"Awesome," Philia whispered. They could *both* communicate with dragons. Laurie would be thrilled. "What should I do?"

"Be wise, Your Highness." His eyes drifted closed.

Philia placed her hand against her stomach, where she had tied the precious jar of antidote around her waist. She didn't like this deal, either. It could be a trap. The dragon could be lying. And even if it was telling the truth, it would cost Philia a half-jar of antidote. She would lose a month's supply of pain-free care, and a postponement of her coming death.

The dragon hissed impatiently.

Philia, how could you? she reprimanded herself. *Think of Will!*

She placed the jar of antidote on the ground in front of her. As soon as she did so, the dragon flicked Will out of its mouth with its tongue. He dropped on his left side, still as stone.

The dragon snarled when Philia tried to approach him.

"Let me take him, please," she pleaded.

The she-dragon gave her a pointed look.

Philia swallowed, then brought up her dagger. She wasn't sure how to do this thing. Where to make the cut or how to know she'd given enough blood. She did know that if she didn't do it, Will and everyone in the medical wing would probably die. From the sound of their voices, Philia guessed that Laurie and at least a dozen warriors were still in the high-ceilinged chamber, trying to rescue her.

She decided on a fleshy part of her right forearm, between elbow and wrist, then pressed the knife into her skin. When the blood started welling, she carefully placed each drop into the dragon's half-open mouth.

A hundred years she stood there, breathing in rotten flesh, swaying like a pendulum, dripping out her life-blood, Will lying motionless at her feet.

The dragon purred in seeming delight, slitting its eyes.

"Good, child. Your offering is well-given. Now listen: your lover will die unless you do as I say. Anoint each of the boy's wounds with the antidote, and then give him the rest to drink from your jar. Once you do this, I will go."

Philia knelt beside Will and did exactly as the dragon had instructed. She anointed each of the three puncture wounds on his right shoulder and back, then sprinkled antidote on the bluish blisters covering his skin. As she worked, a hint of color returned to Will's ashen face. She gently lifted the remaining antidote to his lips.

"Will, please drink this for me? It will heal you." She administered a small amount into his mouth, then watched him obediently swallow it.

His grey-green eyes blinked open. By the Founders, those eyes were beautiful. Like a storm-tossed sea.

She raised the jar upwards to give him the last of the antidote, but Will stayed her hand.

"No, Will, you need this," she urged him, pushing the jar toward him.

At her insistence, he took the jar. But he didn't drink it. Instead, he captured her right hand, kissed it tenderly, and poured the last of the antidote over the deep cut on her forearm. Immediately, her broken skin stitched itself back together, leaving a hair-thin scar.

Philia stared at her healed arm, then back at Will.

He mouthed three silent words to her.

Your lover, the dragon had called him. When her need was great, Will had been the first to come and defend her.

With an ear-splitting roar, the dragon reared its head towards the ceiling. Above them climbed loop after loop of shimmering dragon skin. The dragon quaked, then drove its spiked head through the rafters.

Screams and cries filled the chamber as the ceiling collapsed, ripping the medical wing asunder. The dragon compounded this de-struction by thrashing its body against the walls and support beams, so that the entire chamber, and much of the adjoining infirmary, collapsed around them. Although this dragon had no wings, it climbed quite skillfully out of the infirmary ceiling and disappeared into the midnight sky.

Will wished he could return the Princess' antidote: she needed more of it, sure. Her face and arms were badly scraped and bruised, and her still figure drooped with exhaustion.

He raised his head to the shattered ceiling, noting the damage left by the dragon. One massive wooden beam swung precariously overhead, a dark bar blotting out the starry night sky.

We need to take cover.

"Yes, take cover, puny little human," the dragon hissed in his head. Will flinched at the sound of her searing voice. "Crawl along the floor, like the rats."

The massive beam shuddered overhead, then began its ominous descent.

Will dug his good shoulder into Philia's abdomen and propelled them both across the floor with his legs. They made it one, two, three yards from their original location. The beam swerved once, twice, thrice, above their heads. Beside him, Philia stirred.

Faster, faster!

Cold sweat trickled down Will's temples, stinging his eyes. His arms and legs shook with effort. He pushed himself and Philia forward another two feet. Bright red blood leaked from his shoulder wounds, painting the Princess' garments. Too much blood, perhaps. Too little antidote, also.

So get the Princess out alive—now.

Will strained forward, rallying his body for one final push. But he couldn't move. It wasn't paralysis, exactly. More like a loss of control. At the same time, his vision clouded over with a strange purple haze.

"See how she can depend on you," said the dragon, hiss-cutting into his thoughts.

Let me be. He strained forward a second time, but his body refused to respond.

"Yes, keep trying, boy," the dragon taunted, laughing at his efforts. "Good thing she can find a hundred more just like you."

Every utterance sent searing tongues of fire spiraling through Will's arms and legs. This dragon breathed no outward flames, but her words summoned hell-fire.

Then the Princess' face swam into view, followed by the soft vanilla scent of her skin. Her cherry lips moved in comforting formations as she leaned over him.

"She says it's because of her venom." Philia lifted Will up to a sitting position, and supported him as he sagged against her. "She says I should leave you here and run."

"You should," Will grunted.

Philia frowned at him. "Well, *I* say that I won't leave you. *I* say I'm going to carry you."

Then she pulled his upper body over her shoulder, clutched his legs across her chest, and—miraculously—rose to her feet. The massive beam fell down behind them, raising up a cloud of dust.

"I'm going to carry you, Will Owain," the Princess declared, and then she marched them both through a maze of fallen beams, shattered glass, and splintered hardwood floors.

Her steps were steady, confident, even. "You're lighter than I expected, for someone so strong," she told him.

The fabric of her dress kissed Will's cheek. *And you're far stronger than I knew.*

5

The Aftermath

WHEN WILL AWOKE again, he was resting in his own bed, in his own room at Watch's Headquarters. His pale blue oil lamp glistened in the semi-darkness. Whether a few hours or a few days had passed, he could not tell. He did know that his shoulder did not hurt anymore, and he could breathe freely.

Will's bedroom, or *cell*, had always been a place of refuge for him. The cream-colored ceilings and blue-tiled floors spoke of safety and hope. Above his head, double-paned windows opened out to the Watch's training yard, where he had spent five years learning and perfecting his watchman skills. This cell, and the Watch's Headquarters, was like his second home.

And his home had just been assaulted by a *dragon*.

He rolled himself up to a sitting position on his cot, wincing at the angry feedback from his bruised ribs and back. Once his aches subsided a little, he pressed his cold fingers to his temples to summon his last memory: Philia carrying him. Her surprisingly strong arms had cast him over her shoulder, leading him to safety.

Further back, Will.

Yes. He remembered now.

Several hours after interrogating Ewan, Will had headed to evening weapons training, dressed in his protective gear and chain mail. Afterwards, he decided to visit Philia in the infirmary.

The hallway before her sick chamber had been mysteriously empty, and intense heat had radiated from the doorframe of her room. When he wrenched the door open, he found himself gazing up at Amaranth's image, unfurled over a massive serpent.

A *Navahogg*, the ancient dragon, gnawer of ash trees and tormentor of the dead, had somehow emerged from the floorboards of the Princess' chamber.

To see a Navahogg, the legends said, was to foresee one's own death. After having spent a few excruciating moments within the Navahogg's jaws, Will could understand where this legend came from.

And yet he still lived. The fiery venom had not killed him.

He gingerly touched his right shoulder, where the dragon had impaled him. The puncture wounds throbbed as he rotated his arm in a careful circle. He was sore, yes, but he could move again. And that unbearable burning sensation, caused by the dragon venom surging through his veins, was completely gone.

He shuddered. The venom had dragged his mind down some terrifying places before it completely pulled him under. He would still be in that horrid, twisted underworld if the Princess hadn't saved him with the antidote.

"You healed me, Philia," he whispered to himself, blinking the mist from his eyes. "But at what cost to you?"

A dagger of regret plunged between his ribs, turning his gratitude into shame. The dragon had told Will she had come to destroy the antidote. She had made no secret of her plans. But he couldn't have anticipated *how* she would destroy it.

The Faeries could easily restore a shattered jar of medicine, but they couldn't restore something that had already been used. They couldn't remove the antidote from Will's body to give it to the Princess. Once used, it was lost forever.

This is Lord Amaranth's doing, he thought angrily. *Another one of his cruel games.*

The sentiment propelled him out of bed and onto his two bare feet. He swayed and reached for the wall.

As he stood there, a damp gust of air from the window kissed his cheek—a salty, chill breeze hailing all the way from the Western Sea. All the way from Gwynedd, where his father Madoc waited for Will's return.

But Will wouldn't be going home to his father. Not now. Not with the *Navahogg* on the loose. Not with Philia dying from the Curse. A dragon, summoned by Lord Amaranth in the heart of Headquarters, was a declaration of war. King Bran would be forced to respond. All of the King's soldiers, knights, and watchmen would be preparing for battle.

Will was ready to join them.

"My place is with the King, and his daughter," he decided.

Still, he hadn't forgotten Ewan's offer. His half-brother had promised they could save Fiona: her two loyal sons. And he'd revealed something else…

"The ring!" Will gasped.

He sat down again, then reached under his mattress to pull out the satchel he'd snatched from Ewan. One tug on the leather tie, and a sparkling blue object tumbled into his hand.

"By the Founders…"

It was his mother's wedding ring. A lovely sapphire rose, outlined in gold wire and guarded with emerald cloisonné thorns. His mother had let him hold it once, as a small child.

It will be yours one day, my love, she'd promised.

Even his wretched half-brother had echoed this sentiment. *Mother meant for you to have it all along.*

Will held the ring up to the lamplight and marveled at its superior craftsmanship. "Why did you want me to have this, Mama? What is it for?"

He examined it a while longer.

My mother wore this ring on her fair hand. She touched this ring that I now touch. His fingers closed over it, opened again.

Will jumped at the rumble of voices outside his door. He hastily slid the ring into its satchel, then hung the pouch around his neck, beneath his tunic. Next, he pulled on his leggings and buckled his sturdy leather boots. His stomach growled. He wondered why no one had checked on him yet.

There's only one way to find out.

Will sucked in a shaky breath. Getting dressed had exhausted him. "Here we go," he muttered.

He rose once more to his feet, stumbling forward until he hit the north wall of his cell. The action jostled his right shoulder, making him gasp in pain.

But he refused to pause for long. There was so much he needed to know. How was the Princess? Who had survived the Navahogg's attack, and who had fallen? Had any of the antidote been saved?

He limped over to the cell door. The brass lock clicked as he turned the doorknob. A beam of lamplight stabbed into his cell, followed by a clamor of voices.

Will peeked out through the opening.

Crowds of people. So many tired, frightened people. Older men, women, and children. Standing or squatting restlessly up and down the long, blue-tiled hallway. They were farmers and workmen, cooks and blacksmiths, peasants and villagers. They whispered in hushed tones, and kept glancing uneasily at the high-raftered ceiling.

He pressed his ear against the doorframe to listen. Over and over, in a dozen snippets of conversation, Will heard the same word spoken: *Dragon.*

A short time later, Master Raven entered his room to change Will's bandages. Raven was a middle-aged watchman with dark brown hair, a neatly trimmed beard, and an athletic figure. Like Will, he was shorter in size and stature—ideal qualities for a watchman.

"How does your shoulder feel?"

"Better, but still in a sorry state," Will admitted. "I can't move it much."

Raven's dark eyebrows sprung up. "Owain, any state at all would be better than how we found you three days ago. Almost dead from the dragon's venom, even with the Princess's antidote. Why did you attack before we got there? Why didn't you wait for help?"

Will's gaze dropped to the floor. "I'm sorry, sir." He studied Raven's boots, noting the wine-colored blotches staining the weathered leather. "I saw Amaranth on the dragon's back and attacked him. But it was just an illusion."

"Amaranth," Raven repeated with disgust.

Will raised his head to search his master's tense, worried face.

"What you did was right, Will," his master continued, with a heavy sigh. "You saved the Princess' life—"

"Master Raven," Will interrupted. "What's the matter?"

His master's eyes widened in mild surprise. "Have I become so transparent as all that?"

"No. I've just spent five years of my life with you, that's all." Will couldn't help but smile.

Raven crouched down by the bed, his expression curious. "What gave me away?"

"Well, the blood on your boots for one. Also, the people in the hallway, huddling in fear and whispering *dragon*," Will answered, with more than a little irony.

A spark of cheer warmed Raven's deep brown eyes. "*There's* my old apprentice."

There were three wounds in Will's upper shoulder. Raven hummed softly as he cleaned them, filling the room with the astringent scent of aloe and Faerie's salve.

The top two wounds stung when Raven cleaned them, but the pain soon dissipated. Then Raven reached for the third, and deepest, wound. At Raven's touch, Will flinched and pulled himself forward, tucking his face into his lap.

"Steady now," Raven murmured. "They removed a segment of dragon tooth from this one."

Will gasped and cursed, clawing his fingers into his leggings. He remembered the dragon's searing words, gnawing into his skull, pulsing in horrid rhythm with the venom surging through his veins:

"Useless boy…feed him limb by limb to my young…"

"Will. Will!"

"I'm—here," Will stammered. Slowly, he realized that Raven had finished cleaning the wound, and was now tightening the last length of bandage around his shoulder. He lifted Will upwards, helped him put on his tunic, then fastened Will's right arm into a sling.

"To prevent you from putting too much pressure on your shoulder," Raven explained. "It's just for a few days." He frowned as he studied his old apprentice.

Will hoped Raven couldn't feel the tremors running through his body. He also hoped he didn't look as weak as he felt.

"They want even more from you, Will," Raven said bitterly. "I told the King you need to rest and recover your strength. He agrees. But…" He scraped his boot against the floor, scattering dried flakes of blood across the tiles.

"By the Founders, Raven," Will sighed. "What is it?"

"He's back to his old ways," Raven answered, his words a low growl. "Amaranth is waiting at the front gate of Watch's Headquarters with his nightcallers and warriors. He has thirteen hostages, taken from one of your father's villages that was just raided by his damn dragon. He'll give them to us, alive, in exchange for Ewan, and…"

"And what?" Will couldn't imagine any worse news.

"And an audience. With the King, the Princess, and… you."

"*Me?*" Will shook his head in disbelief. "Why?"

His master chewed his lower lip, as if considering whether or not to answer him. Will guessed that Raven did have an answer, and he wouldn't like it.

Panic coiled around his chest. Even on his best day, Will wouldn't have felt ready to face Lord Amaranth. And today was certainly not his best day.

"Wh-what will happen if I don't go?" he asked hoarsely. Lord Amaranth at the gates. His mother's kidnapper and abuser. Here for Ewan, and the Pendragons, and…

And me.

Raven rested a hand on Will's good shoulder. "Present moment, Will."

"What—will—*happen?*"

"He'll kill the hostages," his master answered flatly. "And if we anger him enough…Amaranth will send the dragon on us for the third time."

"The third time!" Will gasped. "Is that why there's all those refugees in the hallway?"

Raven nodded. "Yes, the Navahogg returned last night, chasing hundreds of displaced villagers– villagers the creature had made homeless. She wrecked most of our main defenses this morning. The Faeries haven't the time and resources to restore them all in just one day. So if Amaranth attacks us within the next few hours…"

"Headquarters may fall," Will finished.

"Yes. We weren't prepared for a dragon attack. We've never had one."

Will swallowed, his throat dry and parched. He gestured for water, and Raven filled a mug and handed it to him. The cool, refreshing liquid cleared his mind. He drew in deep, steadying breaths until his panic receded.

Raven didn't say anything. He just sat there, hands in his lap, watching the clouds devour the sun outside Will's window.

"Yes, Master." Will rested the mug against his knee. "Of course I'll go."

His master shook his head. "The King shouldn't ask this of you. You haven't the strength to defend yourself, should Amaranth's negotiations become physical. Could we find someone else—"

"That's what Amaranth *wants* to see, though," Will interrupted, thoughtfully. "Isn't it? He's wounded us, and now he wants to watch us bleed."

Raven tilted his head. His muscular shoulders drooped, like someone in mourning.

"Your six weeks in Scotland really changed you, didn't they?" Raven said softly. "You left Avalon a boy. Now, you're a man."

Will nodded. "Help me, Master," he pleaded. "I need your wisdom."

Raven's wisdom came in the form of outstanding physical protection. His master wrapped special bandages, woven from spun spider's thread, around Will's injured shoulder.

"They should keep your wounds from reopening, even if you get battered around a bit," Raven told him. "This particular weave is so dense, it will protect you from most knife and sword strikes as well."

Next, a female servant dressed in the King's livery arrived, bearing a long, metallic tunic fashioned from interlocking copper-colored rings.

"Faerie-wrought armor?" Will asked hesitantly. "I'm a watchman, not one of the King's knights."

The servant politely inclined her head. "His Majesty has named you his knight for this mission, and commands you to wear this garment beneath your watchman's attire. It will protect you from attacks, both physical and magical." She held out the tunic and ran her fingers over its gem-studded surface.

"But…it's so fine," Will whispered. "It's covered in precious stones."

The servant shook her head. "These are resin-coated salt crystals, Sir William," she explained, "mined from the sea caves beneath the Capital. They have the power to ward off Faerie curses and spells."

Will glanced at Raven, who nodded.

"Go on, Will. Accept the King's gift."

He held out both arms, wincing at the weight of the chain mail over his bruised skin. The interlocking rings felt cold and precious in his grasp. King Bran had given this to him. The King *believed* in him. He would not send Will out to die.

He thinks we can win this fight—or at least, survive it.

Will drew in a steadying breath, then allowed Raven and the servant to slide the King's gift over his head.

After that, they had to walk to main Headquarters. Raven wouldn't allow Will to walk to the front entrance unattended. He was concerned Will might collapse along the way—a fear which wasn't misplaced. The further they walked, the worse Will felt. Even with Raven's help, Will had to stop three times to catch his breath and wait for his lightheadedness to subside.

The walk, which passed down polished wood floors, blue-tiled walls, and high-raftered ceilings, was usually a pleasant one for Will. This was the main thoroughfare through Headquarters, passing by the mess hall, fencing gymnasium, and inner training yard.

Today, however, the quarter mile journey was slow and grueling. The hallway was lined with displaced villagers and exhausted watch warriors, and the flow of traffic was decidedly against them. Everyone was trying to move away from Amaranth and his army, while Will and Raven were headed straight toward them.

At last, they reached the entrance foyer, a large, high-ceilinged space where they'd agreed to meet King Bran.

Will placed a hand on Raven's shoulder, signaling him to stop. "Wait, Raven. Let me catch my breath before we meet the Pendragons."

In reality, Will needed far more than another breath. The venom still lingering in his veins was affecting his sense of balance and perception. The brighter lighting in the foyer speared into his skull, onsetting nausea and a debilitating headache.

"Can dragon venom cause migraines?" he whispered to Raven, keeping his eyes close to the ground.

"It's…possible?" Raven clasped Will's arm. "Are you sure about this, Will? You still have a chance to refuse His Majesty."

By the Founders, how Will wished he could just return to his cell and rest! He felt he could sleep quite happily there for another three days.

"There are thirteen hostages counting on me, Master Raven. I can't let them down."

All the same, he was still nauseous. Will stumbled a few steps from Raven, then threw up into an empty mop bucket. He braced himself against the wall, so he wouldn't topple over.

He felt much better after that.

Raven passed him a handkerchief, Will cleaned himself up, and then they entered the foyer. The first voice Will heard was the Princess's. She was arguing with her mother about the proper footwear for meeting Lord Amaranth.

"Boots, Mum," Philia insisted. "There is no way I am going out to a fight in *those* wretched things."

The "wretched things" were pink silk slippers, covered with intricate curls of ribbon and lace.

"This is not a fight," the Queen answered, in a hushed, even tone. "This is a diplomatic mission. Is that not so, Bran?" Her warm brown eyes turned upwards, searching for the King.

King Bran himself entered the foyer from Will and Raven's right. He had dressed for the occasion with suitable magnificence: Faerie-wrought armor, a scarlet cape, and an embroidered tunic depicting the Pendragon Rose. His blade *Nevertarnish* hung proudly from a polished leather belt.

The King inclined his head to his wife. "In this case, my dear Vivi, boots *will* serve her better."

Philia smiled at her father, her bright eyes like turquoise jewels. To Will, she was unmatched in beauty. Still, he could see her fatigue.

Will and Raven stepped into the fuller light of the foyer, a windowed hall set behind the wooden doors to Headquarters. Will dropped his eyes to fend off his headache.

Outside, the afternoon was overcast. Dove grey clouds hovered moodily behind the flame-like hues of the tannin pines. These lofty pines changed color and lost their needles each winter. Right now, they were at their peak, casting amber, orange, and crimson shadows across the Watch's courtyard. They also lined the forest edge, where Amaranth would be waiting.

Raven nudged his shoulder, and Will raised his head. The Pendragon family had noticed their arrival and turned to face them. The two watchmen knelt before the King.

"At ease, friends," the King said. "This is not the time for formalities."

Raven and Will arose. When Will raised his head, he got his first good look at Philia. Although she had tried to hide it with face paint, the Princess' skin had lost its normal radiance, and pale blue circles gathered under her eyes. Worse, angry markings crept along her neckline in intricate patterns. Will guessed they were the marks of the Curse, spreading across her body.

"Oh Philia," he lamented. "Forgive me that I didn't stop the cruel brat while I had the chance."

Her sickly face flushed pink. "Forgive me that I couldn't give you *all* of the antidote to heal your wounds." Her gaze shifted to

Raven. "Uncle, is Will going to be alright?"

"I think he can recover, Your Highness," Raven assured her. "*If he's given enough time and space to rest.*" This last line seemed directed towards the King.

His Majesty's face hardened. "Time and a safe place to rest is also what the Princess needs. Which is why they will both go with me." He stepped in closer and lowered his commanding voice. "If we play our hand right, we can free thirteen innocent Avalians, *and* bring the Princess and Owain to a safer location."

Raven's eyebrows sprung up in surprise. "How can that be so, Your Majesty?"

"Yes," added the Queen. "Where could Philia be safer than here, at Watch's Headquarters?"

"The dragon's last attack on Headquarters has proven that this fortress is not impenetrable," the King said. "In fact, Amaranth would likely have destroyed it already, if we didn't have his son Ewan held prisoner inside.

"Amaranth needs his heir to make a legitimate claim for the throne. *We* need to get Philia as far from Amaranth and his dragon as possible." Lamplight shimmered off the rubies in his golden crown as he surveyed each of their faces. "So we shall go out to meet him, bringing Ewan with us.

"At the same time, Lady Courtney and Master Paul will evacuate the villagers and all remaining civilians to Gwynedd, through the western tunnels. We will distract Amaranth as long as possible. And when things become unsafe for the Princess…we will take our flight."

The King smiled and flexed his right hand. The *modrwy* Shekinah sat proudly on his ring finger, glistening with tear-shaped rubies and pearls. For the last 800 years, it had been passed down from Pendragon to Pendragon, up to the present King Bran.

"But what of the antidotes, Your Majesty?" Will asked. "Has the dragon destroyed them?"

The King nodded. "The dragon destroyed all of Headquarters' store of antidotes three days ago, when it emerged beneath Philia's chamber. Our secondary supply, some miles north of here, was destroyed two days past by Faeries loyal to Amaranth. The antidote is produced from a Sacred Wood flower that blooms only in the late spring."

When the King fell silent, Raven continued. "In sum: the current antidote is lost, and no new antidotes can be produced for five months or more."

Everyone turned towards the Princess. She trembled, shrinking a little behind her father.

Can Philia fight the Curse for five months? Will wondered.

"L-lady Agnes never promised the antidote would cure me anyway, Father," the Princess whispered. "She only said it might slow things down a little, or ease the pain." She winced and tugged at her soft leather gloves. "Perhaps…they would only have given us false hope."

Will studied Philia. Her words seemed at odds with the bright, cheerful girl he had befriended in Scotland.

"The antidotes would have granted us more time," the King said. "Time for a new solution or remedy."

And yet Ewan swore there was no cure.

The Princess's wide turquoise eyes met Will's. He saw the ghost of her pain there—a hollow desperation. He also felt a kinship, which eased his heartbreak.

I won't let that wretched Curse take her from me, Will vowed, setting his heart to his promise like steel to the flame. *And I won't let her face Lord Amaranth alone.*

The bellowing of Amaranth's horns wrenched Will back into the present. He reached out and claimed Philia's hand protectively in his own. The King took the Princess's other arm, and then the three marched forward through the opening doors.

6

The Villain's Price

WILL AND THE King kept the Princess safely between them as they crossed the entrance yard, the King flanking Philia's left side, and Will, her right.

"I can't believe Father is letting me go with him!" Philia confided to Will. She leaned heavily on his arm. "I need to do *something*. The dragon wouldn't be here if it wasn't for me."

Will didn't answer. He didn't want the Princess within a hundred miles of Lord Amaranth, let alone a hundred meters.

After a few minutes of walking, the rough, grass-ice-mud mixture of the entrance yard ended at a stone-covered mound of dirt: one of the immense earthen walls protecting Watch's Headquarters. The mound sloped downwards for seven yards, creating a U-shaped exit way into the looming forest beyond.

King Bran of Avalon paused just before he reached the exit. Will and Philia stopped with him. A northern gust of wind cut through their fur-lined cloaks, making them shiver.

"Look Father," Philia cried, squinting into the forest undergrowth. "Here come the hostages!"

Together they peered into the Wood. Amaranth's warriors were leading out a line of dirty, frightened villagers, each tied to the other at the ankle with ropes.

Will started counting: "Five, ten, thirteen," he breathed. "All accounted for, Your Majesty."

The King nodded. "Yes, all thirteen alive, thank the Founders." His expression grew apprehensive. "But first we must reckon with Amaranth."

He raised his left arm and squeezed his gloved hand into a fist.

Four master watchmen answered the King's signal, leading Amaranth's son, Ewan, between them. Judging from the surly expression on Ewan's face, he wasn't delighted about his upcoming reunion with his father.

Ewan and his watchmen guards stopped near their group of three. Ewan's wolfish gaze slid past the King and Philia, landing on Will.

"Time to pay the price," he said flatly. The sharp breeze stirred his flame-red hair. Then his eyes snapped back toward Amaranth's men.

Will stiffened as he recognized the warning.

Don't interfere with my father, Ewan had told him, only days earlier. *He always makes you pay.*

Fear strangled Will's lungs, forcing his breath out in quick, frosty clouds.

I cannot I cannot too small weak useless I cannot

"Courage, Will," Philia whispered, squeezing his arm and breaking his litany. "Remember those poor hostages. Remember the evacuation."

Will drew in a deep, calming breath. The Princess smelled like lavender and vanilla, which he found soothing. How could such a little thing make any difference?

"Yes, Your Highness," he managed to say. "I do remember."

Will was overly terrified of facing Lord Amaranth; the Princess, not nearly enough.

A tall Faerie male, dressed in deerskin leggings and a thick, white-furred coat, stepped out of the tree line. He stood between the King and the hostages.

"My Lord Amaranth, Royal Vicar of Valeria and Duke of the Seven-Faced Fortress, sends salutations and greetings to his beloved brother, King Branaric III of Avalon." The Faerie herald had a pleasant, textured voice, as rich and sweet as honey chocolate. He dipped his head demurely at King Bran, then continued. "My Lord generously offers these thirteen villagers from fierce Gwynedd, in exchange for his son and heir, Sir Ewan David Pendragon."

The thirteen hostages peered towards the King and his company. Will could tell by their dress that they were farmers from his father Madoc's fiefdom. He could also see they had been treated poorly by Amaranth's men. Several of them had burns and wounds, wrapped only with filthy rags. The youngest, a boy about twelve years of age, sniffled as he hugged his left arm to his chest. The arm looked broken.

Will's fists clenched in anger. Amaranth's Faerie medics could have healed that boy's injury in a matter of minutes.

The King stepped forward. "You may take Ewan," he commanded, with simple directness, "once the thirteen hostages are safe with my watch-warriors." He gestured behind and to his left, where a team of watchmen and medics awaited the King's command.

The tall Faerie raised his gaunt chin, paused, then directed his attention to Philia and Will. Flamboyant silver feathers fluttered along the rim of his fur-lined cap.

"You may take the hostages," the Faerie messenger said, mimicking the King's phrasing, "if you proffer the boy, William Madoc Owain, for my lord's inspection along with Ewan. My Lord fears some trickery from the Watch, or that you may offer him a worthless Changeling."

Will flinched at the words "worthless Changeling" but said nothing. He turned towards the King.

"Your Majesty." Will lowered his head. "What will you have me do?"

The King hesitated, but only for a moment. "Go out to meet Lord Amaranth with Ewan. He will seek to humiliate you." A streak of sorrow crossed his face. "I pray you, for the sake of the hostages, and for the Princess…let him do so."

"Father," Philia hissed in protest. "You ask too much of him."

Will shook his head. "No, it's not too much, Philia," he countered, squeezing her hand. "He only asks what is necessary." He shifted his head so the Pendragons couldn't witness his panic and dread.

Not too much, he repeated. *But am I enough?*

Then he remembered the precious Faerie armor the King had given him, and how he had named Will his knight.

The King believed in him. He would not send Will out to die.

Will exhaled, knelt before the King, and laid his blade *Llewgalon* at the monarch's feet.

"Yes, Your Majesty." As he kissed the King's offered ring, a deep calm settled over him. There. He had done it—remained obedient to the Crown. All that was left was to accept Amaranth's price.

Will turned, and saw Philia's face out of the corner of his eye. She was trying, really trying. But he could see the whiteness of her knuckles and the clench of her jaw. She was afraid for him.

He kissed her hand. "I'll come back soon."

Philia nodded, but it was shaky. "Please be careful."

"I will."

He turned back to the line of hostages.

I can do this, Will told himself, crafting a new litany. *The King trusts me. I am his knight, and a loyal son of Owain.*

He walked through the exit and past the Faerie herald. Ewan was released by his guards at the same time, so that the two half-brothers walked nearly side-by-side, together.

He watched in relief as the thirteen hostages were led forward to meet the King, Philia, and the Watch attendants. Just as the hostages reached the King, Will fell under the shadow of the great oaks and tannin pines, where Amaranth waited with his warriors and night-callers.

Lord Amaranth stood tall and thin and striking in the twilight of the trees, virtually unchanged from Will's last memory of him. Snow-white threads of hair wafted eerily about his pale face, and magnificent black and gold armor clothed his slender form. His frosty blue eyes shone with satisfaction, but to Will they still looked dead.

Will's recent injuries had given him a slight limp. As a result, Ewan reached his father a few seconds before him.

"My lord," Ewan said, bowing deferentially to his father.

"My beloved son." Amaranth placed a frigid hand on Ewan's shoulder. "Are you hurt?"

"Not much, sir. The watch-guards barely even touched me." Ewan's sharp eyes flicked towards Will. "Too soft, I suppose," he added with a shrug.

Or too civilized, Will corrected.

"Come, give my son and heir my finest coat, and spiced mead to drink," Amaranth announced pompously. A Faerie warrior and maiden rushed forward. The warrior draped a thick, wolf-skinned coat over Ewan's shoulders, then handed him a steaming goblet from the maiden's serving tray. At Amaranth's urging, Ewan drank deeply from the ornate gold cup.

"It's good, Father," he said, but his expression was guarded. Wary. As if he half-expected the cup to be drugged.

The Faerie maiden took the goblet back from him, then retreated into the crowd of warriors. Once she'd returned to her place behind Amaranth, her eyes lingered thoughtfully on Will.

Does she know who I am? Has she seen my mother?

Amaranth's attention also shifted to Will, who had stopped a few yards from both Ewan and his father. It was bitter cold beneath the shadow of the Wood, and Amaranth's scrutiny was colder still. The damp, wintry air made Will's dragon wounds ache. His fingers itched for his blade, but he'd left *Llewgalon* at the King's feet. Safe from Amaranth's thieving hands.

"And you, Madoc's son," Amaranth drawled, his syllables exaggerated and pitying. "Are you hurt, boy?"

When Will didn't respond, the villain gestured lazily in his direction. "Come closer, Owain. So I may inspect you."

Will's sense of self-preservation urged him to throw his best hunting knife into the lord's throat, then run the other way and never look back. To avoid whatever humiliation Amaranth had evidently prescribed, just for him.

But the hostages were still being transferred to the King's care. And at Watch's Headquarters, the evacuation had only just begun. They needed more time.

Will stepped forward.

"The good King Bran commanded me here," he said evenly. "I come out of obedience to him, Avalon's rightful king. Not to please *you*, Lord Amaranth." He spat out his name like it was so much trash.

Amaranth immediately backhanded him, making Will's ears ring and sending a shockwave of pain through his recent injuries. He sucked in a breath and Amaranth struck him again. Harder. Faster. Hamish had beaten Will severely before in Scotland. But Amaranth had the inhuman strength of the Fae behind his blows.

The villain's third blow knocked the air from Will's lungs and forced him to his knees. In a panic, Will struggled for a breath that would not come. His stomach muscles spasmed as he clutched at his chest.

Breathe, Will. Breathe. But nothing happened.

All the while, Amaranth kept strutting back and forth before him. He swung a long silver chain necklace around his gloved hand, then snapped it across Will's face. The chain bit like a metallic whip, slicing open his cheek. Will was only grateful it hadn't landed in his eye.

His lungs started working again. He gasped and fell forward, his shoulders heaving as he dragged in breath after breath.

Amaranth laughed and pulled Will's woozy head up by his hair.

"What love the good King shows you," he taunted. "Sending you out, alone and unprotected, to satisfy my rage."

He called for his guards, who seized Will's arms and then beat a solid wooden club into his injured shoulder.

A cry tore from Will's lips, and unbidden tears. He felt the wounds anew, as if the dragon was again impaling his flesh. Heard her poisonous words, coursing like hell-fire through his veins. He clung to whatever protection the Faerie armor still offered him.

You should have run, Will, his body scolded him. *While you still had the chance.*

But Will wasn't only here out of loyalty to his King.

"M-mama," he croaked, his voice a broken whisper. "Where… is…my mother?" Had Amaranth brought Fiona with him on this mission?

His adversary either didn't hear, or chose not to answer.

"Look at me, boy."

When Will didn't comply fast enough, he got two more blows to his shoulder. Underneath the King's armor, which was undoubtedly softening the strikes, Will felt Raven's bandages separate from his wounds. Warm blood seeped out into the padding beneath his chain mail.

He raised his eyes to Amaranth's face and repeated his question. Slowly, so the vile, venomous bastard could make out every word:

"Where is my *mother*?"

Amaranth's icy blue eyes expanded. He dragged his greyish tongue across swollen lips, then smiled.

"Aaah. Fiona. So vexing, so frustrating, that after all these years, you have yet to find and save her?" He laughed and jerked Will's head upward until he gasped in pain. Everything Amaranth did seemed crafted for pain.

"You are useless, boy. You will never save your mother, and your loyalty to Bran is pointless. His precious daughter will die, I will seize his throne, and Fiona shall be my queen. And then *you* shall be our palace plaything."

"Take me to her," Will whispered fervently. "Please."

The villain's gaze locked with his. His razor-sharp eyebrows shot up in surprise.

"If I take you, I would treat you just as I have always done," he told Will, with startling directness. "I would use you to make my sweetheart obey me. Never forget that you exist, that you live, only to keep my sweetheart perfectly in line."

"*Shut up*," Will snarled fiercely, as he spat in Amaranth's face. "You can't force someone to love you. If you truly cared for her, you'd let her go."

Amaranth roared in fury. He struck him repeatedly, until Will couldn't see, couldn't hear, couldn't taste anything but blood and guilt and heart-breaking sorrow. When Amaranth was finished, he left Will lying face-first in the mud, his left eye swollen shut, his cheek cut open, his right shoulder on fire.

Will tried to focus through his pain. Were the King and the Princess safe? Had he given the hostages and evacuees enough time to escape?

"We're coming, Will! Take courage!" The Princess' sweet voice kissed his ringing ears, making Will want to weep in relief.

But Amaranth wasn't quite done. He knelt beside Will, a short, curved blade cradled in his hand.

"It's not time yet, to take you to Fiona," he said, soft and low. "But I shall take a piece of you back to her. A little souvenir of our visit, yes?"

Will pushed himself away from Amaranth and the knife. Dizziness and nausea crushed him back into the mud.

"We're coming, Will!"

He heard the chime of blade against blade, and the fierce cries of battle. But the sound was faint, distant. Too far away to stop Amaranth from driving his curved blade into Will's scalp, and harvesting a strip of golden-blonde hair and flesh from the back of Will's head.

Will shrieked, sending out a shrill cry that resonated from his entire body, out into the Wood, into Headquarters, and into the hearts, perhaps, of everyone in the entrance yard. It must have been so. Why else would such profound silence follow his scream?

He grabbed at the back of his head, dipped his shaking fingers into a meaty indentation. His hand came away drenched with blood.

Amaranth stared at him for an endless moment, watching Will struggle for breath and consciousness. When Will's humiliation had apparently satisfied him, he nodded.

"Yes, Lady Jade was wrong," he muttered to himself. "This boy is no threat. He is weak, and I have made him even more so."

The villain folded up his gruesome souvenir—a slice of Will's scalp and his wheat-blonde locks—and wrapped them in a clean white handkerchief. The cloth instantly blotted crimson with blood.

The next thing Will remembered, Amaranth was gone and the King himself was crouched beside him.

"Time to go, my son," the monarch said.

Philia was there, too, her eyes red and puffy from crying. "I'm sorry, so sorry, Will. I've never seen anyone get tor—I didn't… I'm sorry." She knelt down beside him and buried her face in his clothes.

Will wanted to weep, too, and not only for himself. He'd weep for his mother, and for Philia's lost innocence, and for the anger and shame carved onto the good King's face.

His Majesty's *modrwy* ring, the *Shekinah*, shimmered and glowed, surrounding the three of them with pure white light.

"Meshtiwa, shway itsa," the King said in a clear, concise voice. "Reshua, otsudavit!"

At the King's summons, a majestic bird of paradise appeared, three times the size of a man, with a long, feathered tail the color of living flame. The King lifted Will's broken body upwards, then placed him on the creature's back.

Will sunk wearily into a sea of silken feathers. A sweet, soothing sensation overcame him—a most delightful escape from Amaranth's torments. He almost wept. So long, so exceedingly long, since he had felt anything but pain.

Once they were mounted on the creature's back, the bird of paradise rose with a flurry of teal and vermillion wings, each gathering of feathers rainbow-eyed and radiant. Its wings gave off an aroma so strong, Will could almost taste it. Citrus, pine, sage. It revived him enough to speak.

"Where are we going?" he murmured.

"Father's taking us to the rendezvous," the Princess said, on the other side of those vibrant feathers. "But please don't worry about that, Will. Rest."

"Rest now, my son," the King agreed. His *paradisa* sent them streaking through sunshine, leaving trails of sparkling colors in their wake.

At first, Will shared in his companions' relief. But the longer they flew, the more confused Will felt. He tried to remember how he had gotten up into the air, and where he was going, and who was with him.

"Philia," he cried out. "Philia, are you there?"

Two voices answered him, speaking garbled words Will couldn't understand.

He started shivering. All his body heat seemed to flow right out of him, at the same alarming rate that he was losing blood. He sagged against the *paradisa's* quivering neck, trying to soak in its warmth.

Someone touched the back of his head, close to his fresh wound. He shoved them away.

"Don't touch me!" he said. "d-don't touch…"

They didn't listen. Instead, someone held his arms down while the other pressed a fold of cloth against his scalp wound. He screamed and pushed their hands away.

"Philia," Will panted, his breath coming in rapid gasps. "*Philia…*"

No one answered him. He was alone, in a pain too great for his body to feel. All was fire or numbness; agony or emptiness. The emptiness was worse, because it was both real and a lie. It was the villain's true price—refusing Will his mother.

"Mama," he whispered, faintly now. "I'm sorry..."

Later, he drifted off into a fitful sleep. He traversed a thousand starlit dream chambers before he heard a woman calling his name.

"Will?"

He turned and beheld a younger Fiona, the one he remembered as a child in Gwynedd. She wore a flowing emerald gown that drew out the vivid grey-green color of her eyes. Her face was bruised and her arms scratched, but her stance was resolute. As Will watched, she presented her left hand to him, and he saw the ring, Enduri. The sapphire rose, golden band, and emerald thorns.

He rose to meet her, in her place across a forest meadow. Overhead, the sky was brilliant with stars; below, soft grasses and tiny, five-pointed flowers.

Fiona smiled and beckoned him forward with her ringed hand.

"Come, Will," she urged, her voice fierce, practical, real.

He moved to obey, but as soon as he took a step, a wide pool of water yawned open at his feet. He couldn't tell how deep it was, and this filled him with dread.

No sooner had he stepped around the first pool, but another appeared, and another, until there were six pools of water blocking his path to Fiona. Some of the pools swirled in agitation. One appeared black as night in its dregs. Another flashed lightning over its surface.

The last one reverberated with the echo of Will's screams.

He backed away. *Is this real? Is she real?*

But his mother kept beckoning him forward, tenderness and hope in her spring-green eyes.

"Come Will," she called, over the sound of restless waters. "Let me show you how to live."

7

The Color Thief

PHILIA CLUNG TO her father and his *paradisa* as long as possible, before Amaranth's flying steed came between them and sent her tumbling from the sky. Below, she could see that Will was already falling.

Her heart was still reeling from what had happened to him.

She should have known better. If she had learned anything at all from her first week in Avalon, it was to expect violence and suffering at every turn. Especially violence upon people she knew and loved.

Hush Philia, that doesn't sound like you at all. There must be more for you in Avalon than death.

It was an ironic burst of hope for a Princess plummeting ruthlessly towards the ground. As she approached the forest canopy, crisp winter air sliced through the openings of her fur coat, acting like a makeshift parachute and slowing her descent.

"Father!" She screamed, but he was fighting Amaranth many yards above her. Her father rode a *paradisa* bird with teal and vermillion wings. The moment before Philia fell, Amaranth had caught up to them, riding a golden horse with cobalt wings.

But Philia had no creature to break her fall.

"Father, help us!" she cried.

The King immediately shouted out a string of commands. Something about wind and earth, lifting and receiving. At once, the wind responded. It wrapped itself around Philia's body, slowing and taming her deadly descent.

Below her, Will slowed as well. When he entered the tree line, he had time to raise his arms and protect his battered head. The tall tannin pines gathered him in their branches, swallowing him up in fierce autumn color. The rush of the wind was too loud for her to hear if he made any sound.

This is it, she thought hopelessly. *He'll be dead once he hits the ground. And me, with him.*

She shielded her head in her own arms, a foreign despair creeping into her bones. As she passed through the canopy, the branches pulled away from her, as if fearing her touch. A tree swayed aside to avoid her path. Even the soft, downy heather of the forest meadow parted and receded as she crash-landed into the earth. Her father had commanded the wind to come to her aid, but all the Wood's living things refused to break her fall.

Because I'm the Cursed one.

For a grind of time, she couldn't tell where or how she had landed. Everything was dark and disorienting and marked by throbbing pain.

And then, as if to complete the chaos, she heard a childlike voice, squealing in terror.

"Mama…*Mama!!!* No…no. I *won't*—" A series of uncontrolled shrieks. Each cry stabbed into Philia's chest, begging for her compassion.

"Hello?" she called, coughing out a mouth full of dirt. "Can I help you?"

The wind answered her with a soft, grey sigh.

She raised her head and peered into the meadow grasses. "Hello?"

More screams. More sobs.

But then: a soft, tender light rising up from the earth. A luminous radiance, expanding and contracting with each outpouring of misery. Its gentle white glow lit up the heather grass from within, so that each blade blazed an iridescent green, and each flower a striking violet hue.

Her ears heard only the panicked cries of some poor, injured child. But her eyes! They beheld a vision so mysterious and unexpected, it struck her dumb with wonder.

Out of misery, a burst of life.

She tugged down her fur coat, then shuffled across the meadow towards the strange phenomenon.

After a short crawl, she spied a single hand tangled in the grass. It clawed and grasped at the earth, a fair hand covered in crimson, attached to a mottled grey sleeve caked with mud.

"No..." the child cried, weaker now. "I won't let you...death *first.*"

The hand disappeared into the heather, and the cries subsided into weary pants. The mysterious glow shimmered once before fading away.

She wriggled through the heather to find the place where the child should have been. This was how she learned that it wasn't a child at all, but an adult. A still, lifeless adult whose upper torso was soaked in blood.

What an eejit I am, she thought. *It's Will.*

But then where did the child's voice come from?

"William Madoc Owain," she murmured.

"Good," drawled a sickly-sweet voice from behind Philia, one which she had already learned to despise. "The fall didn't kill either of you. Such a shame it would be, to cut the boy's sufferings short. Or to rob the Curse of its greatest victim."

Lord Amaranth lifted Philia from the ground as if she weighed no more than feathers.

She struggled against him, but his Faerie strength and speed eclipsed any self-defense move her mother had taught her.

And the Curse wears on me, Philia admitted to herself.

Amaranth wrapped his arm across her chest to hold Philia still, then gripped her left wrist to examine the mark on her palm.

He had also positioned her so that she could stare down at Will in the heather.

Will's cloak and tunic were ripped and torn, especially about his right shoulder, which had soaked through with blood. She knew it was Will, but the visible side of his face was so swollen from Amaranth's punches, he could have been any young man in a watchman's uniform. Worst of all, she saw the bright red wound where Amaranth had gouged out a piece of Will's scalp. It was about four inches long, and it emitted a copious amount of blood that made Philia sick with worry.

"Oh please," she murmured. "Let me help him."

Lord Amaranth sneered, then jerked Philia away from her watchman. "What's the boy to you, First Princess? All he's done is fail to protect you."

She bristled at this entirely unfair assessment of Will. "Not so. I'm still here, aren't I? Still on my feet and ready to fight, because of that boy."

Her words reminded her of the self-defense techniques Will had taught her in Scotland. Philia made herself small and slippery, working herself out of Amaranth's iron hold.

The Faerie usurper's eyebrows lifted. As soon as Philia pulled away from him, he released her wrist, causing her to sprawl backward in the grass.

Philia scowled and jumped back onto her feet, then drew *Brightwind* with one swift stroke. It slid from her golden scabbard with a clear musical chime.

"Why are you here?" she demanded.

Lord Amaranth watched her hungrily. "I wanted to see you. As you are now, in your prime. While you still have dreams and joy and *life* left in your veins." He took a step forward, his arms reaching towards her. She stumbled away, almost running into Will, who except for his rising and falling chest, could have passed for a corpse.

She shivered, and not from the forest fog creeping into the meadow. Will was the example, it seemed, of how Amaranth treated his very worst enemies.

"Take comfort, dear Princess, that of the two, you are the lucky one," Amaranth drawled, jerking his cruel head at Will. "Someday soon you will taste the delicious, permanent escape of death. For Madoc's son, I will offer no such respite."

Amaranth hadn't killed Will, as Philia had feared at first. He didn't challenge him to an honorable duel, to work out their differences. No, he had simply and ruthlessly crushed him—her *watchman*—until death surely felt more desirable. A tantalizing escape which Amaranth then refused him.

Philia flinched and shook her head. That was another strange, un-Philia like thought.

It's coming from the Curse, she realized. It sat crouched like a shadow at the edge of her brain, feeding her forbidden urges.

Amaranth smiled; a white smile full of sharp teeth. "I came to see everything that Bran is going to lose as I slowly, carefully, steal his only beloved daughter away from him."

She stepped around Will and even farther back from the repulsive Faerie. Will would have told her to flee, but then Philia would have to leave him alone with this monster. No. She would stand and fight.

"For my father," she whispered, raising *Brightwind* aloft. "And my watchman."

Amaranth's grin grew wider. "And she is as brave as she is beautiful."

"Do not mock me," she protested. Then she charged at Amaranth with everything she had.

He lowered his head, as if to receive her blow. Then he was gone, and her stroke met empty air.

Where did he go?

Two strong arms materialized behind her, clamping around her arms and chest.

"Hello, Princess," Amaranth breathed in her ear. She startled in fright and slammed her boot into his leg. He didn't budge. Instead, one of his arms slithered down and forced *Brightwind* from her left hand. Next, he pushed his jagged fingernails directly into the cursed mark on her palm.

At his touch, a violent electric shock ran up her arm, her neck, and into her head with blazing ferocity. She couldn't breathe or move or speak for the burning sensation pressing brutally into her head and behind her eyes.

Her vision faltered and went black. She slumped in Amaranth's arms. For a time, all she was aware of was the Curse and the sound of Amaranth's soft breathing in her ear.

"Stop," she gasped, her voice less than a whisper. "You'll kill me...sooner than you want."

He immediately released the pressure on Philia's left hand. Her vision popped back, and the relief made her weak.

"Fool," Amaranth muttered, as if he was frustrated with himself. "Pity to have you suffer so much without my dear brother here to witness it. The girl has better sense than I do. But see! I was just so excited about my new plaything."

Philia shuddered.

"I'm *not* your plaything," she panted, still fighting for each breath. "And your games stink."

He laughed. "You certainly are one of a kind, aren't you, Princess Philia? I would hate to lose you, if you were my daughter."

Heat rushed into her cheeks. "Aye, my father loves me. Must you destroy every good thing you see?"

"Silence, girl. I want to show you something." Amaranth shoved Philia to the right, where the grassy meadow rolled softly into a labyrinth of trees. The meadow was dotted with a dazzling array of wildflowers. Daisy-like blossoms with ruby-red petals and sky-blue centers swayed in the autumn wind. Orange and yellow buttercups wound across the grassy floor, encircling clumps of wild chrysanthemums. Other Avalian blooms bobbed up and down in the late afternoon glow, their colors shifting as they passed between sunlight and shade.

"Pretty little woodland scene, isn't it?" Amaranth said.

It really was beautiful. Philia admired the flowers' brilliant variety, the mesmerizing spectrum of reds and umbers, turquoise and bronze, pale green and iridescent gold.

"Watch carefully now." Amaranth held up her left hand. "I wonder what would happen if I pressed…here?" He pressed a part of her scar, and instantly, some of the colors in the wildflower grove faded to grey. He pressed another area, and the daisy's red blossoms appeared almost black. He traced a line across the center of her scar, and all the colors vanished.

The wildflowers and grasses kept bobbing in the breeze as if nothing unusual had happened. But the colors, all the gorgeous, vivid colors, were gone.

"How has that improved things for you, Your Highness?" Amaranth asked.

"My colors?" Tears turned Philia's world a gloomy-grey hue. "You might as well have taken the sun and the moon."

"Philia!"

Her ears took note of the sound. She knew that voice. Not sickly sweet like Amaranth's, but good and noble to the core.

"Father!" she called back. "I'm here, in the meadow!"

"Bran," Amaranth hummed with pleasure. "Excellent."

Philia gasped as her father leapt through the undergrowth, his blade ready to strike.

Amaranth snarled at the King, then took one step to the left and disappeared, just as he had done before.

"Father!" Philia hurried to his side, but the King held up his hand.

"Wait." The King surveyed the surrounding meadow, searching for any sign of Amaranth. His hair was ruffled and his garments torn, but otherwise he seemed unharmed.

"Amaranth hijacked our escape," he explained to Philia without preamble. "His flying steed wounded the *paradisa*, so she dropped me and fled. It took me precious moments to discover where you had fallen. Are you hurt?" Philia rubbed the Curse mark, where Amaranth had taken away her colors. "Not exactly."

He gazed at her with weary tenderness.

"My brave one," he said softly. "Keep your hope strong, *and*," he lifted his blade, "your sword ready."

Amaranth reappeared, this time wielding a fine glass blade and charging straight towards the two Pendragons.

Her father swatted away Amaranth's attack, releasing a cloud of shimmering dust as the two glass blades met and clashed. Then the King took the offensive, pummeling Amaranth with the *Giver*, *Romantic*, and *Encompasser* strokes, each with breathtaking grace and skill.

Amaranth snarled and cursed, raining insults on his half-brother as his blade nearly sliced the King's right arm. The King sidestepped at the last moment and pulled back a few steps, panting.

"So…" Amaranth murmured, licking his swollen lips. "We are dueling for the throne of Avalon, yes?"

"The throne belongs to me and my daughter," the King answered, his voice confident and firm. He re-entered the fight, expertly striking Amaranth on his left side and then his right shoulder. The two cuts drew blood, but didn't slow Amaranth down.

Still, Father's clearly the better swordsman, Philia thought.

The Faerie must have reached a similar conclusion. Instead of rushing in for his next attack, Amaranth threw a knife at his half-brother.

Bran dove to the left, and the knife whizzed through the grass, close to Philia.

"Get back!" the King ordered, as he barreled full speed towards Amaranth.

Philia ran and hid behind the copse of heather, where she had discovered Will moments before. She crouched down in the tall grasses.

"Your Highness."

She jumped in fright and whirled towards this new voice.

"Will," she sighed with relief. "Y-you look terrible," she sputtered.

He made a weak effort to raise his head.

"The view from here s'not so bad," he said, slurring his words. He gave her a sunny smile.

"How—how are you *smiling*?"

If possible, Will's grin got broader. "I remained loyal to the King. Mother's still alive. *You're* still alive. So…"

"Life is good?" She crawled over to him, drew out her linen handkerchief, and pressed it to his cheek.

He winced and released a tense breath.

Philia couldn't understand his good mood. Why had he let Amaranth beat him up so badly?

"Do you enjoy being treated so poorly?" she murmured, frustrated. She knew he'd done it for the sake of the Avalon hostages, but she didn't care.

"No," Will answered quickly. "I don't." He tried to lift himself up again, but fell back shaking.

"Hush," she said, kissing his forehead. "Lie still and rest."

The clash of blades grew closer.

Philia whipped her head around to watch. Bran and Amaranth had continued their deadly dance through the wildflowers. Bran's blade soared towards his opponent's neck; Amaranth retreated just in time. The villain retaliated with a stab of his blade and a dagger thrust—the King was too quick. *Nevertarnish* blocked Amaranth's sword and dagger simultaneously. The dagger snapped in two, and the blades struck each other with an explosion of sparkling dust.

"I still reign as King in Avalon, 'Ranth," Bran thundered. "And as long as I live, you shall not lay hands on my daughter again."

Philia viewed her father's face in profile, his silhouette passionate, determined, and sure. Amaranth's profile held a similar resolve, but his dead eyes glistened with cruelty and hate.

"What good is your protection, Bran?" he sneered. "How can you protect Philia from what defiles her on the inside?"

His dead eyes pivoted and bored into Philia's, a murderous glance that rallied the Curse within her body. Searing pain ripped through her fingers, hand, and arm like liquid wildfire. When the Curse's heat reached into her neck and head, she sobbed and curled herself into a tight ball. The lost children of the miserable crowd pressed in around her, clawing, tearing, biting.

Help us, Princess! Save us! the children begged.

"Leave me!" she muttered, swatting their hands away. "Let me alone."

"Philia." She couldn't see Will from inside her huddled ball, but she felt his gentle touch on her shoulder.

"Will," she said. "I—I get it now. Why you were so afraid... of *him*."

His grip tightened in acknowledgment. "I wish..." his voice mirrored the pain she herself was experiencing. "I wish you had nothing to fear."

She peeked at him through the lattice of her crossed arms. With her colors gone, she couldn't readily distinguish Will's blood from his bruises and cuts. It all blended together in a monochromatic tapestry of lights and darks. The handsome contours of his face were distorted by Amaranth's violence, and his usual clean, golden-blonde locks appeared grey and tangled in her new vision.

But these imperfections were just the proof of Will's great love for his people. They illustrated his soul's nobility, and so to Philia, they made him exponentially more attractive. The most beautiful creature she had ever seen.

Philia startled as her ears rang once more with the sound of clashing blades.

Clang! Clang! Clang!

A short distance away, her father disengaged his sword and lunged towards Amaranth's chest, puncturing his opponent's metallic armor.

Amaranth roared, retreating rapidly. Dark liquid oozed from his chest. He'd been too distracted by the battle to disappear in time.

"I will find a way to save her," the King declared, as if continuing a conversation Philia had missed. "Even if it costs me everything."

"It would cost far more than you could ever pay." Amaranth's voice cut hard as steel. "I have placed the punishment of the Way's opening solely on the Princess' shoulders, and she shall pay its bitter price to the full." He spoke it calmly, like someone stating a fact, not an idle boast. "She will die, and you will lose everything, Bran. Just as you did before, at Flaxen Grove."

Her father screamed in bitter fury. "You will not rob me of my family again!"

Chime, chime, chime!

Their blades flashed across the meadow, faster than Philia could follow, fiercer than any duel she'd ever seen.

Clang, clang, clang!

Shimmering glass dust burst forth with every stroke, filling the meadow with clouds of glittering smoke.

The King swung his blade into Amaranth's fighting arm, tearing a gash through both armor and flesh.

Amaranth hissed and retreated until he crouched beneath the Wood's lengthening shadows. The King pressed his advantage with outstretched sword.

"Killing me won't save her, Bran," his adversary snarled, clutching his wounded arm. "Her death is mandated by ancient Faerie law. You cannot undo the Curse, without unraveling the laws of Avalon itself." Amaranth retreated further and further as he spoke, until he was nothing more than a menacing shadow in the deep grey cover of the pines.

"No! I *will* save her!" the King sprung forward, angling his sword towards Amaranth's neck. But the foul villain vanished before the blade struck home.

8

Into the Wild

"Who won the battle, Philia?" Will asked, when the chime of blades fell silent.

She squinted across the clearing. "No one. But my father's alive and well." She nodded. "Here he comes now."

The King ran back across the meadow and knelt beside the two injured young people. His warm gaze fell first on his daughter, then Will.

"Amaranth has left us, at least for the present," the King said, his expression weary. "So let me attend to the two of you."

"Will first, Father," Philia said. "I'm alright."

The King gave her a searching glance, then nodded.

Will still lay awkwardly on his left side, his breaths shallow and his body a minefield of hurts. When Bran shifted Will's position to examine his injuries, the young watchman recoiled.

"D-don't touch me," he said, pushing the King away. He pressed his face into the ground, seeking privacy.

"I fear to move him," the King told Philia. "He may have internal injuries."

Her hand brushed the crown of Will's head. "What we can see is horrible enough."

"It's okay, dear Will," she added. "That beast Amaranth is gone. Father wants to help you."

Will groaned before nodding his consent. It cost him.

When the King shifted Will's body to remove his tunic and armor, he screamed and screamed. There was nowhere else for the agony to go. He lost consciousness more than once.

The next time the pain forced him awake, the Pendragons were talking about escaping and maps and a tincture and whether or not to give it to him.

"Give it to him, Father. Don't let him suffer another minute because of me."

Cool liquid anointed his skin, permeating first his scalp wound, then the dragon wounds. The tincture was cool to the touch, and wherever they rubbed it into his skin, his pain subsided. The brutal throbbing in his shoulder eased to an ache; the burning of his scalp cooled; the cuts on his face lost their sting. The tincture didn't heal him, but it halved his pain and doubled his energy, and when it was finished Will felt life might possibly be worth living again.

"Thank you," he gasped, his eyes fluttering open.

Philia and the King were still next to him, their faces drawn and worried.

"I am the one who must be grateful, Owain." King Bran bowed his head and made a sign over his heart.

Will recognized the gesture. "No, Your Majesty. You owe me nothing."

"Because of your obedience, my daughter and I are still alive," the King said. "I am indebted to you, and with this oath, I vow to repay your good and faithful service."

"Very well, Your Majesty," Will said, his voice soft but clear. "I accept your vow."

The Founders know I need all the help I can get.

A far-off sound reached Will's ears. He strained to listen, heard the sound again: a long, plaintive howl, followed by three shorter, answering growls.

Will cursed inwardly. "Wolves," he snapped.

"Wolves?!" Philia startled and gazed wildly about the meadow.

"Your Majesty, we need to leave this place. The spilt blood will draw them straight to this clearing."

More howls joined the first one. They weren't close, but Will knew that the three of them weren't going anywhere quickly.

"We can't leave now," Philia said in a panic. "You are in no state to travel anywhere."

"We leave," Will panted, "or we die." His chest convulsed, putting terrible pressure on his lungs. The tincture had addressed the external injuries, but the King was right—something was broken on the inside. A couple of ribs, probably. Perhaps more.

"Help me sit up," he ordered, through gritted teeth. Sweat trickled down his brow.

The wolves howled again. *Three, four miles away,* Will estimated.

"Help me *up*." This time, with urgency.

The King hauled him up to a sitting position. Stars danced across Will's vision. Something hard dug into his chest cavity, making it difficult to breathe. He wasn't alive anymore. Just a vessel of pain.

But in this position, Will saw it—the watchman's path.

"Th-there," his good arm pointed towards the southwest corner of the meadow, where a deer path passed between two cedars. "Take that path. Go...to the lake."

The wolves called again, as if they couldn't bear the thought of giving the trio even a moment's peace.

The Pendragons raised Will to his feet. Will's head swam dizzily and all the good done by the tincture instantly unraveled. He moaned softly, then bit his tongue to hide how much this was costing him. Clear streams of water trickled off his cheeks. He realized they were his own tears.

The King and Philia supported Will on either side.

The movement jostled his injuries. Will's head dropped and his knees buckled.

"Will—" Philia pleaded.

"Keep going!" He hissed back. He coughed, spitting out the blood from his torn tongue. Then he planted one foot onto the meadow grass and forced himself to rise again. His body protested, but his legs held.

And the wolves. Those *damned* Albine wolves. They just kept on howling.

Will had no words to describe what that journey was like for him. Every few minutes, he felt certain he couldn't go forward another step. But then a warm, gentle heat would fill him—emanating from where his mother's ring lay in his pouch, against his chest. His arms and legs would gain the smallest increase in strength, and then the trio kept going.

His throat was parched from dehydration and blood loss. His forehead ached like Amaranth was actively pummeling his skull. And his limbs—they were so weak, he knew it was really the Pendragons keeping him upright. Mile after mile.

That, and his mother's ring.

Come Will, she'd whispered. *Let me show you how to live.*

If living feels anything like dying, I think I've learned enough, Mama.

Finally, after six miles and twenty thousand years had passed, the King stopped at the shore of an inland lake. Both Will and Philia collapsed onto the beach, unable to take another step.

The next thing Will remembered, the King was raising a canteen of water to his lips. The water cleared his head a little. Enough for him to close his eyes and listen, profoundly listen, to the Wood.

The north wind rustled through the pines, its voice a soft sigh. Nighttime rodents chittered as they hunted for their next meal. And far out on the lake, Will heard the otherworldly cry of an Avalon loon.

He relaxed, tension sloughing off him in powerful waves. The cry of the loon meant safety.

"It's alright, Your Majesty," he said. "We can make camp. The wolves have not followed us here."

The King nodded. "Indeed, I haven't heard the wolves for the past half hour. Why this is so, I cannot say."

Will gestured at the lake, whose peaceful surface rippled with reflected moonlight. "It's Lake Galadrys, Your Majesty. The wolves won't go near these waters. Master Raven says there's deep, ancient magic in the lake that wards them away."

Philia spoke for the first time. "Does that mean we're safe here?"

Will turned towards the Princess and smiled. "Yes, Your Highness. As long as we stay by the lake, the wolves won't bother us."

"That is good news," the King answered. "Owain, rest here with Philia while I set up camp." The King shouldered their supply bag and headed back into the Wood, leaving Will and Philia alone.

The loon cries ceased as the sleek water bird dived into the murky depths. Lake Galadrys was hundreds of feet deep; ideal for fishing *ryba* and other subterranean lake dwellers.

Will and Philia sat peaceably together, watching the stars shimmer off the lake's surface. A gush of wind touched Will's sore and swollen face. He loved the Avalian wilderness. Forget the Watch's healers and the Faerie's tinctures; the Sacred Wood had always been Will's best medicine.

Soon a new bird cry graced the nighttime air.

"What was that?" Philia asked. She rested her weary head on Will's good shoulder. "Good" being a relative term, of course, after Amaranth's brutal beating.

"That's a nightingale," Will whispered. He hesitated, then rested his own head over Philia's. "In fair times and foul it sings its sweet song, filling the hearts of all who listen." He closed his eyes. "They make me think of my father. The nightingales build their nests in the eaves of Gwynedd Castle."

Philia shifted deeper into the hollow of Will's shoulder. Her head pressed against his bruised chest, but Will didn't mind.

"Gwynedd, by the sea," she said. "Where we played by the castle moat as children, and you brought me roses."

He laughed. "Nay, Your Highness. Only one rose, and a soggy, sorry rosebud at that."

Red rose, he'd cried, dripping wet in his mother's arms. *Red rose for Philia.*

"But you nearly drowned to get it for me."

He kissed the top of her head, breathing in her vanilla scent. "It was worth it."

The nightingale continued its music. A sad, soaring melody.

Philia sat very still against him. "Why are you so kind to me, Will? I'm damaged goods now. The Curse has tainted me."

Her words surprised him. "The Curse is what's happened to you, Philia. It's not who you are."

Philia sniffed. "It doesn't feel like that. It feels like the Curse has poisoned me, and everything I touch. Look at what happened to you, Will, because of me. The dragon, formed out of my blood, nearly killed you. And Amaranth made things even worse. You don't deserve that."

He pressed her close, unsure of how to answer her. "I don't know about what I deserve," he said finally. "But I do know that I love you, Philia Pendragon. Your gentle, tender heart. Your compassion. The Curse hasn't taken those qualities from you. If anything, the Curse has made you more kind."

He pulled in more tight, shallow breaths. So much he longed to say; so little breath to speak it.

"You are so beautiful, Philia—inside and out." He touched her silky brown hair, pushed one curly strand behind her ear. "The Curse wants to hide it from you, but you are *not* the Curse. You are Philia Pendragon, the sweetest, bravest princess this Isle has ever seen."

She gasped, soaking in his words. "Do you really believe all that?"

"I do." He smiled at her simplicity. "Do you know what else I believe, Your Highness?"

She shook her head, waiting.

"I believe you are worth protecting. No matter the cost." His gaze drifted towards the King, who had returned to fill their canteens with lake water. "Your father believes it, too. So keep fighting, Philia. We will keep fighting for you."

Later, after Philia had settled down to rest in their campsite, it was Will's turn to wash. The King helped Will remove his tunic and Faerie armor, so that Will could bathe and scrub the blood and dirt from his clothes. By this time, the gibbous moon had fully risen, giving them better lighting.

"How does it look, Your Majesty?" Will asked.

"The gouge in your scalp is much improved, thanks to the medicine. But..." the King made a sound of disapproval. "Your entire back is black and blue, Owain. And the wounds in your shoulder reopened on our journey to the lake." He rifled through his supply pack, procuring a glass vial with a wooden stopper. "This is a restorative healing tincture distilled by Lady Agnes. We gave you some in the meadow, and I just gave Philia a dose before she retired. I'd like to give you a second dose as well."

Will examined the vial, which was three-quarters full. "Is there enough tincture for us both, Your Majesty?"

"Let us hope so," the King said, his tone firm. "Because I am giving you a second dose tonight, whether you agree to it or not."

9

Mushroom Hunting

THE NEXT MORNING, Philia awoke to a freshly foraged breakfast of merlin berries, wild chestnuts, and her father's *gwemka* bread. Her father and Will had taken the watches of the night, letting Philia rest. The dark circles under their eyes told Philia that neither had gotten enough sleep.

"Tomorrow night, let me take one of the watches," she insisted, in her most imperious princess voice.

Will and the King were too tired to argue. Once the night watches had been settled, the King pulled out his map of the Sacred Wood and laid it in a patch of sunlight. Philia marveled over its detailed cartography and hand-drawn illustrations.

Will squatted beside the map, his intelligent eyes moving swiftly over its contents. He held a traveler's compass in one hand, which he used to mark their present coordinates.

"This shows our current location along Lake Galadrys, Your Majesty," he told the King. He ran his finger along the lake's narrow shoreline. "If we continue along the beach to where the lake meets the Running River, we can avoid the Albine wolves for another day of our journey."

"How far to the River?" the King asked.

"Ten miles."

"And how much further from that point to the rendezvous?"

Will surveyed the map. "Another seven miles. Too much for one day, with two of us injured. I recommend that we set up camp tonight at the river mouth, then continue the final leg of our journey tomorrow."

"Can't we just call another *paradisa* to help us, Father?"

The King shook his head. "The *paradisa* allowed us to escape, but its magical presence also alerted Amaranth to our precise location. We don't have the strength to fight Amaranth or his allies again, so it seems most prudent to stay hidden." The King studied both of them. "How are you feeling, Philia?"

Before breakfast, Philia had rubbed the tincture into her Curse marks, to soothe their incessant burning. Fatigue still clung to her limbs, but she figured she felt pretty good, considering the circumstances.

"I'm tired and sore," Philia said out loud. "Still cursed. But I can walk, Father. I can do this."

The look her father gave her—like a wound to her heart.

"And you, Will?"

"Ready for the journey, Your Majesty," Will replied. If anything, he seemed eager to continue.

After they cleaned up camp, Will led them back to the beach. The sand was hard-packed and ran several yards from the water to the Wood, giving them plenty of room to spread out. A cool mist hovered over the lake, shimmering like the glassy dust from her father's sword as the morning sun cleared the trees. Even in black and white, the sight was stunning.

Soon the mist evaporated, revealing fuzzy cattails bobbing along the lakeshore, and various waterfowl hunting for fish. A pair of swans paddled about the lake, their pure white wings catching the sunlight.

Philia wished she could catch a handful of that sunlight, too, and set it like a lamp in her heart. Surely this day's splendor could compensate for her bleak interior world, which the Curse had painted a foul, murky grey.

Ah, the Curse taunted, *but what will you do once I take your eyesight away?*

Philia shoved the Curse's dark suggestion aside, then hurried across the sand towards her father.

"Father, sing for me." She didn't need eyes to appreciate music. "Sing me a ballad of the Founders Seven."

The King glanced at her in surprise, then turned to their watchman. "Have we need for silence here, young Owain?"

Will gave Philia a thumbs-up, a decidedly Earth-ish gesture. They both grinned at the King's confusion.

"No need for silence at present, Your Majesty," Will clarified. "Not while we're still on the shoreline."

The King smiled down at his daughter, then began:

"Hear ye a ballad of the Founders Seven. Hear ye the tale of Ranger and Bright Eyes, Avalon's true lovers…"

Come to me, my starry night lover
Star-crossed lover, starry night lover
Come to me, my starry night lover
Come slip across the stars!

Her father's singing voice was deep and rich, with the polished quality of someone trained. Philia wondered if she would learn to sing like that, once they reached the Capital.

Voice like bells, eyes like pearls
Lips like roses, hair in curls
Come to me, my starry night lover
Come slip across the stars…

The King sang the story of a man named Ranger and a Faerie maiden named Bright-Eyes, who had lived in Avalon in the early days. And Ranger loved Bright-Eyes so much, he died for her sake on a starless night.

My love's too strong, my starry night lover,
Star-crossed lover, starry night lover,
My love's too strong, my starry night lover
For death to stop its power…

Philia imagined the final scene of the story, when Bright-Eyes and Ranger climbed a great ladder into the heavens, and their love became the Northern Lights that graced the Avalon skies.

Rise with me, my starry night lover,
Our love will light the darkness…

Her father's piercing voice echoed across the lake and through the Wood. The music swept the Curse's lies from Philia's thoughts, and quenched the burning pain in her arm. For a moment, she felt joy. For a moment, she was an ordinary girl walking in the wilds of Avalon, and life was sweet.

Around midday, Will showed them a path parallel to the lake, which passed through the forest.

"We need to do some foraging for tonight's supper, Your Highness." He gave Philia a cheerful smile. "So many treasures out in the Wood this time of the year."

And indeed, as long as Will stayed with her, showing her what plants to search for, Philia found a steady stream of edible flora. Wild mushrooms, peeking out behind fallen logs; currants and chestnuts; wild onions and other herbs.

"Look, Will!" Philia exclaimed, pointing at a patch of mushrooms. "Are those safe to eat?"

"Yes. And well done."

Although they had been walking slowly, Will leaned against a massive oak and let Philia pick the mushrooms on her own. When she returned to the oak tree, Will's complexion had gone unnaturally pale and he was clutching his chest.

"Will?"

Her watchman drooped forward without responding to her cry.

"WILL!" She dropped her basket of mushrooms and ran to assist him. "Father, come help!"

Together they guided Will to a quiet spot beside the path. He made a small choking sound when they helped him into a sitting position, but then fell silent. Perhaps ten seconds passed before she noticed he'd stopped taking in more breaths.

"Father! He can't breathe!"

"Carefully, Philia." The King placed himself behind Will, then slowly lowered him closer to the ground. About halfway down, Will's chest began rising and falling again, and his breath returned in short, stilted gasps.

"I'm—sorry," Will wheezed, clinging to Philia's coat. He coughed, which must have hurt him, because each tight exhale was punctuated with quiet, anguished cries.

Philia felt so helpless, watching Will's distress, but having no idea what was wrong or how to fix it.

"What's the matter with him, Father?"

"Overexertion, I would guess." The King adjusted his hold on Will, trying to make him more comfortable. "And his broken or misplaced ribs. Injuries we cannot see, and the tincture cannot touch." He addressed Will directly. "Where does it hurt, Owain?"

Will laid his hand over the right, middle section of his chest. "Ribs. Broken," he gasped.

Philia judged Will was more alert now, because his cries of pain had ceased. Still, his haggard expression told her he felt no better. He was *masking* his suffering.

"Philia, grab the tincture," the King ordered.

She opened their supply bag and pulled out the medicine.

"No," Will groaned, pushing the tincture away. "No, no, no. *Philia.*"

Not again. Not another "who needs the medicine more" moment. Philia wanted to blame Amaranth for this, but of course the foul villain didn't know about the tincture.

"I'm fine!" she snapped. "Just take the stupid tincture!"

Will clung to her coat and dragged himself upwards, until he found a position where he could breathe more easily. "No...medicine. Not yet. Just...need a break. Then," Three tight gasps. "I can walk again."

Philia looked at her father. Her father looked at the tincture's more than half-empty bottle.

Is there enough for both of us?

"Give him a chance to recover, my daughter," the King said finally, answering everyone's unspoken question. "If Will can then continue on without the tincture, we will delay administering it to him. We still have a long journey ahead."

They rested awhile, drinking lake water and eating from the King's supplies. After half an hour had passed, Will politely asked the King to help him to his feet. Once standing and steady, he limped back to the path, his eyes searching the undergrowth.

Philia half-expected Will to fall over, but he kept his footing.

After a moment, Will took a few steps forward, knelt on the south side of the path, and pushed aside a cluster of ferns. A stone marker stood behind the undergrowth, about two feet tall. Philia watched curiously as Will removed his glove and ran his fingers over the marker. At his gentle touch, mysterious symbols magically appeared on the stone, as if etched by an invisible hand.

"What is it?" she asked.

Will peered at the symbols another moment before answering. "It's a milestone, Your Highness. Used by the Watch and other travelers to measure their journeys." His breathing was still strained, but much improved from earlier.

The King joined them, shouldering the supply pack.

"Five miles more, Your Majesty," Will reported, gesturing at the stone.

Her father nodded, then helped Will back onto his feet. Her watchman's face was drawn but determined as he led them forward.

Philia was angry with him for refusing the tincture, but she was also afraid he might topple over on the path. She got up and walked beside him.

The farther they traveled, the more her limbs ached and burned. She began to long for the tincture herself. But when she saw Will's stoic resolve, she stayed quiet.

I don't care what Father says, she decided stubbornly. *The next time we take the tincture, Will goes first.*

They reached the river mouth by end of day. Will led them to a protected grove, walled on two sides by ledges of limestone, where the Watch often set up camp.

Will propped himself against the nearest ledge and gave the Pendragons directions. He tasked Philia with finding the fire pit, hidden under a pile of autumn leaves.

"And if you search beneath the base of that ledge, Your Majesty, you should find an ample supply of dry firewood." He coughed, his shoulders rising upwards like church steeples. "And...medicine, maybe."

The King knelt down and searched for the opening, a low-lying cave hidden by a curtain of vines and moss. He vanished behind the foliage, then reappeared a moment later with a stash of firewood and cooking supplies.

"No medicine," he told Will. "But these items will be useful."

Philia swept aside the fallen leaves, revealing a tidy firepit. It was encircled by smooth river stones, with a packed dirt floor and slots on the sides for hanging items for cooking.

"How did you know all this was here?" she asked Will.

"The Watch's secrets," he murmured mysteriously. "Assist me, Your Highness?" His words were soft with fatigue.

She came and helped him find a more restful sitting position beside the firepit.

"Much better," he sighed. "Thank you."

Under Will's patient instruction, Philia learned how to start a fire, prepare a forager's soup in the cauldron, and best of all, roast food on a stick.

"We can also use the cauldron to sanitize our bandages and medical supplies," Will explained. "And a fire will keep us warm and merry." He smiled at her, the glowing flames brightening his expression.

"Can we cook the nuts and mushrooms we've been gathering?" she asked.

"Of course." Will pointed at the foraging basket. "Those red ones first, Your Highness."

Philia searched the basket. She saw two types of mushrooms: round and light grey; and round and grey. Nothing looked "red".

"I don't know, Will. Which ones are red?" She rubbed her eyes, pretending she didn't know what the problem was.

"What do you—?" Will stopped when he noticed her embarrassment.

"Amaranth stole my colors from me," she confessed. "In the meadow, after our escape from Headquarters. Now all the world is dreary greys." She hung her head.

The King came to the firepit with a load of firewood. "He's taken your colors?" He stacked the logs, then knelt beside her. "How is that possible?"

She explained how Amaranth had manipulated the Curse marks, so that the colors had vanished, one by one, in the meadow. As she spoke, new lines of worry creased her father's face. He studied both of her eyes intently. "The healers," he whispered, his words brimming with compassion. "I pray they will have some remedy for you."

He opened his arms and she fell into them, consoled by his concern. In the grand scheme of things, surely losing her colors was a small, insignificant thing. But to Philia, it was like the first taste of death.

"I suppose I shall have to become an expert in Avalian colors now," Will told her, offering his sympathies. "Then I can describe our beautiful kingdom to you, so you won't miss anything."

She gave Will a brave smile. "I would like that. Thank you."

Her watchman helped her sort out the red mushrooms for their meal, then put her to work skewering the fungi on long switches of beech. Soon she was resting comfortably by the campfire, turning mushrooms on sticks and listening to the evening birds sing good-night. Will watched over the soup in its cauldron, and the King brought them all fresh canteens of water from a nearby spring.

When the mushrooms were ready, Philia got to take the first bite. She rolled the mushroom in her hand to cool it, then bit deep into its tender, buttery flesh.

"Mmm." Philia licked her lips. She couldn't remember eating anything so delicious, fresh from a fire. "Perfection. Feed me wild mushrooms, plant me beside some spring, and I'll grow roots."

Both Will and her father laughed at her silliness. She hadn't heard either of them laugh in a while, so she decided to keep going.

"I mean it. You two better plant me in the ground, or build me a mushroom palace here, or something." She devoured the next 'shroom on her stick. "Because I am never leaving the Sacred Wood again. Ever. Do you *hear* me?"

She flourished her fungi stick to accentuate her point. Unfortu- nately, the movement sent the last two precious mushrooms flying across the campfire, where they bopped against Will's head.

Will caught both mushrooms and laughed even louder, his eyes twinkling. "As you wish, Your Highness. Everything shall be done just as you command." He popped the mushrooms into his mouth.

"Yes." The King bowed fancifully. "We must do everything in our power to please the royal princess."

She sighed in contentment.

Will pointed excitedly above their campfire. "Look, Your Majesty and Your Highness! Berry-bides!"

Philia gazed up and saw brilliant streaks of light zipping back and forth over their heads. They swooped a few yards above the fire, then disappeared back into the forest canopy.

"What is *that*?" She covered her head with her coat. "Are they giant fireflies, or some kind of bird?"

Her watchman laughed. "Too cold for fireflies, Your Highness. Those are bats. Their wings glow, ah, fluorescent, is that the word? To attract their nighttime meal."

"Bats?" But now Philia could hear the faint flutter of their wings. They didn't glow for long stretches of time, but rather in short, vibrant bursts.

At first, she thought to ask Will what color the berry-bides were. But as Philia studied them longer, she decided it didn't matter. Her monochrome vision only enhanced their stark beauty. Instead of focusing on what she was missing, she marveled at the berry-bides' extraordinary gift of light.

The berry-bides reminded her of a conversation she'd had with Will, a few weeks ago in Scotland.

What did the founders Ranger and Bright-Eyes do, to make those shadows die? she had asked Will.

I suppose they focused on that one pinpoint of light in the darkness, he had answered.

While Philia watched the berry-bides, Will set a pan of chestnuts over the fire.

Once the nuts had roasted, the three of them settled down for their feast: wild onion and mushroom soup, served with waybread and cheese from the camp's emergency supplies; ice-cold water from the nearby spring; and plenty of currants and roasted chestnuts for dessert.

"Not bad." Will nodded his approval. "The Wood yielded its fruits to us today, Your Majesty." He ran his fingers reverently over the earth. "Thanks be to the Founders, and Avalon our mother, who feeds us."

The King made a similar gesture over the ground. "Thanks be to Avalon, our mother."

Philia considered imitating them, but she had learned by now that the Isle didn't like her Curse. After all, a few drops of her blood, cast into the earth, had conjured a dragon.

"Thanks be to the Founders," she said, keeping her hands tucked safely in her coat.

After they had eaten, Will and the King boiled water to wash and sanitize their bloody, dirt-stained clothes. The King gave Philia more of the tincture for her Curse-marks. Then they both convinced Will to place a moderate amount on his half-healed scalp, shoulder, and the area above his fractured ribs.

A quarter of the healing tincture remained.

They had each agreed to take a watch of the night: first the King, then Will, and then Philia.

That night Philia went to bed sleepy and comfortable, wrapped in her father's cloak beside the dying fire. Will settled down across from her, on the fire's north side. Just before she drifted off to sleep, a speck of light caught her eye.

A cluster of tiny, five-pointed flowers. White as milk and pure as moonlight. They had pushed their ivory heads out of the soil, exactly where her watchman's fingers had brushed the earth.

A gift from Avalon, our mother, Philia mused. *The Isle hates my touch, but it loves Will's.*

10

The Miserable Crowd

PHILIA'S DREAMS STARTED off pleasantly.

She strode along the sandy beach of Conwy Bay, searching for seashells in the early morning quiet. When she reached the ramparts of Conwy Castle, her mum was waiting on the steep, grassy hillside with a picnic. They watched the sun rise over the green Welsh mountains, munching on apples and McVite's biscuits from the filling station. Everything was peaceful and serene. She and her mother laughed, while the Curse curled up tight within her, fast asleep.

Soon the morning train rumbled into Conwy town, its rhythmic rattles and squeaks familiar and comforting—but also unbearably loud.

Loud enough to wake a sleeping Curse.

The medieval walls surrounding Conwy disappeared, replaced by an empty gravel plain, bordered only by darkness and a moody, starless sky. Her mother had vanished, leaving Philia all alone in the dreaded Curse-landscape.

She *knew* it was the Curse-landscape because the plain was riddled with the charred, swirling patterns of her Curse marks. She knew it because when her eyes adjusted to the gloom, she saw the miserable crowd.

"There she is—seize her!"

A swarm of famished, neglected children staggered towards her from every side. Their wan faces turned towards her, desperate and pleading.

"Feed us, Mother! Feed us!"

Their emaciated fingers groped at her clothes. She shrieked as a little one dug his teeth into her hand.

"Get back!" she shouted, yanking her bleeding hand from his grasp. "Why are you attacking me? I'm a prisoner here, same as you."

The kids bounced up and down, tugging at her arms, their little teeth flashing in the darkness.

"We're so hungry, Mother. Feed us, feed us!"

Philia thought of the mushrooms, and the roasted chestnuts. Perhaps the children would like those. She reached into her coat pockets, but they were maddeningly empty.

They won't actually eat me, will they?

Another child came forward, his sharp teeth ready to take a chunk out of Philia. She sidestepped away.

If they do eat me in the Curse landscape, what will happen to me in the real world? They crowded around her, small but strong in their desperation. *Will I die here, but keep going on in Avalon?*

The first boy to attack her took another bite out of her right arm. She watched in detached horror as he pulled a small chunk of flesh away with his crimson teeth. Her stomach twisted at the sight.

"Mmm, you are delicious, Princess!" he giggled, as if this was all a game to him.

But she felt the pain in her arm and the tear in her skin. She felt the other children snapping hungrily, too. For her, this was no game. No make-believe.

Run, Philia. Run!

She shouted and wildly waved her arms, hoping to frighten the children away. Two or three pulled back, just enough for her to make an escape. She squeezed past their flailing limbs and clawing hands, her face scratched and clothes torn.

Her legs slipped on the charred gravel, but she didn't stop. She'd learned a page from Will's book. She could be relentless, too.

Thuuuud-crash!

She slammed sideways into a wall of stone. She howled and rubbed her bruised shoulder, launching angry words at the slab of rock.

Somewhere in the gloom, the children giggled. "There she is! Let's eat her!"

Her heart slammed near out of her chest.

"Come on, Philly, come on…"

She probed the wall's grainy surface, searching for a crevice or crack. Any possible means of escape. But there were none.

No way out.

Philia slammed her fist against the wall. Loose pebbles rained down on her upturned face.

"Oh Avalon, our mother, come to my aid," she prayed, remembering her father and Will's devotion, and the tiny white flowers. "Before I was Cursed, I belonged to you. I came from you, and your tender, fertile soil. Remember me now in my time of need."

The children rushed towards her with loud, crunchy steps. She could smell their unwashed bodies, feel their hot breath on her skin. Their hands clamped around her limbs as one, making her their prisoner. Their feast.

Philia fought against them, but there were far too many hungry little ones. She both feared and pitied them. Could she truly blame them for wanting to eat?

Just as she braced herself for gruesome death, a deep, motherly voice resonated across the Curse-landscape.

"Philia Pendragon, you have never stopped belonging to me," the voice rumbled, shaking the ground like an earthquake. "You are still mine, and I will teach you how to feed them. My poor, miserable crowd."

Philia awoke with a start, shaking and trembling beneath her father's warm coat. She wriggled both arms out from under the jacket, examined her flesh for any sign of the children's bites. But her arm was smooth and clear, as if the Curse had never marked her.

Her heart leapt with sudden hope.

Did the dream cure me?

She rubbed her eyes and looked closer. Her skin! Pure, unblemished, and…wait.

Where her right arm had been spotless before, new spider-veined Curse-marks were appearing on her skin. Her left arm, already Curse-marked, now had dozens of new tendrils curving and diving across her flesh. The urge to scratch and rub at the itchy, burning lines grew stronger. But she knew she mustn't. It would make the marks spread even worse, like poison ivy.

With a cry of dismay, she clenched her hands into fists and slammed them into the dirt. Dust and scattered leaf fragments flew up in clouds, blinding and choking her, but she kept on pounding.

The burning was much worse now. After that horrible, vivid dream, when the Curse-landscape and its wretched inhabitants came out to play.

Feed us, Mother!

Exhausted by her mini-fit of rage, Philia curled beneath her father's cloak and drifted into a restless sleep.

When she woke up, it was almost dawn. Time for her to take the third watch.

It was Will's loud, labored breathing that had awoken her. He sat hunched beside the fire, holding his rib cage, moaning with each intake of air. He had that distant, pensive look she'd learned to associate with unmanaged pain.

"Will." She flung off her father's cloak and shuffled to his side. "What's wrong?"

"Rib cage. Sh-shoulder," Will panted. "Everything." The pre-dawn light painted his face chalk-white.

"Would taking more of the tincture help?"

"Not enough, for both of us, Your Highness," he breathed, with almost comical politeness. He spoke as if he was refusing a peppermint, rather than a powerful pain-reliever.

"Take mine, then."

"You won't make it…all the way to camp." He coughed vigorously, his lungs rattling. A feverish sheen glistened on his forehead.

"What? And you will?" She clasped his left hand in her own, ignoring the burn of her Curse-marks. "Amaranth pummeled you to bloody pulp only two days ago. The dragon wounded you three days before that." She swallowed, hating the truth of her words. "You're not exactly in tip-top shape either, Will."

He shook his head weakly.

"You're…First Princess. Much more…valuable than me."

"Will! That is *not* true." Philia's tears sprang out of nowhere. "Don't you ever say that to me again. I—I love you."

Their eyes met, and Will's hand trembled in her grasp. His whole frame softened. Everything from his face to his shoulders to his heaving chest.

"You know that I feel the same." His calm, clear voice. "Don't you, Philia?"

She blinked her tears aside, so she could take in his battered face.

"Yes. I do." She sniffed. "And I also know that you're right, darn you. I can't imagine stepping another foot towards the rendezvous, without taking an ocean of that tincture first."

The children, Will, she was too afraid to say. *They're eating me alive.*

"I'm so sorry, Philia."

She ground her teeth in frustration. "I don't know how to do this," she admitted. "I don't know how to keep going, smiling, *living,* with Death lurking at the door. How do I carry this Curse with grace?"

The first notes of birdsong reached their campsite as Will considered her question.

"Hmm. Master Raven would say, 'if Death is waiting at the door, don't let him in.' His Majesty would tell you to stay in the wild glory of the present moment."

"And you, Will?" she prompted. "What would *you* say?"

The first rays of dawn cut through the trees, washing Philia in light and Will in shadow. A songbird offered a melancholy tune as it soared overhead with a flash of silvery wings.

A nightingale, Philia thought. *The one that means Will.*

"I would say...even if you're dying, you're also living," Will answered. "Feeling all this pain means you're still alive and free. So...I would say, embrace it. *Love* it, even, Your Highness."

"*Love* my Curse?"

"Love that you still live to fight against it—that you still draw breath. That you and I are sitting right here, bemoaning our wounds, sure, but also enjoying the loveliest sunrise I've ever seen in this stretch of the Wood." He turned his head, his noble cheekbones catching the light. The more he spoke to her, the clearer his words became. "By the grace of the Founders, we have this morning."

Will shifted closer. The full pine scent of him filled her with new and poignant longing.

"Your Highness. Since we're both still alive, and also miserable," Will glanced down shyly, "Perhaps a kiss might cheer us?"

She hesitated. It was difficult, to the extreme, for her to think about something as romantic as a kiss, when the Curse had her trapped within its prison of pain. *What if my kiss hurts him?*

"If you don't want to, I understand." Will shifted nervously, rubbing the hilt of his sword. "It's just, sharing a kiss with you…it reminds me that all of this," he gestured at his injuries, "has a purpose. That it's worth it."

Philia nodded. "The watchman deserves his wages."

Will shook his head fiercely. "I—I want to be *more* than a watchman to you, Philia Pendragon. I want to share my whole life with you."

His whole life…

Suddenly, Philia understood why Will had taught her how to forage for mushrooms, cook over the campfire, and listen for loons and wolves and nightingales. He was opening up his life to her.

He took her hands, kissed them, and laid something soft and fragrant in her palms. She glanced down and gasped. He'd filled them with those same white, five-pointed flowers from the night before.

"Come, Philia, see my world." The wind caught his dark blonde hair and sent it cascading across his face. "See how very good it is."

She brushed his wild strands aside, came so close their noses touched. At this range, she could feel his uneven breaths, and when she kissed him, she tasted the salty tears on his lips. She wondered if he was like her, and sometimes cried without knowing why.

They both had plenty to weep about. A villain, a dragon, and an evil Curse. Death's jaws yawning wide around them, and not enough tincture or antidotes in all the world to stop it.

Love it, she thought. *Love how all this evil has forged for me so great a lover.*

"Philia," he sighed. "I feel I could endure anything at all, if it would win me your heart."

"Yes, Will." She affirmed him with gentle kisses. "I know you could, I know it." She sighed. "And I feel I could endure anything at all, if it meant I could be won by you, *Llewgalon*. My Lionheart."

II

A Parting of Ways

When the morning sun climbed above the tree line, Will, Philia, and the King sat in a circle, examining what remained of their medical supplies.

There wasn't much to examine: three sanitized bandage rolls; two jars of antiseptic and fever reducers; and one tincture bottle with a single dose left.

Will's gaze drifted constantly to Philia. *She loves me.* He breathed in, feeling the awful shudder of his broken ribs pressing against his lungs. *She loves me,* He breathed out, tasting the sweetness of her lips. *I know a girl named Philia Pendragon, and she loves me.*

However, accompanying this awesome knowledge was Philia's rapid decline. Her body posture this morning was restless and agitated. At first she had engaged in their planning for the day's journey; but now her gaze had wandered off and she no longer seemed aware of her surroundings.

"It's the effects of the Curse," the King explained to him, with a worried frown. "The longer she has it, the more the Curse will drag her into its shadow-landscape. Each time she passes into that land-scape, her Curse also physically spreads." He placed Philia's scarred hand within his own. "Thus the fresh marks on her arms."

"Shall we give Philia the last dose of tincture now, Your Majesty?" Will asked.

Beside them, the Princess muttered and flinched, as if being as-saulted by invisible hands.

"Without the tincture," the King countered, "can you make it to the rendezvous?"

A nightingale chirped its morning melody, piercing and sweet.

"No, Your Majesty." Will had heard the wolves howling through the night. "The Albine wolves will return once you con-tinue to the rendezvous. With speed, you can outrun them. I would slow you down." He spoke the truth almost happily. He'd promised to endure great things for Philia. Now an opportunity had been placed before his path.

"You wish me to leave you here, alone in the Wood?" The King repeated. His good face hardened into sharp, worried edges. Dread lingered in his turquoise eyes.

"Yes, Your Majesty. The tincture can't set my ribs back in place, and neither of us have the skill to mend my injuries. I need a healer's care to continue, and the only place we can find one is at the ren-dezvous." He paused, out of breath from his explanation. His ribs ached and his shoulder—well, he tried not to think about it. Will didn't need to be a Healer Proficient to know his shoulder wounds were going bad.

The King nodded. "What you say makes sense, Owain. It would be better for you to stay here and rest, in this safe place, while I go ahead with the Princess. I can send a Watch medic team to help you."

"Thank you, Your Majesty," Will answered, surprised and re-lieved that the King had agreed with his plan.

"However," the King continued, "The other issue is your shoulder."

Will looked away. He had hoped the King wouldn't bring it up.

"Let us administer the tincture to the Princess now," the King commanded. "And then I shall examine the wounds beneath your armor."

Will spread the tincture liberally over Philia's arms, noting her visible relief with satisfaction. She had fallen unconscious some time before, and while the tincture did not wake her, it did return the color to her bronze cheeks and cooled her fever. He wrapped some of the bandaging from the King's supply kit down her arms, securing the fabric at the wrists.

They laid Philia to rest on the King's cloak and a bed of fallen leaves.

Next, the King studied Will with a frown. "What am I to do with you, Owain? If I lay you on your stomach, it will crush your ribs. If I lay you on your back, it will hurt your shoulder."

"Examine me as I am, Your Majesty. I'll sit here and lean against the firepit if I need to."

The King removed layer after layer of clothing—cloak, tunic, armor, padding—until at last he reached Will's bandaged shoulder.

Will shivered as the cold hit his skin, his left arm tense and rigid on the firepit. He counted the line of river stones within his view—one, two, three…ten, eleven, twelve.

"Brace yourself," the King warned. "I'm removing yesterday's bandages now."

Will nodded and closed his eyes.

First the King doused the bandages with water, to help release them from Will's skin.

He gasped as the King slowly peeled the bandage away. The

cloying stench of infection made both of them gag.

My wounds have gone bad. Will flinched as the King worked the bandage off his shoulder. *The smell will attract scavengers.* Hot, purple pain tore through his dragon wounds. *Vultures. Foxes. Wolves.*

Will thought he heard the King swear, but he must have imagined it.

"Your shoulder wounds have become infected." The King cleaned his shoulder with a damp cloth. "Did you know?"

Will shook his head. He wanted to lie down, but when he leaned forward, his ribs stabbed into his lungs.

"No," he gasped. "This is new."

"This is magic," the King corrected. "Ancient Dragon magic. You need a healer straightaway, Owain." He opened the jar of antiseptic and poured most of it over Will's wounds.

Will cried out and clutched the firepit until his knuckles turned white. It took long minutes for the stinging to subside into a manageable ache. Meanwhile, Will's body trembled and his skin grew clammy with cold sweat.

The King offered him water and a bite of *gwemka* bread, which helped.

Once he had wrapped Will's shoulder with the last of the bandages, the King helped Will into his tunic. The Faerie armor he folded and laid beside Will.

"I fear the armor would place too much pressure on your shoulder," the King explained.

Will heard a faint wolf cry, and an answering howl. He wanted to tell the King to leave. He needed to tell him. Yet he also feared being left alone.

"Please, Your Majesty, you and the Princess should go. I am sorry I cannot join you." He gave the King directions and lent him his compass and a hunting knife. "You will make it there, Your Majesty. Follow the map and stay on the Path."

"I will send healers," the King promised. "Watch for my people, coming from the south at dusk."

King Bran wrapped his cloak around Philia and lifted her into his strong arms. Will could tell she was truly ill, because she made no protest when the King told her they were going on alone.

"Your Majesty?" Will asked. "May I offer Philia my protection before you go?"

The King's expression softened. "That is your right, as an Owain."

"We are honored to serve the house of Pendragon." Will remembered the words from something he often heard his father say, back at Gwynedd Castle.

The King knelt and laid Philia beside him, so that Will could place his hand over her forehead. Her open eyes looked straight through Will, as if she wasn't seeing him at all.

"I, William Madoc Owain," he began, "give my protection to Philia Pendragon…from any and all dangers," he paused to catch his breath, "from now until the time of my death. May the loyalty of my ancestors, and the grace of the Founders, hold me to this oath."

His hand slipped from Philia's forehead. Relief rushed through him. He had done what he could.

The King now laid his brown hands on both of them. "May the grace of the Founders preserve you, this day and forever, from all evil influences, from fire and water, illness and infection, curses and death. And may we swiftly meet again, to partake of the fruit of the earth, and sing all the ballads of the Founders Seven."

"May we sing them boldly," Will said, giving the customary response. Philia said nothing.

12

The Curse Worse Than Death

PHILIA WAS DREAMING, and there was no escape. The Curse kept her prisoner, and no outside force or internal thought could bend or break its tyrannic reign.

She sat on broken stones in a dry, empty riverbed, while the miserable children played court about her feet. They were exactly like the real children Philia knew. They shifted quickly between kindness and cruelty. They competed for the closest spots to Philia, and for her undivided attention.

In one significant way, however, these children stood apart: they thirsted for her lifeblood. Weeping scars from their bites and scratches riddled Philia's skin, where the children had torn off her sleeves and gnawed her bare arms.

All except little Tamlyn, the girl Philia had helped on the night Ewan gave her the Curse. When the others came to feast on Philia's blood, Tamlyn fended them off with her tiny little fists.

"No! You shouldn't eat her!" Tamlyn said stoutly, pushing the other children away. "She's my friend."

A ravenous boy darted around Tamlyn, snapped his teeth into Philia's wrist. Philia cried out and shook him off, clutching her bleeding wrist to her chest.

The little boy giggled, crimson on his teeth. "But she tastes so delicious!"

And the hungry children kept coming, far too many for Philia and Tamlyn to fend off on their own. Many more partook of her "delicious" lifeblood.

In the Curse landscape, she could endure such things for interminable stretches of time, without fainting or perishing or bleeding out. If they bit too deep, her arm healed back to its original state, ready to be gnawed again.

I never knew, she mused stoically, *how much a person could suffer without dying from it.*

Indeed, when she did wake, the only scars that translated back into the physical world were the puckered Curse marks crossing her body, and the burning sensation that roared through her veins.

These children could, in fact, devour her interminably, with minimal physical consequence, for days on end. Here in the Curse landscape Philia knew hunger and thirst, but these longings never killed her. Rather, they grew and grew, without ever ending her.

The Curse worse than death. That's what it means.

But she wasn't about to let Lord Amaranth and his stupid Curse win. Not after her father and Will had sacrificed so much for her survival these past three days.

During her last stretch of consciousness, she had watched her father and Will administer the last of the healing tincture over her Curse marks. She'd seen the worry on her father's face, and the underlying pain in Will's weary eyes. They were giving up so much to protect her. They hadn't failed her, and she refused to fail them by succumbing to the crowd.

I heard you, Father, she wanted to tell the King. *I know what you are enduring for my sake. I heard your blessing and Will's oath to protect me. I hear. I know. I care.*

Since she could no longer move or speak, the only way to express her gratitude was to live.

And so she had set aside her hunger and thirst, perched herself meekly on a smooth grey river-stone, and invited the children to gather at her feet.

"Listen, children!" she called, extending her raw, bleeding arms in invitation. "Gather round, and I shall tell you a high tale of Scotland and Avalon."

Didn't that work for Arabian Nights? *Surely it can work for me, too,* she decided stubbornly.

"Once upon a time," she began, projecting her voice as her high school drama instructor had taught her, "in a fair green world, both impossibly far and incredibly close to us, a young princess sought a way home to her kingdom. She had lost her mother in a dreadful storm off the Irish Sea, a place quite like the Western Sea—teeming with codfish and sharks and sea dragons.

"The Princess and her mother, the Queen, had set out in their wee fishing boat before the rain began. Thunder rolled and lightning snapped, but neither the rain nor the storm could deter them. For that very night, Arthur's Gateway would open over the Irish Sea, offering them a way home to Avalon at last. With a magical piece of glass called an iPhone, the exiled Princess could scry through the heavy storm clouds, to see the stars as Arthur saw them, when he sailed to Avalon after the last battle. Those same stars acted as noble beacons, guiding the Princess onward to both her kingdom and her father."

The children paused their devouring. They settled down, cross-legged in the empty riverbed, to catch Philia's every word.

"Midnight struck. The gateway opened. It was invisible to the Princess's eyes, but real. So very real. Their stormy journey was destined for success. The Princess extended her arms over the cerulean sea, ready to cross the threshold into another world."

A long silence. Philia kept it, using the moment to meet the eyes of as many of the children as possible. What words would speak best to them? What might distract or even encourage them? Surely this Curse-landscape was not some endless hell. Surely there was some way to escape.

"But that fateful night, the storm was too much. Waves as fierce and tall as mountain giants battered the hull of their fishing vessel. One, two, three monstrous, ice-cold waves. The water pummeled the Princess' body and tossed her out into the open sea."

Tamlyn gasped in horror. Several children joined her. The others murmured nervously, but their attention remained fixed on Philia. Or rather, on her words.

Ah. I have finally found another way to feed them, Philia considered. *I shall feed them my stories.*

"It was her noble mother, Queen Vivien, who saved her," Philia continued in a stage whisper. "Her dear, tender mother drew the Princess out of the water, back towards their listing boat. The women's hope was rekindled. They would cross the gateway. They would make it to Avalon. They would be home in the arms of the King before the next dawn blessed the worlds with its healing rays." She swallowed back her sorrow and regret. "But then, alas! The fourth wave hit."

She had their attention now. Each boy and girl sat captivated, longing for her next words, longing for something real outside their impenetrable misery and darkness. She would give it to them. She *wanted* to give it to them...

"Philia," her father's voice called from the physical world. "Philia, come back to me. Speak to me, or I will lose all hope, and fail even in this simple task of carrying you. Speak, my daughter, or I will perish from this unbearable grief."

The King, she thought. *He is calling.*

"Father?" she answered. But merely saying his name did not change her predicament. The children chomped their lips and watched her with greedy impatience.

The story, Philia. Finish the story.

"The crown of the Princess' head dashed the boat's hull, leaving a long scar," she traced the faint pink line above her ear. "The boat capsized, and the Princess and Queen watched in horror as their vessel slipped beneath the waves. All around, the night loomed dark as pitch."

"Philia," her father called again, his voice desperate. Hopeless.

I'm coming, Father! I'll find my way back.

"...but this wasn't the end," she continued aloud. "The Princess didn't go home to Avalon that day, or the next day, or the next. For months it seemed she wouldn't get what she wanted: her father and her homeland."

Tamlyn inched forward to sit at Philia's feet. Her ebony eyes watched Philia with rapt attention.

"But the Princess kept searching," Philia continued. "She made new allies and friends. She met two brothers, from Avalon. One brother risked his life to protect her; the other gave her the Curse worse than death."

She held up her palm, revealing the sideways "S" pattern carved into her skin.

The children stirred restlessly. Their little heads bobbed up and down, and then as one, they raised their hands.

The Curse of the Way. The Curse, the Curse, repeated over and over, from one tiny palm to the next. So many little victims. Who had cursed these innocent ones, and why?

It's not right. It's not fair.

"The Princess wanted the Way into Avalon, but not its Curse. She wanted the joy, and not the pain. Yet she received both."

Tamlyn waved with the rest of the crowd, then cradled her head against Philia's knee. "I'm glad the Princess was Cursed. Because now you are here, *seeing* me. Seeing us."

The children covered their bloody faces with Curse-marked hands and cried. "No one has even seen us before. No one has ever wanted us here."

Philia's heart expanded within her chest—a sweet, excruciating pain. Like her soul was making room.

"Who are you?" she asked the crowd.

"We are Arthur's children."

"And who am I?"

They smiled at her, hope bright on their faces.

"You are our *mother*."

She leaned way, way down to kiss their dirty cheeks and tangled hair. They needed stories, yes. But what these children longed for, most of all, was *love*.

And this was a thing so simple, Philia could give it to them.

"Philia, come to me!" she heard the King cry.

Before the Princess answered, she pulled little Tamlyn onto her lap. "I see you, Tamlyn. I will *never* forget you."

No sooner had she embraced Tamlyn, when both the little girl and the Curse-landscape vanished from view. The King was carrying her through a sun-dappled pine grove, in the wilds of Avalon, and it was morning.

Something about that small act had pushed Philia back into the physical world.

"Father, I'm here!" She pressed her aching forehead into his soft velvet tunic. His chain mail clinked pleasantly as he trudged forward, with Philia locked securely in his arms. "See, Father? I'm still here, with you."

The King cried out when he heard her.

He staggered towards a flat rock adjacent to the forest path, then sank down onto its solid surface. He repeated her name—*Philia, Philia*—and rocked her back and forth like a child. The King christened her face with his tears, blessed her burning hands with the gentlest kisses.

This was the love that the children had needed; she would shore it all up within her, for when the Curse returned again.

"Philia Branwen," he proclaimed. "I see you." The same words he'd said when Philia returned to Avalon, and he first recognized her face. The words that meant she belonged to him, and to the noble house of Pendragon.

"I'm here, Father," she answered. "Still seeing you."

At least for now. At least for this one, unrepeatable moment.

The sun kissed their faces, and a nightingale chirped its heartbreaking melody. Wind stroked her hair, and sighed softly through the pines. It was the present moment, and within it, Philia felt so *alive.*

Her father held her close as he rose back to his feet. "We cannot stay here. Will said the wolves are closing in behind us." He took his first step forward, his jaw set. "And it is only in Avalon's capital that we have any hope for a cure."

Philia turned her face into his chest, willing her body to grow light as a feather in her father's arms. Imagining she was no princess, but a silver-tipped nightingale, tearing through the Curse's bonds and soaring high towards freedom.

13

Wolf Moon

THE WOLVES ARRIVED just as the afternoon shadows lengthened towards the east.

Their slow approach had given Will enough time to strap his remaining belongings around his waist, bury the campfire with clods of earth, and drag his broken body to higher ground. He had left some of his soiled bandages by the firepit, to throw the Albines off his scent. Or, at the very least, to divide their attention.

He wouldn't have to fend the wolves off for long. The King had promised to send aid before dusk, less than an hour away.

Will propelled himself forward with his legs until he reached the vast root system of an ancient beech. Its smooth grey roots stretched majestically across Will's path, a natural bridge between trees. He smiled when he heard the cheerful murmurs of the woodland spring, which he knew lay nestled behind it.

Get yourself over these roots. Wait by the stream.

It wouldn't stop the wolves forever, but it would delay them.

The swift pattering of pawprints made Will halt and slowly turn his head. Sure enough, he spotted a lone Albine wolf some twenty yards away.

The Wood's Albine wolves were lean and swift. Although relatively small for Avalian wolves—less than three feet in height, and four feet in length—they were the Wood's deadliest predators. They had an acute sense of hearing and smell, great intelligence, and almost always attacked as a pack.

More footsteps. Will froze, spotting two more wolves coming up on the first wolf's left side. He heard pants and growls on the right, and tightened the grip on one of his two hunting knives. A bow and arrow would have served him better, but Will couldn't pull the string back with his wounded shoulder. The hunting knife would have to do.

The first wolf surveyed the clearing, then ran his nose along the ground, stopping at the spot where the King had cleaned Will's wounds. Will was certain he had left plenty of interesting smells there.

The wolf crept along a little farther, sniffing and salivating at the mouth. That was the greatest danger with the Albines. Their acidic saliva could eat holes through a man's flesh, if left untended.

As the wolf sniffed his discarded bandages, Will grunted and hauled himself over the massive tree root. He swallowed a cry as he slipped over the top and slammed his head against a tree root. Pain rippled down his spine in unforgiving waves. His breath hitched in his throat, and for a moment he forgot everything else.

Why did I send the King and Princess away? he thought miserably. *I'm going to die out here.*

The wolves, he reminded himself. *You need to fight them.*

Branches snapped. Will held still; sure enough, he could hear a wolf whimpering.

"The snare," Will breathed, his chest rising and falling with the effort of staying alive. He made a face. Now he'd have to wriggle upward, to check that his snare had indeed worked.

He peeked one cautious eye over the tree root. Sure enough, the first wolf had gotten trapped by the loop of rope Will had hidden beneath his bandages.

One wolf down. Only five, six? More to go.

Good thing Will had a few more tricks up his sleeve.

He didn't hate the majestic creatures; on the contrary, he admired their tenacity and grace. They were small and scrappy, just like him.

However, they also planned to eat him for dinner. So when a second wolf leapt out of nowhere into the clearing, Will hurled his hunting knife directly into its throat. The knife landed exactly where Will had aimed it. The creature staggered forward a few steps closer to Will, frothing at the mouth and leaking orange-red blood from its throat. Then it collapsed to one side, whimpered once, and fell still.

Two down. Will slumped against the smooth bark of the beech tree, panting for air. His broken ribs made each breath so painful, Will could barely motivate himself to keep pumping in more air. Maybe it would be better to stop trying. Maybe it would be better to just fade away.

No, Will. Don't give up!

Help was coming, and Philia had told him she loved him.

Dusk was fast approaching. During daylight, Will had a chance against these wolves. Once the night rolled in, however, they would have another advantage over him: Albine wolves could see perfectly in the dark.

Three, four, five wolves loped into the clearing. Two went to the ensnared wolf and started gnawing at its bonds. Clever creatures. The other three sniffed at the wolf Will had just killed. They howled, one by one, then turned their dark, hungry eyes towards Will. They looked underfed, and thus, more dangerous.

Will lowered himself from the wolves' sight. Crunch, crunch— the sound of pawprints. Soon they were so close, he could smell their wild, canine scent.

Certainly, they could smell him, too.

He propped himself on his left side and kicked out his feet. His boots connected with a long strip of wood, but it didn't budge. He tried a second time, passed out from the exertion, and woke to find an Albine peering down at him from the massive tree root. The wolf panted and growled.

Come, my brothers, Will imagined the wolf saying. *Dig your jaws into this fresh piece of meat.*

"Sorry," Will gasped. "Not today."

He dragged in a final breath, then kicked the strip of wood a third time.

This time, the lever lifted.

It began as a trickle, then a gurgle, then a torrent of spring water emptying out into the clearing. The Watch had long ago constructed the lever-operated dam as a contingency plan for the campsite. The lever shifted the pile of river stones, allowing the spring water to flow freely, at rushing speed.

Will listened to the wolves' panicked howls as the water swept them up in its powerful current.

All the same, it was too late for Will. The other wolves might be hampered by the flow of rushing water, but the Albine perched on the log was out of harm's way. It leapt down into the hollow between the beech roots and crawled onto Will's legs.

Will seized his second knife with trembling hands. But in these close quarters, it wouldn't help him. The wolf would gouge his throat out first.

The slender wolf growled deep inside its chest, its saliva dripping on Will's cloak with a hiss.

But before it could lunge for his throat, an arrow whizzed over the tree roots and sank into the beast's side. The wolf whined and fell to one side without fanfare. Within seconds, it was dead.

A perfect shot, Will thought in admiration.

On the other side of the tree roots, hidden from Will's view, he heard the whizzing of two more arrows, followed by two more animals whimpering in pain.

Who is this archer? He's excellent.

A cheerful whistle echoed across the clearing, and then the magenta rays of sunset outlined Will's rescuer. The marksman leapt onto the massive roots of the ancient beech and peered down at Will. He was tall and athletic, his skin a warm golden color, and a mischievous grin played on his lips. He wore jeans, a plaid flannel shirt, and a voluminous black leather jacket that Will instantly recognized, for it had once belonged to Sir Hamish Lee.

"Dylan?" Will stammered in disbelief. "Dylan Lee?"

The young man startled when Will called his name. He surveyed Will for a long moment, as if trying to piece his identity together.

"It's me, Dyl," Will gasped. "Owain..."

"Owain...*Will?*" Dylan exploded into a colorful arrangement of Scottish profanities. "Damn it, Will, please tell me that's not you under that bloody" –more curse words– "heap of bruises." He sprung lightly down from the tree root, swept the dead wolf aside with his boot, and was at Will's side in a moment.

Will grinned. It was his Scottish friend, the bold and daring Dylan Lee. The last time Will had seen him, Dylan had been lying unconscious across a riding saddle, while his treacherous father Hamish tried negotiating his escape from the King's Watch. Hamish had gotten away, using his Faerie gift of flight to whisk himself and his entire family out of the Watch's hands.

But they must not have gone too far, Will mused. *If Dylan's still here in the Sacred Wood, a week later.*

"You're here," Will said in disbelief. "You're alive."

"Aye. Which I can hardly say of you, you noble eejit." Dylan pulled out a thermos and helped Will take in some water. He drank gratefully, his head clearing a little. "What skiving pain in the arse did you choose to do battle with this time?"

"Lord Amaranth." Will shuddered.

Dylan stopped pouring water and stared. "You're serious."

He peered back at Dylan with a frown. "Honestly, you don't look so great yourself, friend."

Dylan had a spectacular black eye, a long, angry red scrape across his cheek, and bruises along his neckline to rival Will's.

"A parting gift from my father," Dylan said, with a shrug. "We had, ah, a bit of a disagreement."

This was such a gross understatement from what must have actually happened, Will couldn't help but grin.

Aren't we a sorry pair.

"Hey! What are you smirking about? None of this is exactly amusing." Dylan gestured vaguely around the clearing. "Dead wolves lying about, a creepy old forest, two blokes with ugly faces, no YouTube..."

Will laughed. His laughter sounded like a dying cat, but it still made him feel better. Seeing Dylan made him feel better.

"Welcome to Avalon, friend."

"Shut up," Dylan said good-naturedly. "And turn over, so I can see what you're hiding under those bandages."

Will tried turning on his own, then passed out cold for his troubles. Dylan's urgings jolted him awake.

"Good God, you scared me to death. Sorry. Let *me* turn you over and check your bandages."

It was difficult. Will didn't want to frighten his friend again, but the process of rolling onto his stomach sent wave after wave of agony through his bad shoulder and ribs. He moaned softly, both tears and sweat stinging his eyes. When Dylan finally succeeded in flipping him, Will couldn't hide his cries of distress.

"Haggises and hounds, Owain," Dylan muttered. "Tell me you're not dying or something."

"Watch...coming," Will said through gritted teeth. "Help. Medicine. Waiting."

Dylan ignored him. "No. No waiting. Right now, *I* am your help. Because, you see, I nicked a few treasures from Dad's medical bag. Sterile bandages, for example. And pain meds."

"Th–thank you," Will managed to say.

Dylan placed a comforting hand on Will's arm, then got to work cleaning his shoulder and wrapping it with his father's bandages. He also gave Will some Tylenol. The medicine cleared his thoughts and made it considerably easier for him to breathe.

Will soon felt well enough to comment on Dylan's impeccable timing. "Perhaps the purpose of all this was for us to find each other," he said, smiling at his friend. "Laurie is going to be ecstatic."

Dylan, who had been drinking from his thermos, choked and sprayed water all over their hiding place. "Laurie is here?! How did she–is she alright? Laurie is *here*?"

Will hadn't meant to startle Dylan. He had simply forgotten that Dylan didn't know who else had come through the Way.

"Laurie came through the Way first, when she was protecting Philia from Ewan at Faerie's Hollow. The Princess and Her Majesty passed through as well."

Dylan's hazel eyes glinted sharp in the sun's setting rays.

"You said the King left you here in the Wood, to take Philia to the healers." He nodded at Will's shoulder. "Yet you yourself need a healer, too. So what drove the good king to abandon you to the wolves?"

Will closed his eyes. "The King didn't know about the wolves. Exactly."

His companion took another chug of water, gazed out into the gathering dark. "I see. But... *you* knew they were coming?"

Will took a deep breath, something that would have been impossible for him to do minutes ago, before Dylan gave him the painkillers.

"Yes," he admitted. "I did know."

"You knew the wolves were coming and that you were too injured to fend them off. But you *still* urged the King to leave you out in the Wood alone?"

Will hesitated, realizing how wrong it sounded when Dylan put it that way. "Yes."

Dylan slammed his fist into the nearest tree root, then ran his fingers through his dark hair. After a moment's pause, he turned to face him.

"Owain. Will. Answer me, and don't you dare lie. Does part of you enjoy suffering? Does a part of you, deep down inside, in *here*—" he jabbed at Will's heart— "just want to die?"

Will stared at his friend, stunned. A torrid mix of emotions churned through him, murky and undefined. Shock, yes, and anger. But also, a morbid despair.

"No, Dylan. I *hate* being this weak and incompetent. I hate having all this training inside my brain, going to waste, while my shoulder rots away."

"Your shoulder is *not* rotting away—"

"I didn't ask for any of this!" Will interrupted, panting for breath. "I feel pain, the same as you. I want to live. I *need* to. But..." He had been about to say it, but now the words got stuck in his throat.

Dylan waited patiently for his answer.

"Philia is dying, Dyl. The night we came through Faerie's Hollow, Ewan gave her the Curse of the Way." Dylan stayed quiet, but Will could feel the shock rolling off of him. "The healers gave her an antidote, but every drop of it got destroyed by Amaranth. We just barely escaped him, three days past. And Dylan... the Curse. It's—" he stammered, lost for words. "Philia has become so sickly and frail. And haunted, like she's seeing horrible things that we can't see."

Will sucked in another breath. It hurt to tell Dylan, but it also felt good. This had been bottled up inside of him since the night he came through the Way. Now at least his grief was going somewhere.

He drew himself upward, mustering all the dignity of a Gwynedd prince.

"I *do* want to live, Dylan. I just want Philia to live more. And today, she needed a healer more than me."

The night sounds of the Wood intruded on their silence. An owl hooted in the distance, and a restless breeze tangled through the trees.

"Do they have a way to cure her?" Dylan asked, over the rattle of dying leaves. "Out there, in the Capital?"

Will shook his head. "I don't know. If she can last until spring, they can harvest the correct flora to make her a new antidote."

Next spring. Yes. That was it. They would just have to keep Philia alive until spring, and all would be well. It *would* be well. It had to be.

"I love her, Dylan," he spoke plainly. "I'd die before I'd let her die."

"She's *my* fierce cousin," Dylan answered protectively. "I've known her since she was a wee babe. So you can't take all the heroic glory for yourself, mate. I'm going to fight to save her, too."

"Help all you want. I'm not a jealous lover," Will joked. "Besides, I'm completely useless at present. Can't even load an arrow in my bow." He said it lightly, but in truth, he felt ashamed. He knew it was the price he had to pay to win their escape from Headquarters. But it infuriated him all the same.

"Hmm," Dylan said, stretching out his legs. "Not thinking a bow and arrow is going to be much use against an evil Curse. Although if it was, Dylan the angelic archer would be happy to take care of things for you." He patted the bow and quiver on his lap.

"Where did you get those?" Will asked, happy to change the subject.

"They're mine, actually. My dad brought it with him, along with many other useful things." Dylan swept his hair out of his mischievous face. "One moment, I was with my dad in his study, at the Academy. The next thing I remember, I was waking up in the forest primeval, like one of Robin Hood's merry men." He frowned. "Whatever my dad gave to me, it left me with a God-awful headache. Still bothering me now, a week later." He rubbed both palms into his skull.

"Are you sure that headache isn't from the tussle you had with your father?" Will asked.

"Aye," his friend agreed. "I did chew the low-life out for shipping me off to Avalon without asking. I lost my temper, Dad lost his temper, and…well." He sighed. "That night I headed out into the Wood alone, to clear my stupid, hotheaded brain. But I got lost."

Will gazed on Dylan with empathy. His valiant friend must have been terrified.

"Then I heard the wolves. Something inside me said, 'Dylan boy, someone out there needs your help.' I followed the wolves, and they led me straight to you."

Will listened in wonder. "It's like the Wood itself drew us back together."

How mysterious!

"Now, if you really do want to live, Owain, prove it," Dylan ordered him. "Get some shut eye while I bury these wolf carcasses. They reek."

"Careful how you handle them," Will warned. "Their saliva is acidic and can burn through human skin."

"Lovely."

"And also, make sure they're completely dead."

"How do I do that?"

"Cut off their heads," Will explained. "Then throw them in a pile to burn them."

Dylan looked like he might be sick. "Hey, why are you smiling?"

"No reason. Just thankful I'm too weak to help you."

Will rested his head against a bit of tree root, then drifted asleep to the pleasant music of Dylan's grumblings.

When the Watch finally came to rescue them, the night was full come, the moon full risen, and the wolves fully immolated on Dylan's makeshift funeral pyre. If Dylan had not come for him, Will would certainly have perished before the Watch's arrival. His appearance on the scene, at Will's greatest moment of need, was like an unexpected turn in the old tales of the Founders. A welcome grace, completely unlooked for.

Will had spent the last three days in the Wood, feeling all but crushed by the weight of his mission: to bring the King and Princess to safety. The demands of his mission meant that, by the end, there had been no one left to protect Will himself.

But that's not so, he mused, as Master Raven and Dylan lifted Will onto a canvas stretcher. *Someone was watching out for me, and for Dylan, too, the entire time.*

When his own strength had failed him, his beloved Wood, and Avalon herself, had come to his aid.

"Thanks be to Avalon, our mother," he whispered, his hand dangling over the stretcher and reaching towards the earth. His fingers had just grazed the forest bed, when Raven took his hand and pressed it to his bowed forehead. The Avalian plea for pardon.

"Forgive me, Owain, a hundred times over, for coming so late," Master Raven said, his face downcast. "The King did not find us at the rendezvous until early evening—the Wood paths had shifted overnight. Amaranth's doing, most likely. It took all of my considerable watchman's skills to trace the path back to you."

"Forgiveness granted," Will whispered. He glanced between Raven and Dylan, whose faces glowed in the light of Dylan's Earth-made torch. The family resemblance was remarkable. "In any case, it turned out well. Your nephew Dylan rescued me just in time."

Both Raven and Dylan startled.

"Uncle… Raven?" Dylan said first, hesitating over the words. He squinted in the torchlight at the grizzled watch master.

"Dylan Lee? My godson?" the watchman's expression remained guarded.

"You can trust him, Master," Will added hastily. "Dylan's nothing like his father."

Dylan growled low in his throat. "Aye, nothing like that back-stabbing, treacherous, black-hearted bastard," he said, tossing in a few choice curse words to drive home his point. "It's an honor to meet you again, Uncle."

Raven shook Dylan's offered hand. "It's an honor."

The two Lees said something else, but Will's fever was rising, and his rotten shoulder throbbed with fresh intensity. The sound of pain drowned out all other words and thoughts. He shivered on the stretcher, flinching from remembered blows.

"Hang on, son," Raven told him. "The worst is over now."

Will nodded slightly. He experienced a horrid shifting motion, followed by a strange sense of suspension.

The stretcher rising, he thought.

"Don't die, Owain."

And he could not tell if it was Raven or Dylan who said these last words, or neither of them, or both together. By this time, every sound and sense had been tossed like pebbles into the surf, waves pounding every part of him, inside, out, into cruelly polished glass.

When the waves had finished with him, Fiona appeared again, as she had done each night since Will's encounter with Amaranth. She waded the storm-tossed shallows of his splintered dreams, her emerald dress swirling about her legs.

Will addressed her before she could speak. "Mama!" he called. "Why is this happening to me? To us?" He shouted and staggered through the shallows to reach her, but she remained just out of his grasp. "Why have they done this to Philia?"

The pain from both his wounds and his heart threatened to overwhelm him. He knelt in the waves and wept in misery.

"*My son.*" He startled as he felt her hand, soft and cool, on his shoulder. "*You love her.*"

"Y-yes, Mama." A fresh wave bowled him over, but Fiona steadied him.

"*You mirror each other now—pain for pain. Blow for blow.*" Fiona's deep red hair rustled over her shoulder, weaving wildly across her face. "*A sign of your growing bond.*" Her grey-green eyes welled with pity. "*But it will not always be so.*"

Her touch on his fevered skin was an oasis in the desert. "*Have faith, my child. When the time is ripe, come and find me.*" Her face glowed with inner radiance. "*I will show you—*"

Her words cut off abruptly. A searing pain riddled through Will's dragon wounds, like a fiery rod dipped in its venom. It pierced through his entire body, sucking every shattered bit of him into deepest darkness.

When Will opened his eyes again, Raven and Dylan were hauling his stretcher into a large white tent, filled with injured people and the astringent scent of antiseptic.

A field infirmary, Will guessed.

Avalian glass lamps hung from strings overhead, glowing gold, pale blue, and yellow green. Colors thought to promote healing, Will remembered from watch-medic training.

Seven rows of string. Ten lamps on each row. And lined in cots beneath the glass orbs, perhaps fifty patients. Most had burns or broken bones, although a few had puncture wounds like Will's.

"What happened to them?" Dylan asked, with concern.

"The Navahogg," Raven answered.

"A Nava-what?"

"An ancient she-dragon. The same thing that sunk its venomous fangs into Owain."

"Wait! In the past week, Will has fought off Lord Amaranth *and* a dragon? That's..."

"Unlucky?" Raven asked, a bit testily.

"Ah, yes. But also, wicked awesome." Dylan noticed that Will had awoken. "You're one *teuch* biscuit, Owain."

Will smiled a little, then stared dully at the rows of hurting people. "So… many."

"A curse on Amaranth and his dragon," Raven muttered. "Most of our patients are farmers and townspeople, not warriors. The dragon has been burning and ravaging all the lovely hamlets of east Gwynedd."

Will cried out in dismay. "Not… my people." He was about to ask further, when his shoulder exploded with sudden, unexplained agony. His body contorted involuntarily, nearly throwing him from the stretcher.

"*Yes, you pathetic, washed-up princeling,*" the dragon's voice scratched across his brain. "*I shall scatter the bones and ashes of your people over every Avalian waterway. All due to your insolence.*"

"Liar," he retorted. His back arched, then folded, throwing Will to the grassy floor. The ground thrummed against his ear like a heartbeat. Or like a...

"*I'll cast your remains at the feet of your father Madoc...*"

The dragon's words reverberated from the very earth. Both their meaning and the searing sensation that accompanied them flooded him with terror. Vicious heat devoured his shoulder, as if the dragon had reactivated the venom in his veins.

"Will! Tell us what's hurting you, so we can help." His master's voice cut through Will's interior noise. The same as Raven's voice always had, during Will's panic attacks at Headquarters. This was like a panic attack, except the danger was real.

"The dragon," Will gasped, screaming through the dragon-fire. "She's… coming."

It was a guess, but not one Will doubted. After all, he wasn't the only one yelling. Several other patients had started screaming, too.

Raven and Dylan brought Will to an empty cot, and had Will sit on the edge of it. A young watch-medic hurried to join them. She placed a cold compress on Will's overheating forehead, then lifted his tunic while Raven and Dylan held Will still. He wasn't fighting them, but his arms kept twitching uncontrollably, making it near impossible for the medic to examine him.

"What's wrong with… my arms?" he asked. Sweat from the dragon-heat drenched his clothes.

"Nerve damage?" Raven suggested. "From the venom?"

"The venom can cause temporary nerve and muscle malfunction," the medic asserted. She took another cold compress and rested it gently over Will's exposed back. The unpleasant scent of scorched flesh invaded his nose, making him gag. Behind him, Dylan made a gagging sound, too.

"When did he get these puncture wounds?" asked the medic.

"Almost a week ago," Raven said. "And since that time, the boy has hardly rested. Amaranth's officers beat his injury with wooden rods, then Will suffered a fall, and then he trekked sixteen miles through the Wood with His Majesty and the Princess, before this fine gentleman saved him from a pack of wolves. And now, this."

The medic's hand froze over Will's back. "How is he even still alive?"

By this point, Will was wondering the same thing. He had been a strong and healthy person before these injuries, but not *that* strong. He should have collapsed and died from exhaustion or infection days ago.

Someone wants me alive, he thought. *That's all. Someone greater than me still wants me alive on this earth.*

He felt the dragon's rapid approach.

"She's close, she's close," Will repeated miserably.

"Who is 'she'?" Dylan asked.

Sudden understanding dawned in Raven's eyes. "The Navahogg. Will. Do you mean, the she-dragon is coming?"

Will nodded. Why else would all the other patients with venomous wounds, like himself, be crying out at the same time? She had embedded a bit of herself in each of them, and now their bodies trembled at her approach.

The watch-medic had overheard their conversation. "I think you should take the lad seriously, sir," she said. "Two of my patients in south Gwynedd responded the same way not three days ago. The dragon was upon us in an hour." She lowered her eyes. "Not many survived the second wave."

"Where can the patients go?" Dylan asked, urgently. "How do we bring them to safety?"

Master Raven drew quiet. "I'll ask the head medic to transport them to the Capital. The Faerie path shifted in our favor this time. The city is less than two miles away..."

The dragon's heat consumed Will. He was a dried-out husk. A cylinder of ashes.

How am I still alive?

"—bring down his fever with King's rue—"

"Show me how? I can help—" Dylan interjected.

"Here, hold down his arms. This—"

"Dragon sighting, dragon sighting, dragon—"

"...will calm him down..." A sharp needle pricked Will's neck. His head dropped forward, and the lights went out.

PART TWO

The Capital

14

Entrance to the Capital

When Philia's father reached the rendezvous, he did not tarry. He entrusted Philia to her mother and the healers, sent Uncle Raven to rescue Will, and then hurried to the council tent to receive the latest reports on Amaranth.

Philia watched him go, her heart stinging at the separation. If he were not King of Avalon, he would have stayed by her sickbed. *And if I were not Cursed, I would have joined him in the council tent.*

Lady Agnes and the other healers gave Philia a warm, scented bath, then rubbed her Curse-marks with tincture and healing balms. They brought her sweet, cool drinks to counter her dehydration, and medicines to lower her fever, manage her pain, and reduce inflammation.

Philia was grateful for these simple, practical remedies. However, Lady Agnes' medicines couldn't prevent the miserable crowd from yanking Philia back into the Curse landscape from time to time, nor could they restore the colors to her sight.

They also couldn't prevent the nightmares that woke Philia in the early morning hours. She had dreamed this time not of Arthur's children, but of her father, sick and in chains, being led out by Amaranth for public execution. For treason. She saw the atrocities committed against her parents, her friends, and everyone who loved her—all at Lord Amaranth's command.

"All of this will come to pass, and it will be your fault," the Curse taunted, filling her head with the worst possible imaginings. *"Your death will bring this upon your people."*

She awoke weeping, and nothing could console her. Not the pleasant glass lamp glowing by her bedside; nor her mother sleeping in the chair across her tent chamber; nor the intricate embroidered blankets covering her shivering body. None of these comforts could soothe her, because the nightmare was true: if Philia died now, her entire kingdom would suffer. Her father's claim to the throne would decrease, and Amaranth's power and influence would increase. Many people would die, not just Philia.

And Will…Philia feared for him most of all.

"For Owain I will offer no such respite." Amaranth had warned her, in the Wood.

Great tears gathered in her eyes and splashed the Curse marks on her palm.

Amaranth won't kill him. He'll imprison and humiliate Will, for years. Like his mother Fiona.

All this, because Philia Pendragon had a Curse without a cure. All this, because no matter what her parents believed or the healers told her, Philia was no better.

"I have to find a way to live, in the Capital," Philia whispered. "Not just for myself, but for my kingdom."

She thought of Will's words from that morning: *"I want to share my whole life with you."* She wondered if Uncle Raven had found Will yet, and when they would return to the rendezvous. She wondered what it would be like, to share her whole life with William Madoc Owain.

Her wonderings wrapped gently around her, coaxing her at last into a dreamless sleep.

When Will arrived at the rendezvous the next day, Philia was not allowed to see him.

"He's very weak, and his fever is high," Uncle Raven reported to Philia and her mother. Her uncle's face was freshly washed, but his clothes were still dusty and stained from his rescue mission. "The healers are working to draw the infection out of his shoulder. When he's out of danger, he can receive visitors."

Philia nodded, too worried to speak. Even here at the rendezvous, Will was in danger.

"And how are you faring, Your Highness?" Uncle Raven asked.

She resisted the urge to turn to her mother for guidance; the healers and servants were watching. Instead, Philia drew herself upright on her sick bed.

"I'm alive and safe, thanks to Will and my father, the King," she answered carefully. "I hope for a full recovery, once we reach the Capital and its renowned healers."

Inside, she wanted to scream. *I'm not better, Uncle! I'm dying.*

"We'll be making our grand entrance to the Capital in the morning," her mother added, placing a hand on Philia's shoulder. Philia had thought she'd heard Mum crying last night, but there were no tear streaks on her mother's face. The Queen appeared calm and strong. "We look forward to presenting the First Princess of Avalon to our beloved kingdom."

Her mother sounded sincere. *But what are you really feeling, Mum? What do you feel as you watch your child die?*

Uncle Raven smiled and bowed. "Excellent, Your Majesty. I do have some good news to report." He placed his head outside the tent flap and waved his hand. "Come on in, you two."

Philia squinted into the sudden light from the tent flap. She could just make out two tall, shadowy figures in the entranceway.

"Laurie?" Before anyone could stop her, Philia was scrambling out of bed, pushing past the servants, and running into the embrace of her friend.

"Philly!" Laurie squealed, squashing Philia in one of her signature monster hugs. "You made it! You're alive!"

"Philly" was the nickname Laurie had given her in Scotland, when she first met Laurie at her uncle's Knightley Academy. They had been best friends ever since.

"No, *you're* alive!" Philia said gleefully. "You made it out of Headquarters okay."

"Mostly." Laurie brandished the sling on her left arm. "I broke my arm in a few places, while we were evacuating the villagers. The dragon dropped a tunnel roof on our heads."

"Very impressive. Do you like my latest Curse marks?" Philia gestured at her neck and jaw.

"Holy neeps and tators, lassie. You'd win the Cosplay prize for best scarring, hands down." The jealousy in Laurie's voice was tangible.

Philia laughed. The best part about Laurie was that she meant it.

"Ah, to heck with the Cosplay," her friend continued boldly. "You and I are on a *real* adventure now. Right, Philly? Look what they let me wear!"

Philia took in Laurie's Avalian garb—a light tunic with dark leggings, knee high leather boots, a flamboyant cloak, and a shiny leather belt equipped with sword and dagger.

"Aye, Laurie, this is a real one, alright," Philia replied. "No more Comic Cons for us."

"No more Comic Cons? But I wanted to go as Dylan the Devious Demigod again," a familiar voice whined.

Philia peered over Laurie's shoulder and gasped. "*Dylan?!?*"

An easy laugh and a flash of bright eyes and teeth told Philia that her cousin was truly here. Dylan offered her an embrace almost as enthusiastic as Laurie's.

"Oy, cousin," he said, pulling away to examine Philia. His smile faded, just a little, when he gazed at her face. Then he whistled. "Laurie's right. Those scars are wicked awesome." He sobered. "But I am sorry, Philia. Will told me they're also wicked painful."

Philia half-laughed and flexed her stiff fingers. "They burn, Dylan. They *burn*." Somehow, dramatizing the hurt helped her feel a little bit better.

"That's the spirit, Philly," Dylan nodded his approval. "Gotta laugh so you don't cry."

Philia liked that. "Wait…did you say that you talked to Will?"

Dylan glanced at Laurie, who rolled her eyes.

"Fine, you can tell her," Laurie groused. "But don't compliment him too heavily, Philly. His 'mighty deeds' are already getting to his big head."

"What in the worlds did you do, Dyl?" Philia asked.

In epic, self-glorifying detail, Dylan explained how he'd single-handedly rescued Will from a pack of Albine wolves, hauled his friend seven miles in a stretcher—"Raven may have helped a wee bit, too"—and then bravely convinced an ancient dragon to turn tail before devouring the camp infirmary.

"Will and the other patients could sense the dragon coming," Dylan said, rubbing his hands together as he warmed up to his tale. "They were yelling and thrashing on their sickbeds, poor lads. So, after I helped the medic get Will comfortable, I took a stroll outside the tent to look for this Nava-what beast."

"The Navahogg?" Philia suggested politely, both alarmed and amused by Dylan's story.

"Aye, the Navahogg. Anyways, I found it."

"You mean, you found *her*?" Laurie corrected.

Dylan glared at her before continuing. "It was the most massive living thing I've ever seen. Head as tall as a house. Spikes as long as my father's best sword. And a scream more terrifying than Laurel-head on a bad hair day—"

"Hey!" Laurie protested.

"Even our old Scottish Nessie couldn't face up to that thing," he added with a shudder.

"So what did you do, Dyl?" Philia asked curiously.

His expression sobered. "For a long moment, I was too terrified to move. I was in the shadow of the treeline, so the dragon couldn't see me. Then it—*she*—pivoted her head in my direction. She sniffed the air, like she was hunting out a scent or something. I strung an arrow in my bow, aimed for its open jaws. And then…"

Both Philia and Laurie gazed at him expectantly.

"She turned her tail and slithered away to the north, before I could so much as tell her, '*get tae*'."

Philia sank onto the chair by her bed, considering her cousin's words. "But what made her go away?"

"I don't know." Dylan shrugged. "Uncle Raven thinks the dragon was summoned north to Gwynedd Castle."

Gwynedd, by the sea. Will's birthplace and hometown. The place he grew up with his father and mother and a much younger Ewan.

The place where he almost drowned, picking roses for six-year-old Philia.

Red rose, he'd cried. *Red rose for Philia!*

"Gwynedd?" Laurie repeated. "Heaven help us. Will's people have suffered enough already." She fell into the canvas chair beside Philia. "Most of the people in the rendezvous are refugees from Gwynedd."

Philia massaged her now throbbing forehead. The pain darkened her vision for a few seconds, then returned to its default colorblindness. She considered sharing her color loss with her friends, but decided against it. The moment was heavy enough.

"Once we enter the Capital, my father will name me as his legal heir," she shared instead. "My father can rally the High Avalian Court to fight against the dragon. Then we can help the people of Gwynedd. And," she added softly, "we can seek a cure for me, too."

Everything will be better in the Capital.

Laurie and Dylan exchanged glances.

"Just focus on getting better, Philia," her best friend said, offering her a hug.

"We need you, lass," Dylan agreed.

The next morning over breakfast, Philia's mother brought up the topic of traveling to the Capital.

"I feel we should leave immediately," her mother said, twirling a silver spoon through her oatmeal. "You're feeling well enough to ride now, and we shouldn't delay your medical treatment in the Capital." She took a bite of oats and cream, then laid down her spoon. "What do you think, Philia?"

Philia nibbled on a few tart merlin berries while she considered her mother's question. She wasn't feeling wonderful, but her mother was correct: she *was* strong enough to ride. The simple remedies she'd received in the rendezvous had returned some of her strength.

Her mother frowned, mistaking Philia's silence for doubt.

"I'm sorry to ask this of you, Philia." The Queen reached out and clasped her hand. "I know the ride will be wearisome, but my heart warns me that we shouldn't wait. The Curse will soon worsen, and when it does, I want you to receive the best possible care."

Philia met her mother's deep brown eyes, remembering a similar conversation they'd had in Llandudno Hospital, when their situations had been reversed. When it was her mother who'd needed intensive care, and Philia who had to make a difficult choice.

"The healers have been so helpful here," Philia said, "but you're right, Mum. I'm not going to get any better waiting around in this camp. Let's ask Father to take us to the Capital."

Her mother smiled, the relief plain on her face. "Thank you, my dove." She leaned back in her chair. "But before we go…"

Philia swallowed, wondering what unpleasant task she'd be asked to undergo. Maybe wearing a fancy dress?

"…let's finish this *pomcha* juice. It's simply exquisite."

"*Mum*! Okay, fine. It *is* pretty amazing."

They filled their glasses to the brim, then drank down every last drop. The juice's mellow citrus tang warmed Philia's belly and soothed her aching limbs. The taste echoed deep inside of her, sounding out her earliest memories. When she was a child carried about in her mother's arms, without a Curse or a care in the world.

"Mum," she sighed. "I'm sorry to place this burden on you. I'm sorry about the Curse, and me…*dying*, and everything."

The Queen gazed into her lap, her thick lashes blinking rapidly. After a moment, she shook her head. "Not now, my dove. I-I can't. I can't give up hope." She rose, jostling the table so that their empty glasses clinked. "I'll leave now to ask your Father."

She left the room without a word, but Philia could hear her gentle sobs. To Philia, it was the saddest sound in all the worlds.

By mid-afternoon, the three Pendragons and their royal retinue were riding out to the Capital. Laurie and Dylan were part of the King's Company, bickering occasionally, but overall on their best behavior. Will was not with them; Master Raven had taken him and the most critically injured dragon patients to the city the day before.

The King rode beside Philia and the Queen during the two-mile journey, explaining the sights along the path and instructing Philia on the area's unique geography.

"Here to the east is the King's Heartland," her father said, gesturing at the rich river valley ahead. "It contains the most fertile soil anywhere in the Otherworld. Most of our nation's wheat, barley, and flax comes from this territory, as well as grapes, cherries, pomchas, and apples."

"Avalon, Isle of Apples," Philia said, fingering the intricate agricultural patterns on her velvet skirt. Today she wore a traditional folk costume representing the twelve territories of Avalon. Her dress was bulky but beautiful, embroidered with stalks of wheat, clusters of grapes and apples, and of course, the white Pendragon rose, symbol of the royal household. Her sword *Brightwind* hung from the belt about her waist.

Their party made good timing on the road. It was still morning when they rode past a cluster of cottonwood trees, and watched the city come into view.

Cair Tintagel, capital of Avalon, was built upon the last solitary mountain before the great Running River poured out into the sea. The city was the soft cream color of lamb's wool, a ribbon of glistening limestone spiraling up the obsidian mountain of Manu. From her mother's maps, Philia knew that the River ran through and around and under the city, pouring at last out of mighty aqueducts into the depths of Ascension Bay, far below. Philia heard the sound of roaring waters from where they rode, still some distance from Rainbow Falls.

"This is the holy city," the King told Philia, his gaze fixed on its sunlit walls. "Here the Founders Seven first took counsel with each other, when they founded our noble kingdom. Here they built a new Round Table, to secure justice and equity among both human and

Faerie lords. Here the Founders once dwelled in Branwen's garden palace, at the city's summit—where Heaven kisses the Earth."

As her father spoke, Philia observed a few clouds dipping down and "kissing" the mountain top, before scattering across the King's Heartland below. The local weatherman in Conwy could probably have given her a scientific explanation for it, but Philia was certain she liked her father's description best.

Soon the gates to the first and lowest level of the city loomed ahead. The Capital had five levels in all, each spiraling up the mountainside with artful skill and grace.

Philia craned her neck to find the King's palace on the summit, but couldn't make out much more than a cluster of stone buildings.

"Must we ride all the way to the top?" she asked. Their short journey had already exhausted her. "With all the people watching?"

Her parents exchanged worried glances.

I guess I'm not the only one wondering if I can make it to the palace.

A flurry of movement caught her eye. Laurie had drawn her horse up to Philia's side.

"Chin up, Philly." Laurie gave her friend a bracing side-hug. "Now's your chance to show these Avalon peeps just how amazing you are. Their best first princess EVER!"

Dylan, who had somehow acquired an incredibly stylish set of riding clothes, followed close behind. "Aye, lassie, stay strong." In a lower voice, he muttered, "Don't let Amaranth and his foul Curse win. You can make this journey. You can be the heir your people need."

The Queen turned and smiled at Philia and her friends. "This is what you've wanted for so long, my dove," she reminded Philia. "To be the princess and protector of your people." She nodded towards the Capital's mighty summit. "Today is just another step toward your goal."

Philia pushed her shoulders back and forced herself to sit upright in the saddle. Her horse's ears perked up, as if sensing the emotional shift of its rider.

It's now or never, Philly.

"I can do it," she spoke aloud, her gloved hands tightening over the reins. "I *will* do it. For Avalon, and my people."

The King nodded, then raised his fist to the sky. The gatekeepers received his signal.

With the rumble of mighty drums and the cry of trumpets, the city's great stone doors groaned open. Philia's stomach lurched when she saw the vast crowd of people lining the streets.

"Hail Philia, Daughter of Avalon!" The King shouted, stirring up the crowds. "High honor to Princess Philia Pendragon, heir to the throne of our people!"

The crowd cheered with excitement.

Watch warriors and knights rushed to either side of the Pendragons, clearing and guarding their path through the gates. Then they entered in.

The people roared and the bells rang. Flower petals floated down from the sky, covering Philia's dress and adorning the city streets.

This is what I was born to, Philia thought. *This is who I am.*

15

The Rose Garden

WHEN IT BECAME clear that Will's condition was not improving, the King personally arranged for his transfer to the palace infirmary. Here, Will's injuries could be treated by the finest healers in the Capital.

Will leaned heavily against the medic assisting him. Lord Periwyn, the King's Healer Proficient, had numbed his upper back and shoulder, and was now stitching his dragon wounds closed. All three of them had ripped open, either during Amaranth's beating, or Will's fall from the *paradisa*, or from the wear and tear of their long journey. At this point, Will couldn't remember the details. All he knew was that he wanted to get better. The pain was unrelenting, and the exhaustion was worse.

"These wounds—they cause you much fatigue?" asked Lord Periwyn.

Will nodded mutely, then stiffened at the pull of thread through flesh. "Yes, sir. When I try to walk, my legs won't hold my weight. Someone has to help me."

The Healer asked him many more questions. Will liked his calm manner. Perhaps he might find some relief at last.

He thought of Philia, who had made her triumphant entrance into the city earlier today. He shared the same fervent hope for her—an antidote for her Curse, and a full and complete recovery. That was why they had endured so much since returning to Avalon, was it not?

Lord Periwyn started stitching his last wound.

Will groaned, all but collapsing against the medical assistant. *How can it still hurt so much?*

"My apologies, Sir William," Lord Periwyn said. "We have anesthetized your wounds, but since this is a magical injury, we cannot completely numb all sensations."

"I understand." He flinched as Lord Periwyn sealed his third and worst wound.

"The watch-medics found a dragon tooth in this one," Will explained. Although the wound was now disinfected and closed, it continued sending signals of distress through his shoulders and back.

Lord Periwyn walked around the examination table. He studied Will with concern. "What's your pain level, my lord?"

"High." Will swallowed. "Very high. Is it because of the venom?"

"Possibly. We are learning more and more about this new dragon's venom each day."

Am I a test subject, then?

"Drink some water, my lord," the medical assistant offered, not unkindly.

Will drank the glass of water greedily. It slaked his thirst, but he felt no better. Sudden chills ran through him, followed by feverish heat.

"Worthless, useless boy," the dragon's voice hissed in his head. *"Good thing she can find a hundred more like you."* He shuddered as her acidic words seared through his veins.

His vision blurred, then surged back in overly intense focus. He could see every spider-thin crack in the hexagon-tiled floor. Every grain of dust and debris swept into the corners. His ears also perceived the slightest of sounds—the healers' heartbeats, and the voices of two watchmen changing guard, several doors away. And one other, far more intimate sound.

"*Come, Will,*" Fiona called, louder and clearer than ever. "*Come, don't be afraid...*"

Will wasn't afraid. Not exactly.

"I want to come, Mama," he whispered aloud. "But I don't know how."

In his mind's eye Will saw her, young and breathtakingly beautiful in her shimmering emerald gown. Green stalks of wheat burst from the earth beneath her feet. The wheat shot upwards, sprouted leaves and ears of grain, then wilted and died with each of Fiona's steps. Grow, die, rise again.

"I will show you," his mother promised. She was smiling, even though her arms bore brand-new scars, and her cheek held a bruise the exact size and shape as the one imprinted on Will's face.

Amaranth's hand, Will thought. *Leaving Amaranth's mark. I have to stop him, and find her.*

"But where are you, Mama?" His voice echoed across the infirmary. The sound drew him back into the present moment.

Will blinked and looked around him. Everything was the same—the moonlight sifting down from the ensconced windows; the expressions of concern on the healers' faces; and his gaunt reflection in the room's looking glass.

The small pouch around his neck grew warm against his chest.

It holds Enduri, he remembered. *My mother's ring.*

With great tenderness, he placed a hand over the pouch, thinking, hoping, and longing for his mother. That he might at last come find and save her.

As he clung to that little scrap of cloth, clutching the hard outline of *Enduri* in his palm, he felt the Dragon's venom driven forcefully from his body. The warmth of Enduri filled his whole being, so that there was no longer any space in him for the dragon's cruel influence. There was now too much life in him for the dragon's deathlike venom to withstand.

The debilitating pain and fatigue instantly left him, along with the hard, bitter ache of his three shoulder wounds.

He shook his head, pulled in a deep, full gasp of mountain air. He felt like himself again. Fresh, strong, and vibrant. Fully alive.

"My lord, this session has done you much good," the medic assistant exclaimed, with an encouraging smile. "See how the color has returned to your face!"

Will smiled in response. He felt better than he had in weeks.

"I'd like to walk back to my quarters in the Watch's household," he said, with supreme confidence.

The two healers gaped at him incredulously.

"Let's see you walk across this room first," Lord Periwyn suggested.

Will pushed himself off the examination table, using both arms equally without any pain. A few moments ago, that would have been impossible. Once he was steady on his feet, he took his first step. Then another. When he reached the looking glass, he turned back to face the healers.

"My thanks to you, Lord Periwyn." Will bowed in gratitude. "At first, I felt no better, but your treatment has truly restored me."

Lord Periwyn bowed his head respectfully, but his expression remained inquisitive. "I gave you the best treatment within my power."

The medic brought Will his garments—an undershirt, sea blue tunic, and deep indigo vest that draped all the way to his knees, buckled at the waist with a black and silver belt. Although Will was still a watchman, he had been named the King's knight, and so for the time being must wear the garb of the Order of the Rose.

Lord Periwyn clasped Will's elbow before he left the infirmary.

Will shifted to face him, his wheat-blonde hair drifting across his battered face.

The Healer studied Will curiously. "I gave you the best care within my power, Sir William, but I am not the one who so swiftly healed you of the dragon's influence. Some higher power has done this to you. A deep, strange magic." His eyes flicked down towards Will's tunic, where Enduri lay hidden in its pouch.

"Do you know of any outside power that could be responsible for your restoration?" Lord Periwyn asked.

Will didn't answer. He suspected that Enduri had everything to do with his restoration, but he wasn't about to share that information lightly.

I need to find Mama, first. I need to understand what Enduri is.

For even if Enduri was the source of his healing, Will could by no means control it. He'd been deeply ill for a week, in far more desperate circumstances, and the ring had not restored him then.

"Be wary, Sir William." Moonlight barred the physician's earnest face. "Restoration magic always comes with a cost."

Will nodded respectfully. "Thank you for your care, and for the warning, my lord."

They parted ways, leaving Will with a restored body and a hundred unanswered questions.

During their first night in Cair Tintagel, Philia and Laurie explored the palace halls near Philia's lush apartments. Their trek led them to a secret garden adjoining the King's private chambers. Pillars of winding ivy and sculpted shrubs led them to a stone balcony, which overlooked a lower courtyard filled with trees and plants of all kinds. It was November, so nothing was blooming.

Nothing but white roses.

From where Philia stood on the balcony, the roses were tiny pin-points of light in a garden of dying, barren things. Like pearls cast over the barren earth, or stars fixed across the midnight sky.

"Laurie, look!" Philia gasped, pointing towards the white flowers. She wrapped her cloak tighter around her body as a chill wind brushed her cheek. "They're just like the roses from Mum's book." She meant *The King's White Rose*.

"They're gorgeous, Philly," Laurie agreed, leaning against the balcony beside her. "Everything about this place is as bonnie as a fresh Highland morning."

"Oh!" Philia exclaimed. "There are people down there."

Two people, in fact. A man and a woman. They were holding hands, and when they came to the white roses, the woman lowered her face to breathe in the scent of the blooms.

"Two Avalian lovers," Laurie sighed, dropping her chin over folded arms.

The woman straightened and turned toward the man.

"Those are my parents!" Philia said, startled. The retreating figures were dressed so differently she hadn't recognized them at first. "Which means…these are my parents' roses." She looked towards Laurie in delight. "Do you remember that scene my mother wrote in *The King's White Rose*? About how all the flowers in King Bran's garden wither and die each winter, except for the white Pendragon roses?"

"Of course I remember." Laurie sounded slightly offended. "It was those roses that kept the King's hope alive, that he might see his beloved again someday."

"Today is that day, Laurie! See?"

Far across the courtyard, her parents drew closer, their arms encircling each other perfectly. They fit into each other's figures as if they'd been made for each other. Her father leaned down to kiss her mother.

Philia let her gaze drop. Tears surged into her eyes before she could stop them and trickled down both cheeks.

Laurie threw her arm around Philia. "Why are you crying, Philly? Is it the Curse?"

She shook her head. It was difficult to explain. She had longed for her parents' reunion for ten years, but now she wept to witness it.

"No, not the Curse. I…Laurie, they're so beautiful together. See how they complete each other?"

"Aye. Just like my parents do," her friend agreed.

Philia traced her fingers along the stone ledge of the balcony. The Curse marks on both hands rippled across her skin. "Do you think something like that—that fierce kind of love—could ever happen to me?"

"I hope so," Laurie replied, after a moment's consideration. "I hope it happens to me, too, someday."

Philia leaned against her. "Oh Laurie, I'm so sorry. About you getting stranded here in Avalon, of course."

"Philly, if ever there was a place I wanted to be stranded on, it would be here." Philia was struck by her friend's calm tone. "President of the Avalon Fan Club, remember? So far, I've already gotten to battle an evil half-brother with a poisoned blade, travel through a magical portal, battle a she-dragon as big as a house, and sample the finest cuisine since last year's Knight Fest. Never a dull moment here," she ended cheerfully.

Philia grinned at that. "Aye. But I'm still sorry, Laurie. About you getting separated from your family."

Laurie's face fell. "I miss my family awful, and Scotland, too." She let Philia give her a hug. "But at least I've got you, Philly. And now… Dylan." She hesitated. "Man, was I glad to see that self-conceited son-of-a-Haggis."

Philia had to stuff her face into Laurie's shoulder to stifle her laughter. "Where on earth do you come up with this stuff? Son-of-a-Haggis?"

"Well." Laurie huffed. "That one's literally true."

Philia thought of Laurie and Dylan dancing at the Masquerade Ball, like Michael Jackson heroes.

"You and Dylan would be great together," she commented. "My cousin's big head is in constant need of deflating, for one."

They giggled in the twilight. Philia watched her parents leave the garden for the King's private quarters. Up and down the corridors, servants began lighting lamps in the halls and windows of the palace.

"What about you, Philly?" Laurie asked. "Any secret crushes you'd care to reveal?"

Images swirled in her head, one after the other, painting vivid scenes against a threatening landscape.

"I should think by now it's no secret," she whispered.

Her friend nodded. "That Gwynedd boy who loves you."

Who loves me enough to die for me. Philia chewed the inside of her cheek. *Again and again and again.*

"What if one day...he sacrifices too much, Laurie? What if one day he faces death to protect me, and doesn't return?"

Laurie squeezed her hand. It comforted Philia, even though it hurt.

"You can't worry about that now, Philia," she whispered. "First you need to fight your own battle. You need to beat this Curse."

Philia stared straight ahead, watching the shadows of her parents through the chamber curtains. They were dancing—a mellow, waltz-like dance.

She blinked and lowered her eyes. She would never know that kind of enduring love. The healers predicted she would be dead by spring.

And yet her heart! It had been pierced and cloven in two by the devotion of Will Owain. Her heart saw him: the too-pale cast of his selfless face; the tender fierceness in his grey-green eyes. Amaranth and his allies kept piling death on both of them, the Princess and her Watchman, and it was only a matter of time before they succumbed beneath its crushing weight.

And yet Will—loyal, relentless Will—he never stops.

It was what she loved about him, and also what she feared.

"Will Owain," Laurie said approvingly, interrupting her thoughts. "A jolly good choice, Philly."

Dylan had said much the same thing, back in Scotland.

"No, it's not, Laurie," she sniffed. "Not now that I'm going to—" Her tears returned, and this time she let them fall. She shook with barely contained sobs.

"Philly? Tell me how I can help you."

"I just want to be alone for a while," she sniffed. "Okay?"

Her friend hesitated, then dropped her arm from Philia's shoulder. "Alright. But I'm going to tell the servants where you are. You shouldn't be alone right now."

Philia rubbed her aching head and sighed. "You're a good friend, Laurie."

Laurie gave her an affectionate bump on the arm. "Ooh, a free compliment. Thanks!"

Night settled around Philia after Laurie left the balcony. Cold white stars pierced a black velvet sky. Across the rose garden, the lamps in the King's chambers went out.

"Chin up, Philia," she told herself, echoing Laurie's words.

Her weary feet carried her back to her own apartments. She passed through dimly lit alcoves with thick marble pillars and luxuriant curtains, exquisite even when viewed in black and white. Lady Agnes and two healer apprentices had prepared a steaming mineral bath for her, as palliative treatment for the Curse's pernicious scarring.

Philia would have preferred to go straight to bed; their procession into the city had exhausted her. But Laurie had reminded her that getting better was Philia's way of fighting against Amaranth. The least she could do was accept the healers' treatments.

She lowered herself into the steaming, acrid-smelling bath, a recessed pool constructed directly into the floor of her apartments. The water gave off an unpleasant smell, like rotten eggs, which her servants tried to cover up with roses, lavender, and other floral scents Philia didn't recognize. The clash of aromas made her head pound and her stomach churn with nausea, which the hot bath did little to alleviate.

"The healing qualities of the Capital's mineral baths can decrease your Curse-scarring and ward against infection," Lady Agnes explained. "It will also soften the skin so we can remove some of the markings."

Philia's forehead furrowed in confusion. "How can they be removed? The scars go all the way down."

Lady Agnes paused, her gentle hand frozen over the misting waters. She'd pulled her rich, wavy hair behind her head, so that it cascaded down her back. "We must do what we can, Your Highness. With the things we can both see and touch."

Philia nodded, swallowing back both nausea and another round of tears. The smell was awful, but the heat did soothe her. When she came out of the bath half an hour later, the scars on her body had faded, just a little.

"Rest now, Your Highness, and do not fear to hope," Lady Agnes said. "I will do all in my power to keep our anointed First Princess alive." She curtsied and exited Philia's inner apartments.

Once all her servants had left, Philia curled her hands into fists, then rubbed her nails along the ridge of her scars. *Stay alive, Philia Pendragon. Your first mission here is to live.*

She collapsed onto her bedroom chamber's soft feather mattress and soon drifted into an uneasy sleep. Pure white roses, ringed with thorns, haunted all her dreams.

16

The Ascendance Ceremony

Three days later, on the morning of her Ascendance Ceremony, the Queen and her servants woke Philia long before the dawn. Today she would be presented before the entire Avalian High Court, and crowned heir to the kingdom of Avalon.

Philia's morning began with a soak in the hot mineral springs, followed by a vigorous scrubbing of her Curse marks to minimize their outward appearance. Next, her ladies-in-waiting applied salves, creams, and powders to perfect her complexion, and gels, combs, and wax to fix her wavy locks in place. By the time they'd finished, Philia felt like a European supermodel prepped for the runway.

"Is this what matters most to the court, Mum?" Philia complained. "How *pretty* I look?"

Her mother pulled a pin from her mouth and deftly adjusted the hem of Philia's gown.

"It's not what matters most," the Queen replied, "but on your Ascendance Day, it is what matters *first*." She gazed up at her daughter. "It's essential that you look the part of a Princess."

Philia turned to study her reflection in the looking-glass. The servants had sprinkled metallic dust over her face, arms, and hair, giving Philia a literally radiant appearance. Her floor-length gown (turquoise, Mum had said), was belted around the middle with a thick swath of iridescent cloth. Pearls and diamonds rose from the base of the dress in stylized swirls, so that when Philia walked, it would look like she was churning up waves on Avalon's sandy shores.

The Queen rose to her feet and rested her delicate hands on Philia's shoulders. "Think of your fine appearance as your armor. A shield protecting you from the power-hungry members of your father's Court." Her mother's voice took on a note of warning.

"Some of Avalon's nobles wish your father had no heir, so that Amaranth could inherit and give them the lands of their kinsfolk. The courtiers will pretend to love and admire you, but they are *not* your friends."

Philia squirmed with apprehension. "Ugh. Then what should I do, Mum?"

"You will have to earn their respect with courtesy, love, and when necessary, fear."

She picked at the fabric of her gown. "Can a pretentious dress and makeup really do all that?"

The Queen laughed. "It can certainly help." She squeezed her daughter's hand. "For now, just show them what I already know: that you are fit and worthy to serve as Avalon's heir."

Stinging pain ran up Philia's arm at her mother's touch. *Don't let Mum see.*

"Yes, Mum." She smiled through gritted teeth.

Maybe this elaborate get-up is for the best, Philia thought. *With all this face paint on, hiding my Curse will be easy.*

The Queen smoothed Philia's gown, then rose to her feet. Layers of silk and taffeta rustled and sighed as the two women embraced.

"Philia my child, remember this: you are a *gift*," whispered the Queen. "To me and your father, as well as your kingdom. In every way, you are… precious." Tears sparkled like gems on the crown of her mother's lashes.

"Thanks, Mum. I'm ready now."

Mother and daughter swept out of the dressing room, arms linked and steps in unison. Servants and ladies-in-waiting curtseyed at their approach, then swept aside the embroidered curtains leading to the hallway.

"Who are my escorts, Mum? Father said I would need them."

"Ah," the Queen answered mysteriously. "You will be in the best of hands."

As they exited the palace chambers, two gentlemen stood waiting in the hallway, dressed to the Avalian nines. They turned at the women's approach.

"Uncle Raven! Will!" Philia hadn't seen either of them since her arrival in the Capital.

"Vivi," her uncle said, bowing respectfully. "Philia."

The Princess grinned and gave the seasoned watchman a fierce hug. "Thank you for coming," she exclaimed, "and for taking care of him." She parted from her mildly startled uncle and found herself face-to-face, and eye-to-eye, with Will Owain.

As far as she could tell, Will had recovered brilliantly. His face had returned to normal, and if his bruises were still there, Philia couldn't see them. She wondered if Avalian men wore coverup. His new uniform made him look so handsome, Philia blushed.

Good thing no one can see that either, with all this face powder and glitter dust, she thought, laughing inside.

She had no way to know what colors Will was wearing, but he looked so striking in greys and whites and blacks, it hardly mattered. His face was serious, but the cold worry in his eyes thawed and softened as she drew near.

"Your Majesty, Your Highness." Will said. Both he and Raven bowed deeply. "A harvest of blessings to each of you this fine festival day."

"And may the rain fall richly on your fields," Philia answered, remembering the correct response. She curtseyed, spreading her turquoise gown outward. Her movement made the coral beads sewn into the dress's hem clink musically against the floor.

When she offered her gloved hand, Will kissed it.

"Your Highness," he whispered.

Her gaze flicked to the back of Will's neck as he leaned forward. A discreet bandage covered his recent scalp wound. It only hardened Philia's resolve.

I must win these Avalian courtiers to my father's side. So that beast Amaranth does not steal the kingdom, and bring down ruin on all whom I love.

When Will raised his eyes, she held his gaze.

"I do this for my people," she said, her voice soft. "I do this for you."

His eyes widened in surprise.

"I will go into the Court and win the loyalty and love of the people. And then Lord Amaranth will *never* be allowed to hurt you again." As she spoke, she acknowledged his scalp wound with the slightest touch of her hand.

Will's cheeks darkened.

"Heal, Philia. Get well and live." His clear voice roughened with emotion. "That is all I ask, Your Highness."

He offered her his arm, and Philia gratefully accepted it. Warmth and strength rushed through her when they touched, as if he was supporting her with some invisible, life-giving force.

She wanted to ask him about it—was it Faerie magic? Her imagination? Maybe both?—but they had no privacy here. Two servants shuffled just behind them, holding up Philia's train.

One hundred steps ahead, as her high-heeled boots went tap-tap-tap against the polished tile floor. Will's steps fell near silent beside her. She breathed in his pine and sea salt fragrance, enjoyed the gentle support of his arm beneath her own. She felt safe with Will.

Like nothing and no one could harm her, here with her loyal watchman at her side.

The doors to the Great Hall opened wide. A chorus of stringed instruments announced the arrival of the royal house. The King stood waiting for them beside the doors. He smiled at Philia, then took his Queen by the hand and marched proudly up the center of the hall. Cheers and applause reverberated across the chamber.

When the King and Queen reached the royal dais, an impossible distance away, her parents stood before their thrones and turned towards Philia and Will.

"Now presenting Philiamaria Branwen Pendragon, daughter of King Branaric III and Queen Vivien, heir to the throne of Avalon." A thin, wispy Faerie called out in a musical voice. "All hail the Princess, on her Ascendance Day!"

Lord Cecil, the royal Protocol Proficient, waved Philia forward. He stroked his jet-black beard and reminded her to smile.

Philia took a deep breath and pushed forward, Will walking meekly at her side. As they entered, the hall thundered with the sound of the courtier's cheers. The Avalian lords stomped their boots and pressed their feathered hats to their chests. Ladies curtseyed, then peered curiously at Philia behind pearly, silken fans. The courtiers wore such a ridiculous collection of jewels and finery, it made Philia a little dizzy. She smiled wider to hide her distaste.

As she walked, the coral beads of her dress sang like tiny bells across the sea glass floor. The High Court welcomed her with perfumes of all kinds—deep and spicy cinnamon; light and airy lavender; rich and noble cedar; fresh and sweet rainwater and roses.

The scents conjured up a flurry of old memories. Philia remembered playing here as a child, racing down the galleries to press her tiny fingers against the Hall's gorgeous stained-glass windows. Next, a birthday memory, when every vaulted beam was decked with evergreens and winter berries. But also, her sitting cross-legged on the throne, watching her father's soldiers carry in the wounded from a battle with Amaranth. The fresh floral scent of the Hall had quickly taken on the stench of blood.

As a small child, that last memory had frightened her. It was her first glimpse into humanity's propensity for violence and war. Today, however, the memory only strengthened Philia's resolve. She was nearly seventeen now. She'd been cast into the midst of bloodshed many times, and survived. Soon she would learn the ways of her father's Court and fight for a lasting peace.

The Faerie herald was still proclaiming Philia's many titles. When he finally finished, he took a deep breath and introduced Will.

"…Escorted by William Madoc Owain, heir to the princedom of Gwynedd and the Western Isles, protector of the King's Watch, ward of the Mystic Way and the Faerie lands, guardian of the northwest shores, and keeper of the royal porpoises."

Philia blinked, then glanced a question at Will. His lips turned upwards in amusement.

"Yes, Your Highness. The porpoises are real."

The image of Will tending to a brood of royal dolphins filled the Princess with delight. In her excitement, she forgot what she was supposed to do next.

Thankfully, Will remembered. "Here is where you leave me, Your Highness," he whispered. "Lord Cecil informed me that you are to take three steps forward, then curtsey and kneel before the King and Queen. When His Majesty asks if you are willing and able to accept your title as First Princess, you may say yes."

She squeezed his arm in gratitude. Her watchman was still protecting her, here in the Court.

Will bowed and left her side, joining the crowd of lords and ladies.

Philia raised her head and took three confident steps towards her father.

An ornate hardwood kneeler, coated in lacquer, had been positioned before the King's throne. Philia knelt, then nodded at her lady servants to arrange the long train of her dress. She knew that when the train was completely extended, the fabric would depict the apple tree from Avalon's national flag.

The imagery was clear. Her father was King, and Philia was his fruit. She was his firstborn daughter and rightful heir.

The next part of the Ceremony was a blur of words and formal blessings. Her father took incense, sealed in a silver censer, and spread its sweet, holy perfume all about Philia, and then out into the Court.

The King handed the censer over to a servant, then came and stood before Philia. His expression was appropriately regal and composed, but kindness still shone in his breathtaking eyes. She longed to see their blazing turquoise color, once again. She longed to view her father, and indeed this entire spectacular Ceremony, in all its multi-colored glory.

Hush, Philia, she scolded herself. *You're lucky to be present here at all.*

The excitement of the Ceremony had distracted Philia from the Curse, but now it reminded her of its presence with hot, stinging pains. She clenched the kneeler and pressed her lips together tight.

"Do you accept your future inheritance, my daughter?" King Branaric III asked. The courtiers fell silent, listening intently.

"Yes, Your Majesty," she answered, projecting her voice so that it rang out through the hall. "From this day forward, I dedicate my mind and body to the fair and just government of Avalon and its peoples, both human and Fae. I swear this oath before the Founders Seven, before the King and Queen of Avalon, before the High Court, and before all the inhabitants of the Enchanted Isle."

It was a long speech. Philia hoped she had remembered all the details. It was too late to fix them now.

"May the grace of the Founders bless you abundantly, my daughter, and hold you to your oath," the King proclaimed, his expression proud. "As King, we accept your oath, and vow to instruct you in the fair and just governance of Avalon. We swear also to instruct you in morality and natural piety, so that Avalon's future queen will be adorned not only with precious jewels and fine robes, but the noblest virtues and the most righteous deeds."

Philia swallowed, feeling the immense responsibility her father had placed on her shoulders. It was not enough for her to be a good Queen; she would also have to be good, pure, and noble of heart.

"We swear this oath before the Founders, this noble court, and all the peoples of Avalon," the King said, concluding his speech. He turned toward the Queen, who rose from her throne and came to stand at the King's right hand.

Following an ancient tradition, a child of about ten years of age presented the King with the tiara.

The tiara had been polished so that it glowed in the morning light. Its metallic strands were woven together in Celtic knots and studded with countless miniature gems. Fresh white roses, chrysanthemums, and other blooms were pinned all about the crown's wire frame. Their sweet, floral scent was almost overpowering.

The King raised the tiara. Both sunlight and the hall's glass lamps reflected off its polished surface.

Philia lowered her head, her heart pounding fervently against her chest.

Yes, she thought, her words a prayer. *I accept my inheritance. For the sake of my father, my mother, my watchman, and all of Avalon's peoples.*

The Curse blazed through her arms, searing even into her chest. Apparently it was not pleased with her choice.

But the Curse could not stop the King from placing the floral tiara on Philia's head, nor prevent him from presenting Philia to the royal court.

"Behold, Philia Pendragon, First Princess and heir to the throne of Avalon!" The King cried out.

As the courtiers cheered, the King leaned in close to her and smiled. "I'm so proud of you, Philia Branwen."

She nodded, blinking back tears.

I'm here in Avalon, with my father. He's just claimed me as his daughter and named me his heir.

For a moment, she allowed herself to indulge in the miracle of it all.

Then she raised her eyes and turned with her father to face the people.

17

This Golden Hour

PHILIA PEERED DOWN into the woven basket from the city's Harvest Festival, examining its delectable contents. Four mini-loaves of spiced *gwemka* bread; a bottle of honeyed mead; dried plums and apricots; and a strongly scented ball of cheese. Last of all, her friend Laurie had tossed in an assortment of hand pies, each with stalks of grain adorning their crisp, flaky crusts.

The Princess swallowed back her Curse-induced nausea, trying in vain to stir up her appetite. Laurie expected her to try all these delicious goodies, and enjoy it.

Thankfully, something else drew Laurie's attention.

"Look, Dyl!" Laurie squealed, jumping up and down in delight. "Harvest...*hats!*"

Philia, Laurie, Dylan, and Will all turned to the marketplace's center, where a festival vendor had arranged a most magnificent display of head coverings. The vendor's shop was overflowing with felt and leather hats, each adorned with outrageous feathers, curling ribbons, blinding jewels, and whimsical layers of lace and taffeta. Simpler designs were displayed on the left, while more elaborate and obnoxious hat concoctions stood to the right, presumably for a higher price. Several well-to-do ladies and gentlemen were already making a beeline for the shop.

"Haggises and hounds, my lady," Dylan said, his hazel eyes igniting with hat-loving fervor. He extended his arm to Laurie. "Shall we go, lassie, go?"

"Aye!" Laurie looped her arm in Dylan's, and off they galloped towards the hat paradise. They had to bump past a few well-indulged merchants to secure the first place in line.

"Oh." Happiness bubbled up in Philia's chest. "Just look at them, Will."

"They pair so well together," Will agreed. This evening, he was dressed in urban watchman's clothes—a pale grey camouflaged cloak and tunic that blended well with the Capital's architecture. "Shall we find a table, Your Highness? Your basket looks heavy."

She nodded, and they found an open wooden table on the marketplace's north side, close to the food vendors. The aroma of roasting hazelnuts and baking fruit pies made Philia's mouth water. Will placed her basket at the table's center, then sat beside Philia and gently lifted her fingers to his lips. His touch sent warm sparks of energy zinging through her body, like an anti-Curse.

"Philia," Will stammered, after a moment's pause. "There's something I'd like to do for you. Something I'd like to try." His eyebrows furrowed with apprehension. "I don't know if this will work, but a few weeks ago, it helped me. It *healed* me, when nothing else could."

The sights and smells of the city marketplace dimmed as Philia absorbed his words.

"Something that healed you?" she repeated dumbly. "You mean, like a medicine?"

He shook his head, sending golden locks cascading across his forehead. "No, Philia. Not a medicine. A *modrwy*. A ring."

Philia frowned, not understanding. "You don't wear rings."

"No." Will laughed in agreement. "But I wear *this* one all the time."

He reached beneath his tunic and pulled out a small leather pouch. Inside the tiny purse was a beautiful ring, with a gem-like rose, cloisonné thorns, and an elegant metallic band.

"This is *Enduri*," Will explained. "My mother's wedding ring." Hope and pain flickered across his face. "I confiscated it from Ewan's pocket, the night we passed through the Mystic Way."

"Oh! That was weeks ago."

"Yes, Your Highness. I had it with me the entire time we traveled from Headquarters to the rendezvous. As you know, my condition only worsened with each new danger we faced."

Philia squeezed Will's hand, her heart aching at the memory. By the Founders, how her watchman had *suffered*.

"But my father's healers helped you get better," she said brightly. "They found you a remedy, at last!"

"I did find a remedy, Philia. But it didn't come from the healers." Will lowered his eyes. "Sir Periwyn, the King's healer, said that a 'strange magic' had restored my strength."

She listened closely. "You...think it was Enduri that helped you?"

"Yes, Your Highness. I do."

The city's lamplighters passed nearby, illuminating the candles on their table.

"Do you...think it could help me, too?" she whispered, so only Will could hear.

"Shall we see?" he asked. When she nodded, Will placed the ring directly over her Cursed palm, then pressed her hand to his heart. His eyes drifted closed, and his face tightened in concentration.

Ah. That same electrifying warmth and heat. Like a lightning bolt leaping out of Will's heart and into her own. Strength rushed through every part of her body, sweeping the Curse aside like a mighty broom. Nothing, not even the Curse worse than death, could stand in Enduri's path.

Will gasped, his breaths coming in short and strained. She felt the terrific pounding of his heart against her fingers and the ring.

He poured so much life into Philia, she could scarcely endure it. Yet she didn't pull back.

Hold on, Philia. Let Enduri scrape every remnant of your Curse away.

But then, the crowd. Her poor, miserable crowd. When Enduri's power entered the Curse-landscape, the children reached out their hands towards its light and warmth.

"Feed us, Mother!" The children shouted. *"Share your good health with us!"*

With her newfound strength, Philia willed the light to pass onto the children. But instead of reviving the crowd, Enduri's power seemed to drive them mad, all over again. They turned towards the Princess with gnashing teeth and clenching hands.

"Look, the light is inside *of her!"* The crowd moaned. *"If we drink her blood, we will be strong like her!"*

Philia cried out as she watched the children, whom she had worked so hard to love, stalk towards her across the Curse-landscape.

"No! My children, let me tell you a st—"

No stories! They shouted. *Only blood!*

They dove towards Philia and took their first bite.

She screamed, jerked her hand away from Will, and dropped Enduri to the ground. It rang once against the stone pavement before Will snatched it up and buried it beneath his tunic.

Philia wasn't certain of her own appearance, but their healing attempt had clearly taken a lot out of Will. His blond locks were plastered to his forehead with sweat, and his eyes glistened with intense effort.

"Will—"

"Philia—"

"Are you okay?" They both asked at the same time.

"Yes, I'm fine," she answered first. "In fact, for a short while, I felt…*normal* again."

"Normal," Will repeated, a sweet smile on his lips. Childlike joy sparkled in his eyes.

"Oh Will. Dear Will," she tried to explain.

He panted for breath, looking for all the Isle as if he'd just ran a marathon. If Enduri did have any magical powers of its own, it still required Will for its engine.

"Do you feel any better?" he asked, between breaths. He reached for her hand again, but she gently pulled it away.

"I did, for a few moments," she said. "But…Enduri did not cure my Curse. It's still there."

"Still there? II-how do you know?"

"I know."

"But *how?*"

"I just know." Philia couldn't look at his pure, selfless face. She would fall even more in love with him, and that would break their hearts further, on the day the Curse took her.

"Philia, please. Don't—leave me."

She choked back a sob, stubbornly turned away. "I don't want to leave you, Will. I don't want to leave Avalon at all."

His fingers brushed against her cloak. His touch was warm, but this time in a regular, non-magical way.

"What I meant was, don't leave me right now. I've missed you, here in the Capital."

Philia shuffled back to face him, enticed by his honesty.

"I haven't seen you like I used to, these past few weeks." Will's breathing had slowed, and he spoke calmly. "I want to…spend more time with you."

Philia blinked. "Are you *courting* me, Will Owain?"

His expression grew earnest. "You're going through Feldspar's seven hells right now. Let me be there, with you, through the fire and flame."

She stared at him, marveling at how quickly he'd moved from disappointment to unflinching support of her person.

"Hey watchman," she whispered. "How is it you grow more attractive every time I see you?"

This question confused her poor warrior enough for her to steal a kiss from him. Well, maybe she didn't *steal* it. He seemed to enjoy it plenty himself.

This kiss was different from the ones they'd had before. There were no tears this time; no promises, and no dreams. It was simply Philia and Will, at a harvest festival in the Capital, loving deeply in the present moment.

18

A Midnight Meeting

It was Decembre. The Healer's medicines had not helped; Will's Enduri ring had not helped; all the salves and tinctures and home-made remedies of the Capital had not helped. Her parents and the healers had urged her to try medicine after medicine, until Philia felt like a human guinea pig.

"No more remedies tonight," Philia told Lady Agnes, when she offered Philia a powerful sleeping draught.

Her Healer Proficient hesitated, her face weary. "The draught will help you, Your Highness. It won't heal your Curse, but it will provide relief."

"*No.* No more treatments tonight." She'd tried *Arthur's Slumber* before. For the span of a few hours, the *Slumber* made Philia forget her Curse. Unfortunately, it also made her forget almost everything else.

"But how will you get any rest, Your Highness?" Lady Agnes argued. "The Curse keeps you awake at night."

"I don't care," Philia said, crossing her arms. "If I don't get any sleep tonight, fine. At least I won't be a snoozing zombie."

Lady Agnes relented, and that night Philia went to bed without medicine.

The palace bells chimed softly, announcing the midnight hour.

Philia tossed and turned in her mighty four-poster bed. At night, her Curse marks burned too fiercely for easy rest. The marks now stretched from her head to her abdomen.

Worse, for the past week, Philia had awoken in total darkness. This blindness would last up to a half-hour. So far, Philia had waited until her sight was restored before she called her servants to help her bathe and dress. But one day soon, the healers and Philia's parents would discover the truth.

"One day soon, your sight will not return at all," the Curse smugly informed her.

She groaned and stuffed her face into her pillow, as if that would silence the Curse.

The shuffle of footsteps made Philia raise her head.

A servant stood in her bedroom entranceway. "Someone to see you, Your Highness," she said, curtseying deeply. "He says it's urgent."

Philia sat up and smoothed her nightgown, instantly intrigued. "Do I know this person?"

The servant bobbed her head. She was young, with springy blonde curls. "Yes, Your Highness. It's the handsome one."

Now Philia *really* had to know who her mystery visitor was. "Please. Let him in."

The servant zipped out of the room, returning with a not-so-tall young man, dressed in the garments of the King's knights. He was silent and his ocean eyes shone lustrous in the lamplight.

Usually, Philia would've risen to greet Will, but she hadn't the stamina. Instead, she stayed where she was and smiled at him.

"Did my father or the Watch send you here?" she asked, knowing her watchman to be a man of duty.

Will shook his head, a ghost of a wince crinkling his eyes.

"No. Your Highness." He glanced at the servant.

"Thank you very much," Philia told the young girl. "You may wait for us outside, in the antechamber."

The girl curtseyed, cast one final curious glance at Will, and then stepped outside. The antechamber was not far; Philia fully expected the girl to eavesdrop.

There's nothing to be done about that, she reasoned. *And we will neither say nor do any shameful thing to give her reason to gossip.*

After the servant had left, Will stood there listlessly, soaking in the sight of Philia as if he couldn't get enough. Like a man parched with thirst, arrived at an oasis, just inches from the water's edge.

"Here." She raised her right hand, gloved to protect her sensitive, Curse-marked skin. "Let's go to the inglenook. The windows there overlook the entire City."

Will crossed the tiled floor, which shimmered beneath him, and helped Philia rise to her feet.

Dizziness made the room tilt, and her legs grew weak. Will offered his other arm to support her.

"Should we stay here instead?" he asked.

Philia slowly shook her head. The dizziness was already clearing. "No. It is always this way now. The feeling will pass."

Nodding, Will waited a moment before leading her over a floor mosaic of the tree of Avalon, ripe with apples. Philia pushed aside a curtain of translucent gauze, revealing the inglenook: a small, enclosed balcony with padded benches, towering Gothic windows, and a view of the Capital to take one's breath away.

"By the Founders," Will gasped. His neck craned upward to gaze at the net of Decembre stars twinkling over the city. She watched him, wondering how many more times she'd have the privilege of *seeing* him.

"Thank you for coming, Will," she said, after a while.

His gaze dropped from the sky. "Shall we sit down, Your Highness?"

"Yes, please, I'd like that. I've wanted to show you this room ever since we arrived in the Capital." They chose a spot on one of the benches, then leaned back against the stone walls. Thanks to the little stove burning in the room's center, it wasn't cold.

Philia was grateful for the warmth. Cold air made her hands ache and cramp, so that by the end of the day, she could hardly use them.

"The Watch didn't send me here," Will said. He shifted so that his body was turned toward Philia, but not touching her. "I came because I wanted to see you. And in case you wanted someone to be honest with."

She laughed. "Oh I do, Will, I do. Even if I wasn't Cursed, a Princess's life is mostly pretending, isn't it?"

"If that is so, you are pretending quite well, Philia. Every courtier I spoke to at the banquet last night had nothing but fine words to say about you."

Philia sighed and rested her head against the wall. She'd far rather rest her head against Will, but then she wouldn't be able to see him.

"According to my parents," she murmured, "the courtiers rarely, if ever, say exactly what they mean. Most of their public words and actions mean more than one thing. They like to nest insults inside of their compliments. And other times…they're simply lying."

She swallowed and squeezed her gloved hands together. The pain sharpened her senses, keeping her alert. How many more days would she have like this? When she would still be well enough to converse?

Will must've been thinking along the same lines. "What say the healers, Philia? Have they hope for a cure? Are they helping you?"

Philia hesitated, chewing the inside of her lip.

Look at him. Look at that good, honest face. Remember how he has delivered himself over to the enemy three times already, so that you might live. You must give him the truth.

"The healers are trying many treatments, to help me manage my symptoms," she said. "Some of them help me feel better. Without them, I wouldn't be able to leave my chambers, or perhaps even my bed." She swallowed, her eyes getting hot and prickly. "But there is no way to cure me. The Curse is fatal."

Distress paraded across Will's face. "*No,* Philia. Tell me it isn't so."

"I will do no such thing. I will not lie to *you,* of all people." She sucked in a shallow breath, but the tears flowed. "I am dying, and the healers say I will not outlast the winter."

Will's fingers clenched into fists, making his knuckles glow pale in the starlight.

"B-but…what about the antidote?"

"It's all gone, Will. Taken or destroyed by the dragon. Even the antidotes here in the Capitol were destroyed by Amaranth's spies before we arrived." She shrugged. "They were experimental, anyways. The healers knew it could slow the Curse down and extend a victim's life. But they've never cured anyone with it. Not yet."

"Not *yet,* Your Highness?" Desperate hope curled in Will's question.

She nodded. "It's too late for me, but since we arrived here, my father and I have diverted new funds towards further development of the antidotes. I guess Father is still harboring the belief that the new antidotes will cure me, but my only hope is that it might help…other victims."

Will turned and stared moodily out the windows. She caught sight of his bandaged scalp wound, Amaranth's parting gift.

"How are you so sure there is no cure?" he asked, his inquiry stubborn and fierce.

"Because," she dragged in a breath, accepting the red-hot waves of Curse-pain running through her body. "I can feel the death in me. Feel my body, mind, spirit dying on the inside. The light fading. The heart slowing. The pain that comes and comes and comes, relentless, unending, unstoppable, so that at night, when I'm all alone, I'm tempted to let myself sink into that agony and put an end to it. So I don't have to go on anymore. Not because I don't want to live, but because I'm already dead."

Will caught and clenched her hand. It hurt, but she didn't let go.

"I'm a dead girl walking, Will. A dead, dead girl. All the life in me is a fraud and a sham. Mere illusion."

"No, no, *no*." He kissed her forehead, her cheek, her hair. "What you *feel* is an illusion, Philia. You are alive and real."

She screamed in silence. "Will! All this…*Curse* inside me. It's too much. I'm drowning, and who can save me? Who can even understand me?" Her distress dimmed her vision, so that she now sat in complete darkness. She reached out a hand and pressed it against Will's chest. His quick heartbeat pulsed beneath her fingers. "No one can help me. Not the healers, not the servants. Not even my own father."

Will pressed his hand over hers, deepening the feel of his heartbeat. So lively. So strong.

"I don't know if I can help you, Philia," he admitted. "But I do think that I might understand. May I tell you a story?"

Despite her dire musings, Philia smiled. "A story? Yes, Will. Please tell me a story."

"It's true," he warned her.

"All the better."

He nodded. "You spoke of feeling dead inside. Beyond anyone's help or understanding." His voice was calm, like a windless day at sea. "I've been there before, Philia."

She studied his pale features, lit dramatically with both fire and moonlight.

"After Flaxen Grove, my father was often away, searching for Fiona. When he was gone, I'd wait and wait for him to come home, so he could help me train and ride together, as we used to. But whenever Father returned from another fruitless search, he'd act as if I wasn't there. As if I didn't exist to him." Will's noble face grew sober. "I know now that it was his grief for Mama that made him act this way. But as a young boy, I blamed myself. I decided I must've done something wrong, although I didn't know what it could have been." Will swallowed, his expression hard. "Eventually, I decided the problem wasn't anything I'd done—*I* was the problem. I was the reason for everything wrong in my world."

"That's it!" Philia exclaimed. "That's what the Curse feels like, as foolish as it sounds when you speak it out loud." She reached out her right hand towards Will. "But what did you do?"

He stared off into the flaming brazier. His fingers picked away at the border of his tunic.

"I stopped eating. I pulled out chunks of my hair. And once—this is what ended it—I threw myself down the castle stairs. Fifty-seven limestone steps, and a solid stone floor." Guilt and confusion crossed his face. "I was ten years old."

Philia gasped and covered her mouth in horror. "Oh Will. Why would you…? Did you fall on purpose?"

He flinched as if her inquiries were blows. "By the Founders, Philia. All your questions."

She blushed at his reprimand. "Oh goodness! I'm sorry, Will."

He tilted his head, stared deep into the fiery brazier. "I…don't know why I did it. I remember landing at the bottom of the stairs, but I don't remember what happened just before."

"That—that sounds *awful*."

"Yes. The healers didn't think I would recover. I broke this bone here," he pointed at his collar bone, "both my arms, and one leg. And multiple blows to the head." Will tapped his forehead, his beautiful eyes grey with misery.

"That's when the castle folk started calling me the 'idiot prince'." He shrugged with false indifference. "They accused me of attempted suicide, of giving up on them and my princedom. Since I couldn't remember what had actually happened…" he swallowed, raw pain in his words. "I struggled to defend myself."

Philia imagined ten-year-old Will, struggling to survive his injuries, accused of cowardice and madness by his own people.

"That's cruel," she said. "They mocked your grief."

"They could not understand it," he said. "And I would not want them to."

"Don't say that," she spit out, with more heat than she'd intended. "It's… *good* to want to be understood." She lowered her eyes and studied Will's hands, which were still worrying away at his uniform. He was going to bore a hole right through that cloth.

William Madoc Owain. She savored both the name and the person in her mind. *Prince of Gwynedd. Skilled watchman. A warrior with a heart of gold.*

She risked a glance at his face, read the dejection and shame in his eyes.

William Madoc Owain, she thought again. *The idiot prince. The failed apprentice. A motherless child accused of self-harm.*

He was all and both those things, wrapped up in one person. With a story in him so terrible, it made her heart recoil in disgust. With a nobility in him so great, it filled her spirit with admiration. Both, and. Light, dark. Greatness, brokenness. A noble, tragic soul.

If he can be all those wounded things and still be so marvelous, Philia considered, *then maybe it's okay for me to be both, too. Maybe I can learn to live with my Curse, as abominable as it may be.*

"I shouldn't have told you that story, perhaps." Will sighed. "I should've told you of rainbows, and Northern Lights, and the pure white sands on Gwynedd's shores. Gentle, beautiful things. Like you." His grief-stricken face cut her heart in two.

Philia did not know how to answer, so she did the only thing she could think of: she held him. She scooted close and wrapped her aching arms around his. Her face pressed childishly into the curve of his shoulder as she clung to him with all her strength.

You exist to me, Will. And you are very, very much loved.

Night and day, she heard the cries of a mob that she could not satisfy, whom she could not placate. It wasn't the violence of the crowd, but her inability to help them, that tormented her most.

But Will was real, and she could love him.

His breath fell hard on her ear, and his body trembled as he returned her embrace. Just for one glorious moment, where Philia knew only the all-encompassing warmth of his arms and the familiar scent of his skin.

"Your Highness." His voice was husky as he gently pushed them apart. "We have no privacy here."

She nodded, remembering the servant waiting outside in the antechamber. Yet she ached to be in his hold again. It was a sweet, hopeful ache, and nothing at all like the Curse's dismal throbs.

Will leaned back against the bench.

"My father was there the day I fell, Philia," he said. "And afterwards, he changed. He stopped leaving Gwynedd to search for my mother. He gave me his full attention and the gift of his time. *He's* the reason I made a full recovery from my injuries. Ever since that day, he's truly been the best father a son could ask for."

"It will be a great honor to meet him someday." She could hear how much he treasured his relationship with his dad.

And no wonder! When he's paid such a price for it.

"I should return to my quarters, Your Highness. Raven will be looking for me."

She nodded and rose from her seat. "Thank you, Will."

He stood up as well. "I haven't done anything. Except bring you more grief."

"Oh, but you have. Very much. You reminded me that everyone has their own burden to bear." She gave him a cheerful smile. "When I return to my royal duties tomorrow, I shall do my best to endure the ones that have been given to me. It will never be too much for me, I think."

She leaned upward and kissed his cheek.

Philia's resolve was tested only a few mornings later. She woke up so ill, she couldn't get out of bed. Her limbs were so stiff and inflamed, she couldn't raise them from the mattress.

This is new, she thought grimly, blinking in the Curse's blindness.

She heard the servants preparing her bath in the next room. The peaceful scent of rose petals, lavender, and mint wafted into her bed-chambers, urging her to climb out of bed and soak in those warm, healing waters.

By the Founders, I am so lucky. Tears leaked from Philia's sightless eyes. *I'm a princess in a medieval kingdom, and my parents are the King and Queen of Avalon. My servants bring me breakfast and give me baths. I have my best friend Laurie, my cousin Dyl, and the world's most handsome watchman for my boyfriend. My life is awesome.*

She tried again to rise. This time, her shoulders and legs responded a little, so that she could turn onto her left side. But the movement sent violent currents of pain through her upper body, taking her breath away and completely blinding her. She slumped back onto the sheets, exhausted.

Before, Philia had been able to push through the Curse, to rise and get ready using her own willpower. But not today. Today, her body had stopped listening to her.

Fear bubbled up inside.

You'll never rise on your own power again, the Curse whispered maliciously. *They'll have to carry you everywhere. A weak, pathetic princess, sliding slowly into the jaws of Death.*

"Oh shut up," Philia murmured, both terrified and annoyed.

You know what's coming, the Curse's voice sent a ripple of agony through her body. She moaned and clawed her arthritic fingers into the bedsheets. *You know the destruction waiting for your people when my lord Amaranth arrives at the city. Bloodshed, chaos, and death.*

"Don't you ever," she muttered through gritted teeth, "have anything…*nice* to say?"

Her words left her gasping, but they also improved Philia's mood. She could still fight back.

She tried rising again. This time, her body responded and she turned over, reaching out her hands as she slid off the bed. A luxurious woven rug broke her fall.

"Your Highness!" One of the servants ran into the room, dropping instantly to Philia's side. Two more servants followed. When they raised Philia to a sitting position, she groaned and nearly fainted.

"Call Lady Agnes," the first servant ordered. "Quickly now!"

The chief healer arrived moments later, trailed by her two apprentices. The servants carried Philia into the bathing chamber, stripped the Princess of her clothes, and lowered her into the water. It was a humbling experience, but also necessary, for Philia could no longer do those things for herself.

She soaked in the hot water, breathing in the soft fragrances and fingering the bubbles and foam crossing over its surface. Gradually, her eyesight returned and her limbs began to relax, so that she could tread the water with her arms. The Curse never seemed to bother her as much underwater.

Too bad I can't greet all my Court visitors from the bathtub, she thought, almost smiling.

"Do you feel any improvement, Your Highness?" Lady Agnes asked anxiously. She knelt beside the water's edge to examine Philia's Curse marks. "You've developed some new scarring since my last visit, two days past," she noted.

Philia nodded. "The bath has helped me, my lady," she said. "But today I was supposed to join my father at the Round Table. How can I meet the King if I can't walk?"

"We can provide transportation for you, Your Highness," Lady Agnes assured her.

Philia felt a pang in her chest. She wished her mother was here. The last few days, the Queen had been tangled up with meetings and councils. Amaranth was gathering an army and approaching the Capital. Both her parents were working day and night to prepare the city for a possible siege.

Philia longed to join them, but the Curse kept her mostly confined to her rooms. Her vision failed more each day, and a strange mental fog hung over her thoughts, distorting her judgment.

I need to join my father today. Philia drew in three deep breaths, drawing in as much oxygen as her lungs would allow.

"How am I going to do this?" she wondered aloud.

A hesitant expression passed over the healer's face. "I do have one solution, Your Highness."

Philia glanced up in surprise.

"It won't make you better, or slow the Curse's progress," Lady Agnes warned. "And taking too much of it can be addictive."

The Princess frowned. An addictive medicine?

"However," the healer continued, "you *could* take a dose of Heart's Ease. It would allow you to move about and function for short periods of time—such as during an hour-long Round Table session."

"Heart's Ease?"

"Yes, Your Highness. It's a powerful painkiller. Shall I prescribe you some?"

The Princess studied the healer's kind face, read only compassion and concern in the Faerie's eyes. Still, Philia hesitated. *A powerful painkiller… potentially addictive.*

But she could join her parents. She could visit Will and her friends. She could enjoy, perhaps, her last few weeks in Avalon.

"Yes," Philia answered, making her decision. "Let me try a dose, and then have my servants prepare me for my meeting with the King."

19

Winter Siege

WILL STOOD GUARD on the outermost wall of the Capital, searching the river valley for Amaranth and his army.

Keeping his gaze open and soft, Will surveyed the terrain from east to west, checking for movement on either the main road or the fields. Last night's snowdrifts dotted the valley like glittering piles of sugar. Today's fresh falling snow accumulated on top, casting an opaque sheen over the surrounding countryside.

Will frowned beneath his watchman's hood.

"I don't like the low visibility out there, Master," he confided to Raven, who stood guard a couple of yards away. "The weather's fair enough for Amaranth's army to travel, but it's not clear enough for us to get a good view."

Master Raven ran his gloved hand along the length of his bow. "If Amaranth's out there…today would be an ideal time for him to attack."

Will pulled his lens-captor up to his eyes and examined the distant tree line. The westernmost stretch of the Wood ended about a mile from the city walls. That was where Amaranth was expected to appear, and where the last of Gwynedd's refugees were expected to escape.

Will had received the increasingly desperate messages from his people in Gwynedd. They spoke of the devastation the Navahogg had wrought on the wheat and barley crops. The loss of livestock and the farmer's fears of famine, and starvation.

At the urging of Will and the other Gwynedd nobility, the King sent emergency food and aid to the north. As the situation worsened, the King had adjusted his approach, encouraging Gwynedd refugees to retreat to the safety of the Capital.

And Will's countrymen had come. Men and women, young and old, high-born and low-born. All alike were welcomed, fed, and housed in the city. Will had visited the refugee camps, seeking out family and friends, and distributing blankets, medicines, and provisions. He was looking for his father, but still, Madoc had not come.

"Hurry, Father," he whispered into the wind. "Gwynedd's become a death-trap."

He turned the lens-captor towards a colossal oak tree, a mile from the city walls.

"Master Raven!" he exclaimed. "Movement on the northwest front!"

Raven drew his own lens-captors, turned to where Will was pointing. "Well done, Owain. Coordinates?"

"Three hands west from due north. By the grandfather oak. It's a…" Will squinted into the shimmering snow. "A soldier on horseback. One of ours?…yes. It's a knight from my father's house."

Will's heart thrummed loudly against his chest. The weary knight galloped towards the gates as if an entire army pursued him.

"A messenger from Gwynedd!" Raven raised a turquoise flag above their viewing post, signaling the wards of the city gates to attend to the new arrival.

"Describe the tree line to me, Owain." His master pointed where Will should turn his lens. Sure enough, massive movement surged along the forest's edge. Will spotted knights on horseback, foot soldiers, and servants. Riding in the center of the pack, near the front—

"Father," Will gasped aloud, his chest flooding with relief. "It's Lord Madoc, riding with his Gwynedd warriors."

"Yes, I see him," Raven answered, sounding pleased. "I'd recognize that shaggy lion's mane anywhere."

His father Madoc's wheat-blonde hair swirled about his face as he urged his troops towards the gates. He led his men with his signature steady confidence, a quality Will had long admired.

"More details, please," Raven pressed.

"My father is leading the 4th regiment of the Gwynedd cavalry, along with some of his infantry. He's keeping the soldiers together. They look exhausted, Raven. Like someone's been pursuing them."

The Gwynedd regiment rode closer, keeping a tight formation, although a few injured stragglers strung out behind the group. The soldiers were close enough for Will to hear their shouts to the city wards.

"Lord Amaranth is coming! Prepare to close the city gates! He's brought an army to reckon with," Madoc called.

At his father's warning, Will turned his lens-captor back to the western tree line.

"He's here, Raven," Will said, careful to keep his voice steady, like his father's. "Lord Amaranth's just arrived on the northwest front."

Lord Amaranth, suited in gleaming black armor, stood visible on the north horizon. A grim line of mounted warriors spread out to either side of him, their black and gold banners snapping in the wind.

"Lord Amaranth!" All along the city walls, the watch warriors raised the alarm. "Enemies on the northwest front!"

Amaranth's army was both magical and diverse. Dark faeries

clothed in spider-thread armor rode a strange assortment of fantastical beasts. Human warriors, on both foot and horseback, marched a short distance behind. As Will watched, the army parted down its center, allowing a group of female nightcallers, draped in their signature maroon robes, to claim the front line.

"He's brought his nightcallers with him," Will reported to Raven. "They're leading pairs of Albine wolves into the river valley. We should warn my—"

Raven was already sending out the signal. "Albines to the northwest!" He bellowed. "Madoc, look to your injured!"

Will kept his gaze on the army, gasping in horror as a nightcaller released both of her wolves. The vicious beasts loped straight towards the closest Gwynedd soldier, a wounded infantryman who'd fallen behind the regiment.

That soldier was me, only a few weeks ago. Food for wolves…

"No!" Will dropped his lens-captor about his neck, then drew and released two arrows consecutively with his reinforced bow.

Two clean shots. Two dead wolves with arrows through their hearts.

A few Gwynedd medics noticed the commotion and rushed back, placing the injured soldier on a stretcher and hurrying back towards the regiment. Will admired their simple courage and skill.

Meanwhile, the first Gwynedd soldiers had reached the main city gate. Will estimated it would take up to a quarter of an hour for his father's troops to enter the city.

The resounding cry of drums and trumpets reverberated across the river valley.

That must be Amaranth's signal to attack, Will thought.

Raven released his first arrow, taking down another Albine wolf. He directed Will to do the same. "The Albines pose the greatest immediate threat to our warriors," he explained.

Will nodded, sending out three rounds of arrows. One struck a wolf in the leg, another through its heart. The third would have struck home, but the wolf shot forward unexpectedly, causing Will to miss his mark.

Luckily, Raven finished off that one.

They weren't the only archers in action. Dozens of the Watch's sharp shooters targeted first the wolves, then the closest enemy fighters.

Will glanced back at the Gwynedd regiment. One third, perhaps, through the city gates.

Yet Amaranth and his army still gained. The villain's own long-range archers took position behind a copse of trees and rained arrows over the city walls.

"Take cover!" Raven roared.

Raven and Will ran to the nearest fortified tower, where they continued launching arrows through slits in the sandstone walls. More archers soon joined them.

Half of my father's troops are through the gates, Will noted, sparing a glance to the east. *And still he refuses to enter.*

Instead, Lord Madoc held his mounted position just outside the gate.

"Quickly now, ye loyal dogs!" Madoc shouted, urging his soldiers into the city. "To safety, and the King's protection!"

The eerie battle song of the nightcallers wafted over the battlements. Amaranth's nightcallers and their wolf escorts had just reached the end of the regiment. One wolf avoided the Watch's arrows and clamped its jaws around a Gwynedd soldier's neck.

Will turned away, sick to his stomach. Then he dragged in a breath, loaded another arrow, and shot the same wolf in the chest. It was too late to save that soldier, but at least he wouldn't be devoured by wolves.

"Lord Amaranth in range!" Raven shouted. "On my mark, warriors! One, two, three…*release!*"

A dozen carefully launched arrows soared towards Amaranth.

Will studied the curve and speed of the arrows as they whizzed across the sky. Would any reach their mark?

Across the battlefield, Amaranth observed the incoming threat. He raised his black and gold shield.

Most of the arrows struck the usurper's shield. One glanced off his helmet; another embedded itself in his thigh. He pulled out the offending arrow and flung it aside.

"To safety! To safety!" Madoc kept shouting.

All but fifty Gwynedd soldiers had entered the gates.

"Why the blazes is Madoc still waiting outside?" Raven growled. He seized Will by the shoulder. "Owain. Go tell your father to get his sorry arse inside, this instant!"

Will didn't need to be told twice.

"Yes, sir!" He saluted and sprinted towards the main gate.

After marching down a spiral staircase, Will entered the covered tunnel leading to the main gate. The tunnel smelled of human waste and mold, and Will hated it immediately.

Chaotic shouts battered his ears, and the pounding of feet. Will swerved to one side as three messenger boys zipped past him, clutching letter satchels to their chests.

Twenty yards further, the tunnel lurched beneath Will's feet, sending him stumbling into the slick stone wall.

Will righted himself and kept going, but almost immediately, the ground shifted again. This time, it didn't stop shaking. Will crashed first into one wall, then the other, bruising his right shoulder so badly, he dropped to the floor from the pain.

His shoulder. The venom. The dragon.

HER.

"Hello again, William Owain."

Will gasped and wrapped both hands around his throbbing head. The dragon's cruel voice ripped right through him, dragging burning waves of agony through his entire body. He kept inching forward. If Amaranth had brought his dragon, then Will had even greater reason to warn his father.

"Get out, get out," he moaned to the dragon.

"*Weak, useless boy. If only the Master would let me eat you.*"

Her words etched into his skull like white-hot flames. Will's upper body failed him again, so that he slammed downward on his chin, his teeth gashing into his tongue. He spit out blood and wriggled ahead. Pale winter light. Not far. Not even ten feet away.

The tunnel shuddered. Loose stones dropped from the ceiling.

Outside, Will heard his father calling to his men.

"*Now Madoc,*" the dragon hissed. "*For him, the Master has given me no such limitations.*"

Will fell again. By now, he knew it was impossible for him to move whenever the dragon spoke. He just had to lie there and take it.

"*And Madoc's blood will be so clean, so pure...*"

"No," Will gasped. He shoved his legs out to force his body closer. Thankfully, a messenger boy noticed him, and helped Will drag himself out of the tunnel.

"Thank you," Will panted, before collapsing against the battlements.

"Don't mention it, my lord." The messenger boy disappeared back into the tunnel.

Will gazed downwards. His father Madoc was directly beneath him, guiding the last wounded soldiers through the city gate.

"Father," he groaned.

The dragon laughed in Will's mind, the sound gouging into his insides like poisoned claws. He curled forward, pressing his abdomen against the stone turret to keep himself upright.

"Father." So quiet, Will couldn't even hear himself.

"*Noble blood, sinews, tendons, TEETH,*" the dragon sang.

"FATHER!" Will screamed, waving his arms to get Madoc's attention. "Take cover! *Dragon!!!*"

Madoc looked up and saw his son. The earth stirred and mounded beneath him. He grabbed the last wounded soldier and charged inside the half-closed gates.

Will sighed in relief. Blood trickled from his nose.

Boom, boom. The dragon corkscrewed out of the ground, slammed its jaws into the city gates, closing and nearly splintering them. She struck again with a force so massive, Will and every other warrior above the main gate slid backwards, over the edge, and down onto the medics and soldiers crowding the first level below.

Just before Will made impact, the dragon hissed:

"Let the feast… begin."

"Will."

He came to slowly. His shoulder was aching, and he wondered why.

"Will, my son. Speak to me. Please."

He opened his eyes, winced at the sudden sunlight. His tongue felt heavy in his mouth, and he could taste blood.

"Father…"

"Will, my boy." His father grinned down at him. His shaggy grey and gold hair fell all about his face like some wild halo.

Tears of relief budded in Will's eyes. *He's alive. He's okay.*

"Can you sit up?" Madoc asked.

Will paused. "I think so."

His father helped him up, then embraced his son. Will embraced him back. He hadn't realized how much he'd missed his father until that moment. He hadn't seen Madoc since the past summer, before the King's mission sent Will to Scotland.

"My soldiers are being attended to here," his father said.

Will looked around, saw that they were in the streets of the city's first level. Tents were set up along the street, where the healers and medics were caring for the Gwynedd soldiers, as well as the warriors injured in the fight against Amaranth.

"Lord Amaranth," Will panted. "The dragon—what happened, Father?"

Madoc nodded grimly. "Amaranth is setting up tents along the tree line, out of the reach of the archers and crossbowmen."

"He's preparing a siege, then?"

"It seems so."

"And the dragon?" Will tapped his fingers gingerly over his right shoulder. The venom pain had ceased.

"You warned me just in time." Madoc examined his son with pride. "My last soldier and I made it into the city gates, and then the gatekeepers bolstered the doors with stone barriers."

"Hasn't the dragon tried to burrow under the city?" Will asked. "She can tunnel underground."

"It's a 'she', is it?" Madoc commented, casting Will a curious glance. "Well, she can't burrow beneath this city. The Capital is built on a foundation of solid rock. That's why they built the city here in the first place—it was during an age when dragons were trained for warfare on the Isle."

Dragons? Trained for warfare? Will must've slept through that history lesson.

"However, we can and should discuss these happenings with the King," Madoc continued, rising to his feet. He offered a hand and helped Will stand also. Will felt a bit dizzy and battered, but well enough to walk.

Madoc waved down two of the stable boys. "Quickly! Two horses for the lords of Gwynedd!"

They rode to the palace level with impressive swiftness. When they reached a good vantage point, Will turned to survey the city and its surroundings, hundreds of feet below. Madoc pulled his horse beside him to do the same.

"Those are all Amaranth's troops, Father?" Will asked, pointing towards the northern tree line.

Madoc nodded. "He gathered quite a few allies in the north this winter. I fear he might have the strength to form a proper siege and attack of the Capital."

"We should not delay then." Will's hand rose instinctively to his scalp wound. It had healed, in a way, but it left an ugly scar and his hair had not grown back. Knowing Amaranth's malice, Will doubted it ever would.

He intended to brand me. Mark me as his property. Will thought of his mother, and Ewan, and their constellations of scars. His stomach turned in revulsion.

His father noticed and gently took Will's hand. "Where did you get that awful wound, Will?"

Will shifted in his saddle. He'd rehearsed explaining this to his father. Somehow it seemed much harder with Madoc staring him straight in the eye.

"Amaranth made the cut," he admitted. "It was the price we paid to escape him, at Watch's Headquarters."

Madoc's grip tightened over Will's. Anger and worry ignited in his blue eyes. "Does the King know of this?"

"Yes, sir. The King gave me the command to go out to Lord Amaranth alone."

"*Bran,*" his father muttered ominously, his righteous fury building. "What were you thinking?" He clapped Will on the shoulder and pivoted his horse towards the palace. "Come now, my son. Looks like we have quite a few *lovely* topics to discuss with His Majesty today."

Will grinned and drew his horse beside his father. "You may not like it, Father," he said, "but the King was right."

Madoc dismissed Will's opinion with a mighty snort.

"If I hadn't gone out there, as Amaranth wanted, the Pendragons and I would probably be dead," Will persisted.

But his father shook his head, urging his stallion to greater speed. "Next time His Majesty needs someone to play the victim," he huffed, "it better not be my son."

Will and his father Madoc entered the Round Table chamber, to find it half full. Will had been in the room several times before—once, to welcome the Princess to her new position beside King Bran; thrice for the weekly state-of-the-kingdom meetings; and twice more for war councils.

If this current Round Table wasn't a war council yet, it was about to become one.

"Your Majesty, announcing the arrival of Madoc Owain, lord of Gwynedd and the Western Isles, and Will Owain, his son and heir," the herald at the door proclaimed.

Every eye in the chamber turned towards the two Owains. Will felt self-conscious in his dirt-stained watchman's attire, but such was the nature of their visit. They had come in haste to warn the King.

When the King saw them, he immediately rose from his seat at the opposite end of the table. Every lord, lady, and knight rose with him, bowing their heads as the King left his seat and strode to embrace his friend.

"Well met, Madoc," the King said.

"Well met, Your Majesty," Madoc answered. The two embraced and joked about each other's latest grey hairs. Much to Will's trepidation, his father *also* mentioned that he'd like to speak with the

King later—in private.

"Very well," the King said, looking slightly terrified. "But for now, Madoc, come and join our council."

He escorted Madoc and Will to the Gwynedd section of the Round Table.

The Round Table was an intricate wooden contraption formed of twelve interlocking wedges, one for each of Avalon's territories. The Table's three concentric circles could be removed for smaller councils, or added for larger ones. Today, the Table was in its middle setting, providing two seats per territory.

Will waited for the King and his father to take their seats, before sitting beside Madoc.

"What news do you bring, my friend?" the King asked from his throne chair, confident and relaxed. Will glanced around the room and saw that this was a gathering of his closest allies.

That's good, Will thought. *They'll be more likely to offer good counsel and support.*

Madoc cleared his throat. "Your Majesty, Amaranth and his army of Fae and nightcallers have laid claim to Gwynedd Castle in the north."

Will stared at his father in grief and shock. Their home castle, taken by Amaranth?

"Our Gwynedd soldiers held out long and mightily against Amaranth's warriors, but we had no way of stopping the *Navahogg*." Weariness lined his father's features. "Gwynedd was overrun when I left it, four days past."

A collective cry of dismay swept around the Table.

"Not beautiful Gwynedd!"

"Who shall guard our northwest borders?"

"What is this *Navahogg*? From whence did it come?"

"And what of Amaranth, Lord Madoc?" the King spoke over the commotion, silencing his courtiers.

Madoc inclined his head. "After Amaranth's army took over Gwynedd Castle, I led my remaining knights and soldiers through the secret paths of the Wood, while hotly pursued by a contingent of his army. We reached the city gates just in time."

"The gates are closed then, Lord Madoc?" asked a count from the Northern Moors.

"The gates are barred and sealed," Madoc confirmed. "The *Navahogg* damaged the city gates, but so far it's been unable to break through." He directed his next words to the King. "Several of my watch warriors have reported that the *Navahogg* prefers to remain close to the earth. Unlike the dragons from the old tales, this one does not seem to possess the gift of flight."

The King nodded, considering Madoc's words. "We are still ignorant of this dragon's full capabilities, or if it has an agenda outside the orders it takes from Amaranth. Although we haven't seen the *Navahogg* in flight, it would be wise to take precautions. Sir Leonore?"

"Yes, Your Majesty." Sir Leonore, an older gentlemen, was the chancellor of the Capital.

"Double the city's defenses on the two lowest levels, and prepare the city for aerial assault."

Next, the King turned to his two attendants. "Send word to the lower level to bolster and reinforce the city gates, and the weaker sections of the outer wall. I also want the Gwynedd refugees evacuated to the Capital's south side."

"Yes, Your Majesty." The attendants bowed deeply, then hurried from the chamber.

"Does Amaranth then have the power to take this city by force?' asked Lady Kirsch. Will had met her a few weeks ago in the palace fencing hall. She was nearly six and a half feet tall, strong as an ox, and a stunning swordswoman.

Madoc shook his head. "I'm not certain, my lady. What news is there from Valeria and the east?"

"No news yet," Lady Kirsch replied shortly. "We wait."

The King placed his weathered brown hands on the table. "Let us send out the Watch to gather what intelligence we can, especially along the Running River. Amaranth will need the aid of his Valerian allies, if he truly wishes to threaten the Capital."

"I brought most of my regiment with me from Gwynedd," Madoc reported, his voice soft. "About thirty percent casualties, and my men are exhausted from their escape through the Wood. But given some time to recover, they will fight valiantly for you, Your Majesty."

His father's loyal words moved the King.

"My deepest thanks, dear friend." King Bran raised his face, so that the stained-glass windows splashed golden color on his noble brow. "We will need the good efforts of every man and woman, and a spirit of unity to defeat our kingdom's enemies. Let us stand firm against Amaranth and all our foes. For the glory of Avalon!"

The council members rapped their fists against the Round Table. "For the glory of Avalon, and the flowering of our nation!"

Will wished the Princess could see the courtiers' fervor. But if Philia was not here, it meant she was too ill to leave her chambers. She was fighting her own battle, within.

Enduri failed to heal her before, Will thought. *But maybe my father can help.* It was a desperate hope, but Will clung to it.

"No respite for our enemies!" The King's clear voice rang across the chamber. "We will defend the Capital, as noble sons and daughters of Avalon!"

20

Branwen's Day

AMARANTH'S ARMY HAD settled in for a long winter siege of the Capital. The Princess's Curse continued to advance. But Branwen's Day still came, on the second day of the second month, and the city still celebrated, as if in defiance of the rising darkness.

That evening Will traveled back to his quarters, weary and drained from a long day on the outer walls, to discover green and gold lanterns on the city streets. Before he'd even reached his apartment, a messenger boy came sprinting down the halls, bearing a letter from the Princess.

Her message came on pale green parchment, sealed with the royal insignia. Inside was written:

To Will Owain:

I awoke and discovered that today was a good day. Let's use it together, to do something marvelous. Choose our location, and I will meet you there after dusk.

With deepest affection,
Philia Branwen Pendragon, First Princess of Avalon

"After dusk?" Will mused aloud. "That only gives me an hour's time."

His exhaustion instantly left him. He thanked the messenger and skipped down the palace halls like a child on holiday. Because if Philia was well today, it *was* a holiday. And she wanted to spend her good health with him…

When he reached his apartment, Will washed up, changed his clothes, and sent a servant to inform Philia of his chosen location.

And soon he was with her, escorting Philia from her royal carriage, at the Capital's largest ice-skating rink. The Princess had been so ill all month, Will could hardly believe he was walking beside her.

"The city is filled with lights tonight," Philia whispered, hanging comfortably off his arm. Lamplight reflected in her bright eyes, casting a healthy glow on her cheerful face. Her hair was drawn up in a spiral of braids and curls, but her garments were less formal: a soft blue coat and a headache-inducing orange scarf.

No ball gowns tonight, but Will couldn't stop staring.

"Your Highness," Will said, inclining his head towards the rink. "Would you care to go out on the ice?"

Philia eyed the rink, which was filled to the brim with townspeople. Speed skaters ducked around couples holding hands, while little children scooted and giggled, dangling from their parents' arms.

"I do, Will." Her eyes widened with longing. "But not today."

He felt the weight she placed on his arm with each step and came to a halt. "Shall we rest, Your Highness?"

She nodded and offered him a gracious smile. "That bench by the ice would do nicely."

Together they walked to the bench and sat down. Philia sighed and placed her boots on the seat, then hugged her knees to her chest.

They both turned to admire their surroundings. The ice-skating rink had been decked with green and gold lights. Shimmering snowflake banners hung from the lamp posts, and musicians of all kinds gathered along the sides of the rink, beguiling the crowd with traditional folk songs.

Branwen's Day celebrated the marriage of Avalon's first founders and rulers, Prince Manu and Princess Branwen, some eight hundred years past. Manu was the lost son of the legendary King Arthur, and Branwen, the daughter of a Faerie chieftain. Their marriage united Avalon's Faerie and human clans under the banner of the house of Pendragon, giving birth to a new nation: Avalon, Isle of Apples.

"The snowflakes are painted silver, blue, and gold," Will explained. Philia liked when he shared the colors she could no longer see. "The bench is deep green, and that musician's hat is, um… I think you'd call it burgundy." He'd tried studying his colors this winter, since their strange names brought Philia so much pleasure.

"Aw, burgundy," she said. "How I miss you! You, and all the other colors." Her gaze slipped from the musicians to Will's chest, as if secrets could be discovered in the folds of his coat.

"The jacket's grey, just like you see it," Will said, uncertain of her mood. "And the shirt is dark blue."

"As blue as the night sky, and littered with silver stars." She reached over and opened his coat. Will had spent a small fortune on the outfit from one of the Capital's finest tailors. He'd needed clothing fit to be seen in the King's court—or out in public with the King's daughter.

"It's very fine." She rubbed the shirt's fabric between her fingers. Will shivered, and not just from the winter chill. "I forget sometimes that you are not only a watchman, but a prince."

"A minor prince, Your Highness," he said.

"Your father's provinces include the Way by Land, the Watch's Headquarters, and the wealth of the Western Sea," Philia answered. "There's nothing minor about your inheritance."

"And do those things please you?" Will frowned. He disliked all this talk about titles and power. Especially since Amaranth had so recently laid claim to most of Will's inheritance.

But not for long, he promised himself, echoing his father's sentiments. *In the springtime, Gwynedd will rise again.*

Philia met his eyes. "Now that I am the kingdom's heir, Father tells me those things should matter more to me," she admitted. "But that's not what I think about when you draw near. I see the boy who has stood by me and saved me, time and again."

He caught her hand and kissed it. "Just as you have saved me, more than once."

"Will." Her soft breath caressed his cheek.

"You know I would do anything for you, Your Highness. Anything at all."

"I know."

"You don't understand." Anger sharpened his tone. "I cannot just sit here and watch you die. It's— killing me, too."

She paused, lips slightly parted, her turquoise eyes huge and lovely on her oval face.

"I long for you, Philia. I think of you every hour of the day, waking or sleeping. I'm a fool, I know. You need a man who is your equal, who can protect you." He had tried to protect her. By the Founders, how he'd tried! "I have failed you again and again, and I'm sorry."

A gentle breeze passed between them, carrying the scent of roasted chestnuts and Philia's lavender perfume.

"No, Will, you haven't," she said calmly. "In fact, you've given me the thing I needed most."

He blinked at her in confusion, but she only laughed.

"I need you to be vulnerable, Will. Otherwise, I'm going to die even faster."

"*What?* Why?"

"Whenever I can help you, it helps me. It keeps me alive a little longer." She removed the gloves from her hands and examined her Curse marks. "There's something I didn't tell you last time when we talked about the Curse. I told you how badly I felt, but not *why*. There's a reason, Will." Her breath fogged in the wintry air, filling the space between them.

"Tell me, please." A shiver passed through him.

Philia dropped her bare hands into her lap. The evening was bitter cold, but she didn't seem to feel it. "When the Curse affects me most, I have this dream. A kind of vision, I think."

Will shifted on the bench.

Visions and dreams, he thought irritably. *A plague on them!* His dream visions showed him his mother, but not how to reach her. They taunted him, but failed to deliver what they promised.

"In my dreams, I see this miserable crowd, covered in darkness. They stand in an awful wasteland where nothing grows. And I'm in their midst. The crowd is made up of little children, Will." She shuddered and half-closed her eyes. "They are hungry and thirsty, but there is nothing for them to eat or drink. So they turn to me, whom they call their *mother*."

Will stared at Philia, riveted, trying to understand.

"They turn to me, and they…devour me. The children bite my arms and take my blood and— they do it again and again. Endlessly." He felt the vibrating tension in her body, the strained catch in her voice. "I cannot die there, in the Curse-landscape. And no matter how hard I try, I cannot help the children, either. They want me to save them, but what can I do? Not even my own body and blood is enough for them."

Philia's description was horrifying, but as someone who had witnessed her outward sufferings these past three months, Will readily accepted her words as the truth.

"Do you know them, Philia? The children in the crowd?"

"I know them *now*," she said, her eyes alight with compassion.

"There's little Tamlyn, for one. She never bites. Instead, she listens to all my stories." Her shoulders shook with silent distress. "But it doesn't matter, Will. I pity them *all*. I feel responsible for them, somehow. Like they're counting on me to set them free."

"Oh Philia." He stroked her hair, then kissed her forehead. Ice skaters and passersby were ogling them, but Will didn't care. "For a heart as tender as yours, that must be the worst kind of torture."

Even worse than being eaten alive, he added silently, holding her close.

She lowered her eyes in silent agreement. "This is what will kill me, in the end," she confessed. "One day my body won't be strong enough to take it any longer. Then the Curse will claim me, and I will join them forever, the miserable crowd."

Forever.

The Curse of the Way, Ewan had called it. *The Curse worse than death.* If Philia was correct and the Curse continued even *after* death…

Then I must find a way to save her. No matter the cost. Everyone died eventually, sure. But the sweet Princess didn't deserve to be tormented forever.

"These…children. The miserable crowd." He hesitated. "Are they real?"

Philia pinned him with a steely gaze. "Is the Curse real?"

It was real, and Will needed no vision but Philia herself to see it. The Curse had exhausted her, changed her. The Philia he knew and loved still sat beside him, clasping her hands, curling her legs beneath the folds of her soft blue coat. But this other, ugly thing had joined her: a cruel, malevolent presence. It drained the color from her cheeks and painted charcoal smudges under her eyes. It sucked the heat from her fingertips and stole the quickness from her limbs. She was lovely, she was ghastly, in the lamplight of the Capital.

Oh, Philia!

He leaned in close, to keep his words private. "The Curse's vision may be real, but there is something even more real than all your affliction and pain." Will seized both her hands and buried them in soft kisses. "See, know, *feel* my love. This also is real."

Her cherry lips parted, released a single gasp.

"Everything that the crowd will not take, I give to you," she declared. "I give you my blessing. My embrace. My..."

Will lifted his head and pressed his mouth against hers. All he'd wanted was to kiss her again, to taste her sweetness and return to that place of paradise called Philia Pendragon.

When at last they broke apart, warm color brightened Philia's cheeks.

"I want *you*, Will Owain. You, and no one else. I want your lion heart."

"Take it, then," he said. "It already belongs to you."

Their second embrace lasted longer than their first. Sea salt, cherry lips, wheat hair, glowing eyes—adoration. Love pulled forth into action.

If I love her, I must show her, Will decided. *If I love her, I must end this Curse for good.*

They sat quietly on the bench for some time. The night deepened, and more skaters poured onto the lamplit ice rink. Over the ice, the lanterns sprinkled glittery puffs of Faerie dust onto the skaters below. The city children especially loved this, and kept circling around for more sparkles. After a while, one of the lanterns burst open, releasing a gorgeous display of emerald and honey-yellow butterflies.

Will described all the colors to Philia. The night was frigid, but neither of them seemed to feel it. Not the Princess tucked in close beside him, nor Will, with such a priceless treasure resting in his open arms. Her breathing was more even the longer they stayed there, and the pain less prominent on her face.

"Thank you, Will," she whispered, resting her head contentedly on his shoulder. "Staying close to all this light and joy—it helps."

"Does it make you happy?" he wondered aloud, anxious to please her.

She furrowed her brow. "Not exactly. But it reminds me that it is possible to be happy, and what happiness looks like. And," she added, pointing towards the children gathered under the opening lanterns, "that not all my children are miserable."

My children. The expression spoken with such love. Philia's "children" were all the peoples of Avalon.

"If only the miserable crowd could see what you are seeing," Will said. "If only you could take some of this light and joy back to them."

She glanced at him, a smile warming up her haggard face. "Oh, Will. What a marvelous idea."

The next thing Will knew, the Princess was ordering him to take as many of the lanterns from the skating rink as he could carry. At first the lamplighters gave him dirty looks.

"Please," he said, "it's for Princess Philia."

They helped him willingly enough after that. They even found extra lanterns, so he could leave the ones at the skating rink for the children to enjoy.

Soon Will and Philia were traveling back to the palace apartments in her royal carriage, their compartment filled with colored lanterns. Philia giggled as one exploded prematurely, littering Will and his fine clothing with Faerie dust. Will coughed and burst into laughter.

"This is so ridiculous," he muttered, so the carriage driver wouldn't hear him. "What are we doing, Your Highness?"

She gave him her most radiant smile. "You'll see soon."

Once they reached the palace apartments, Philia led Will and their lantern assortment to the royal infirmary. They hung a few of the lanterns in the infirmary common area, where some of the patients were playing card games or stringing glass beads for jewelry.

"The Princess brings you these lights, in honor of Branwen's Day," Will told the patients.

"May the Founders bless and keep you," the Princess said, leaning heavily on Will. "And may they restore full healing to each of you."

The patients accepted the gifts with delight. One patient, a weathered old sergeant with his arm in a sling, had tears in his eyes.

"Thank you, Your Highness." The sergeant saluted her and then beat his uninjured hand upon his breast. "May the Lady Branwen bless you and provide full healing also, for *all* that ails you."

Philia paused, examining the man. They exchanged a knowing glance—two Avalians with a common lived experience of suffering.

"Thank you," she whispered finally. "Thank you, a thousand times."

When they had finished in the infirmary, the Princess led Will and their remaining lanterns to one more place. It was a room beside the infirmary that Will didn't immediately recognize. But when they turned on the lamplights, he saw a vast grey curtain hanging across the space. It was a Faerie Cloth, used by Fae healers to check for illnesses of the mind and heart.

"Why have we come here, Your Highness?" he asked.

Philia examined the cloth like a warrior sizing up her foe.

"We have come for the miserable crowd," she answered. "This cloth is the place where I can find them."

Will hesitated. "Is it…safe for you, Your Highness?"

"No," she answered cheerfully. "But I'm already good as dead. What can it hurt?"

He voiced his disagreement, then wedged himself between Philia and the cloth. "No, Your Highness. I won't allow you to put yourself in danger."

She planted her hands on her hips and glared at him.

"You can't stop me. Not this time."

Then Philia ducked under his arms and placed both her hands on the Faerie Cloth.

Philia's fingers pressed into the Faerie Cloth, probing its cool, silky texture. The miserable crowd had hurt her last time she viewed them this way, but Philia had learned a lot more about pain since then. The past three months had increased her tolerance for these kinds of horrors.

What's a few singed fingers, in comparison to an eternity of wretchedness?

The crowd multiplied across the long cloth, their young, haunted faces embroidered in whites, greys, and blacks. At least, they appeared so in Philia's colorblind vision. It made them look all the more like poor, orphaned ghosts.

Behind her, she heard Will's sharp intake of breath. "So many of them," he whispered.

At that moment, Philia loved him more than she'd ever loved anyone, because she heard Will's compassion. He pitied these children, too.

I am the crowd, and the crowd is me, she thought with blazing certainty. *I am the unwanted one, the cast-aside, the broken, fatherless child. The exiled and abandoned one. The children and I are the same.*

Dozens of delicately threaded faces now appeared on the cloth, filling every square inch of fabric, from floor to ceiling and wall to wall. It was like addressing a grand audience at the theater, or a massive Zoom meeting, or...

A princess addressing her most vulnerable subjects. And why do the poor and needy come to a Princess?

"Mama, Mama!" The youngest children cried. Little boys and girls with knotted hair, dirty faces, rags and tatters on their too-thin frames. "Help us! Save us, Mama!"

"Yes, I will help you," she promised. "Tell me, little ones. What can I do?"

The children watched her. Some of them reached out little embroidered fingers to touch her flesh and blood hand. This hurt and burned Philia, but she kept her connection. She was stronger now. She could take it.

"I brought something for you," she told them, smiling at each of their faces. "Something to make you happy."

She glanced back at Will, who was holding the remaining lanterns from Branwen's Day. He understood, and brought the sparkling, shimmering light-wonders to her.

Philia pried one hand off the cloth, so she could take the first lantern's brass handle and draw it up to the cloth's surface. At first, nothing happened. The miserable crowd seemed unaware of the lantern's physical presence.

The Princess chewed the inside of her cheek, considering the situation. On a sudden intuition, she drew her free hand in a circle across the cloth. As she twirled her hand, the crowd shifted around her movements, so that an empty space appeared on the fabric. Before the children could fill the gap, she placed the first lantern inside.

"May the Founders bless and protect you, this joyous Branwen's Day." Philia recited the blessing with all her heart and mind and strength. "May the Foundress Branwen bring you abundant healing and a new springtime of the spirit."

A pleasant warmth gathered under her hands, then flowed gently into the Faerie cloth.

"I bless you, Arthur's children. I bless and do not curse you. I bless you to break your Curse, shatter your chains, release your bonds. Come now, my children. Be free!"

She took the next lantern and placed it into the cloth. This time, both lanterns interacted with the children, shining pure, bright light on their forlorn faces. Sparkles and glitter fizzed out of the lanterns' crevices, sprinkling the children and making some of them giggle.

Little Tamlyn, in particular, gasped with awe and pleasure. Her delighted smile transformed her tiny face. Health bloomed in her cheeks and her ebony eyes reflected the lantern light.

When Tamlyn's fingers grasped the first lantern, the lamp lost its original physical form and converted into a vivacious embroidered design. The threaded lantern then exploded, showering the children with glowing butterflies, wildflowers, and tiny starbursts of light. The miserable crowd, threaded in dark greys and blacks, brightened to soft dove greys and whites.

And Tamlyn, eyes piercing, watched Philia in silence. Glitter and sparkles cascaded about her. The other children stopped staring hungrily at Philia and instead gathered around the lanterns.

Will stepped up beside Philia and helped her pass three more lanterns through the cloth.

"Do you think your blessing opened some kind of portal to the Curse-landscape?" Will asked Philia.

"I'm not sure. But I hope so." She smiled, watching the children dance merrily around the festival lanterns. "It's certainly made us harbingers of light."

"Just like Branwen was," Will whispered, his words soft and reverent. "And Ranger and his Bright-Eyes. Pinpoints of light, in the darkness." She couldn't see his face, but she felt his grief. "That's you, Philia. That's *you*."

Meanwhile, Tamlyn's gaze was fixed on Philia. "What else can you give me?" she asked.

Philia studied the vivid Curse marks on Tamlyn's skin, the despair in her eyes, her defeated posture.

She also saw a faint glimmer of hope.

"I don't know how to cure you, Tamlyn," she admitted. "I can't even cure myself. But I will give you all the things that have helped me live this long."

Tamlyn sniffed and rubbed her nose on her sleeve. "*All* the things?"

Philia gazed back at that child, the one that was *her*. This child, and the other ones, desperate for relief. Could she see them now and tell them she had only one thing to give?

"I will give you everything, Tamlyn," she said. "*All* the things."

"Philia…" Will said anxiously, but this time, he made no attempt to stop her. He had *seen* the children now. He was on Philia's side.

And Philia had everything with her, in a purse provided by Lady Agnes. The purse held everything Philia needed to show her face in public. Peppermint and sage sachets, for her morning tea. The medicine Heart's Ease, to reduce pain and inflammation, so she could walk. The thick salves that reduced the appearance of her Curse-marks. Honeyed kava sticks, so she could concentrate at the Round Table. Even her face powder, which hid the charcoal smudges beneath her eyes.

Each thing, everything, all the things. She'd give them all away.

The children had taken the lanterns and carried them to the four corners of the cloth. They were no longer a miserable crowd, but a joyous one.

"We did that, Will," Philia laughed. She blinked away her tears. "We made these poor children smile."

"*You* did this," he answered, drawing his hands around her waist, and his chin on her shoulder. She leaned her head against his cheek. His sea salt scent washed over her, and beneath it, the aroma of pine.

The place where Will's face touched hers became wet and salty with tears.

"Don't go, Philia," he whispered, his arms holding her tight. "Please don't leave me."

She didn't reply. Will wouldn't like what she was about to do. No, not at all.

But I must do it, now, she decided. *I must, I must.*

Philia kissed his cheek, then drew out the purse beneath her jacket.

"I love you, Will." She passed the purse through the Faerie Cloth, into Tamlyn's open hands.

With childlike eagerness, Tamlyn opened the purse and examined its contents. As Tamlyn picked up each item, Philia felt life and energy flow out of her body and into the cloth. This energy transferred first to Tamlyn, then radiated outward, until every child on the cloth began shining with peaceful, threaded light. Their Curse-marks started to diminish, their pain-etched faces softened, and the dirt and grime cleared from their bodies and clothes. One by one, their faces took on a near-angelic expression of relief.

Philia swayed, and her vision faltered. Will held her upright. She focused all her remaining energy on keeping first one hand, and then the other, pressed firmly against the cloth.

Her vision sputtered a second time, then returned. The children were still healing and radiating light. Philia was fading, but it was worth it. The children would soon be free.

And then, with silent, devastating violence, the embroidered image of the *Navahogg*, the ancient She-Dragon, gnawer of ash trees and tormentor of the dead, stitched itself onto the far left corner of the cloth.

Philia screamed. Behind her, Will screamed, too, his voice twisting with inexpressible agony.

"Venom. Dragon. *Her…*" he rasped. His body wavered like a tree about to be felled.

The *Navahogg* was far too big to be fully depicted on the cloth. Its embroidered presence was all jaws and spikes and venom and teeth.

"*Greetings, Philia Pendragon,*" it hissed, fangs flashing and tongue flicking.

"Go away!!!" Philia shouted. "Leave my children alone!"

The children had all fled to the right side of the curtain, their happy expressions replaced with terror. Tamlyn curled up in the furthest corner, crying.

The dragon's round, Viking shield eye followed the children. She flicked her tongue once more about her teeth.

"*Poor Nava is starving, here in your nasty Curse-landscape,*" said the dragon.

Will moaned and slipped towards the Faerie Cloth, but Philia just managed to push him away. Dylan had told her that Will could sense the dragon's presence, but she hadn't known that Will felt the dragon like *this*.

"*You made me a tasty treat,*" the dragon hummed. "*And now poor Navahogg must EAT…*"

Her watchman collapsed to his knees. Philia would soon follow. Her vision was already fading.

The dragon opened its mouth. The children trembled. And then the ancient creature surged across the curtain, devouring every last one of the children whole. Its coal-black scales turned the Faerie cloth to midnight.

"*And now, Philia,*" the dragon spoke into her thoughts, "*I shall devour you.*"

"N-no!" Will gasped, from his place at Philia's feet. With a great cry, he pulled her fingers from the Faerie Cloth.

A headache swelled behind Philia's eyes, accompanied by the familiar, but never welcome, agony of the Curse. Now that its marks had spread across her entire body, the Curse consumed her from the crown of her head to the base of her feet. She dropped to the floor.

Nothing. She saw nothing. Not the cloth or the dragon. Not Tamlyn or Will.

Will caught her before she hit the ground. His arms still shook from their dragon encounter.

"Philia. Philia, speak to me," he pleaded.

She slumped in his arms, her head sinking into his trembling shoulder.

Her last waking memory was the voice of her watchman, calling and calling her name.

21

The Green Blade

IN THE WEEKS after Branwen's Day, Lord Amaranth and his army set up camps on every defendable side of the Capital. The greatest number of enemy tents were staked out two miles north of the city, along the Wood's southernmost borders.

Ever since the incident with the Faerie cloth and the dragon, the Princess had been on bedrest. Will came to visit her whenever he wasn't on Watch duty, but Philia hadn't woken in days. Will had spent much of his time organizing and distributing provisions to the soldiers, refugees, and civilians living within the city walls.

It's the only useful thing I can do, while Philia is fighting for her life, he thought.

But tonight, Raven had sent Will home to rest.

From his father's palace balcony, Will could just make out the campfires burning in the northern encampment. Amaranth and his generals were staging the siege from up there, safely out of harm's way until the bloody work of combat was over.

Will startled at the sound of his father's footsteps.

"There you are, my son," Madoc said, clapping a hand on his son's back.

"Just where you left me," Will joked. "Were you in the war council, Father? Is there any news?"

"Indeed." Madoc leaned against the balcony railing, his face pointed grimly towards the enemy camp. "Amaranth's army has blocked off all the city gates, even the southern entrance. His soldiers also found two of our auxiliary supply warehouses. They took what they wanted and then set the rest of our goods on fire."

Will winced. "The other journeymen and I spent the past week filling up those warehouses," he said. "That's going to hurt us here in the city. Badly."

His father grumbled in agreement. "Amaranth tried to lay siege to the Capital before and failed. He's... smarter this time."

Amaranth. The name burned like acid in Will's stomach. His mother's tormentor, and the giver of Philia's death sentence. The way his Philia was suffering right now...

I have to stop him.

There was a loud pounding from deep within their apartments, followed by the creak of a door. The two Owains turned as Laurie came sprinting towards them. Her usually sanguine face was streaked with tears. She halted a few steps away.

"Lord Madoc," she gasped between breaths. "Sir Will. Come. Please come. Philia's dying. Lady Agnes says tonight will be the last night." Her eyes met Will's. "She hasn't said anything for days, but I know she'll want you to be there. She loves you, Will."

His father turned towards him.

"It's true," Will answered his unspoken question. "She loves me, and I, her."

Madoc answered by stomping off into his bedroom, opening his wardrobe, and putting on his finest tunic, the one embroidered with the Owain house crest. He found another one for Will and helped his son place it over his head.

"Then we must go to her, giving her the very best of what we have," Madoc announced. Laurie eyed them curiously. "We must come to her as the faithful hounds of Owain, ever loyal to the house of Pendragon."

The soft wool tunic brushed lightly against Will's skin, the grey and blue colors that meant honor, and family, and home. Now when he went before the Princess, blind though she was, he would meet her with his head held high.

Tall beeswax candles, embedded with sea glass, stood sentinel at the four corners of the Princess' sickbed. Hundreds of red and white rose petals had been scattered across her bed sheets. Their presence infuriated Will. Fallen rose petals were for the dying; his Philia was meant to be full of life.

She's not really going to die, he told himself. *This is just a trick.*

The King and Queen sat together on the far side of the canopied bed, the King supporting his grief-stricken wife as they both clung to Philia's pale hand. The Princess lay on the bed, propped with pillows and breathing with great difficulty, her face a ghastly whitish-blue and her sightless eyes staring straight ahead.

Will knew she could not see any of them, or perhaps even hear them. He came to her side and took her other hand. At least she might *feel* that he was near.

Her hand was cold as marble, and it did not stir within his gentle grasp. It had been long days since Philia had last responded to his touch. Their happy, golden hour had long since passed, and now Will and Philia were alone even in their togetherness.

Laurie trudged woefully to the foot of Philia's bed, to sit beside

Dylan, who was playing soft music for his cousin's vigil.

Madoc brought a chair for Will to sit on and then handed him a book.

"Here, I found this little treasure sitting on the dresser," he said. "Maybe you can read it to her? I've heard the Princess loves stories."

Will glanced at the book with surprise. It was a little blue volume he'd planned to give Philia on Branwen's Day: *Songs and Ballads of the Founders Seven.*

"It's good, Father," Will reassured him. "It's just what she would like best."

Madoc nodded gravely, patted Will on the shoulder, and then crossed the room to pay respects to the King and Queen.

Will stared down at the little blue book. The last thing he wanted to do right now was read Philia a story. He'd much rather take the Curse by the throat and hurl it into the fathoms of Ascension Bay. Lady Agnes had told them Philia only had hours to live. It was no longer the time for telling stories, but for making them.

But then the Princess' head turned towards him.

He watched her, afraid even to breathe, lest he miss anything.

"Philia," he whispered into her ear. "Do you want to hear a story?"

She squeezed his hand.

"Okay," he stammered.

Will opened the little blue book. He searched the table of contents for the story that would most please her.

"Chapter Three," he read aloud, addressing the story to Philia. "The Legend of Ranger and Bright-Eyes." He turned the page. "Once upon a time, the Lady of the Lake and the Lord of the Stars had a beautiful daughter named Bright-Eyes. She was graceful as a swan and her skin shone like the stars above, with lovely subtle wonder..."

Philia made no sign that she could hear him, but still he read on. Will found comfort in the perfectly crafted words on his tongue, the wandering rhythm of each line, the passion behind each syllable.

"They had taken his Bright-Eyes away from Ranger," he read. "The dark faeries wove such spells upon her that the burning light in her body and soul dimmed to utter darkness. Without the light, she could not live. 'Tonight, I will die,' Bright-Eyes whispered into her beloved's ear. 'But I will die loving you.'"

Philia's hand tightened over Will's. He rubbed his eyes dry so he could keep reading.

"Now Ranger had heard a story once from his father, about how an act of great and selfless love could save a soul from death. He wondered to himself what kind of great and selfless act he could perform for his dying Bright-Eyes.

"Ranger was a wise young man, and he knew that the measure of love is to love without measure.

"'I must love until I can love no more,' he said to himself. 'And give until I have nothing left to give. Then I will know that I have indeed loved enough to save my Bright-Eyes.' And he greatly desired to do this selfless deed, but his human heart trembled and wavered and his whole body shook with terrible fear. For he knew that if he gave everything, he would never see the face of his Bright-Eyes again."

Will paused, his gaze long on Philia.

"But then the Lady of the Lake, Bright-Eye's mother, came to give him good counsel. 'Now, brave Ranger, take thee this token, which I have made to aid thee.' And she presented him with a blue rose, its stem covered with a hundred cruel thorns. Such was his love for Bright-Eyes that he willingly took it, although the thorns wounded and pierced his hand through and through..."

His voice faded to nothing when he saw the illustration on the right-hand page. It depicted a majestic blue rose, glistening like a gemstone in the deep waters, and guarded by eight enamel thorns. A band of pure, spotless gold circled beneath the rose and thorns, forming the whole into a ring. In the Welsh, a *modrwy*.

His hand clutched the satchel beneath his tunic. The book dropped into his lap, the ring's illustration shimmering in the candlelight.

Will, you fool, he reprimanded himself. *What are you still doing here? It's no longer the time for telling stories.*

Philia's grip tightened on his hand.

"I'm here," he whispered, turning to face her.

She shifted her head a little on the mountain of pillows, and Will imagined that she was calling his name. He leaned over until his lips kissed her left ear. A single tear fell from his cheek to hers.

"I am going now, Philia," he told her. "But I will come back for you. Until I return..." He swallowed the lump in his throat. "Stay alive."

He rose from Philia's side and stepped out of her chambers.

Will wandered the hallways alone, until there were no servants or healers or nobility in sight. He retreated into a quiet recess, where he discovered a garden courtyard. Most of the flowers and plants were dead. It was mid-March: late winter in northern Avalon. The gift of frost still came most nights, to paint icy pictures over fields, trees, and stone.

Yet the temperature in this tiny, cloistered space—a secret garden with four walls, lined with stone arches and covered walkways—was mild enough to allow some floral growth. Even during this most barren time of year, when all the earth of Avalon lay wrapped in deepest slumber.

So when Will entered this hallowed place, he found it was not completely bereft of life. Tiny violet crocuses poked their heads out of the soil, their oval petals and striped foliage magnificent in their simplicity. Beneath the dead branches of hibernating rosebushes, be-hold! Delicate pink rosebuds on spring-green stems, which bowed meekly in Will's silent presence. And further in, ringing the stone wall of a circular fountain, half-buried beneath fallen leaves, grew tiny, five-pointed flowers. Percivals. Their petals cream-white and flawless. Their presence, sweet consolation. A miracle.

He had searched both the Wood and the Capital for these flowers, ever since Fiona first appeared to him last Novembre in his dreams. He'd scoured all the parks and greenhouses of the Capital, seeking any sign of these elegant blooms. He'd found none.

Until the night his beloved was about to die.

He crouched down and placed his fingers beneath a cluster of percivals. The petals were tough and unyielding in his grasp.

They were also, in this barren place, a sign of life.

Will sat back. A shadow passed over the courtyard, as the full moon dimmed beneath a shred of cloud.

He fished out the satchel. A firm tug around his embroidered collar, and the pouch pulled free.

The Enduri *modrwy* now rested in his palm. His mother's wedding band and, according to the *Ballads of the Founders Seven*, also Ranger's magical blue rose.

"If I put this ring on, I will see Mama again," Will spoke aloud.

Philia's deadly white complexion filled his interior vision.

"Mama, help me," he whispered.

He slipped the ring onto his right hand. It fit perfectly.

As soon as he put on the ring, his mother's face came into view. Fiona appeared in the snow-melted water of the fountain, the outlines of her figure shimmering with magical golden light.

Will gasped at her nearness. He could see every detail of her features: sharp cheekbones and wide, expressive eyes. Long, rust-colored eyelashes and tousled flame-red hair. Her bruised face hinted at recent cruelty, but her grey-green eyes were so fierce and strong, she did not seem the victim.

"Will, my son," Fiona said, her voice a startled whisper. "I see you."

"I see you, too, Mama," Will said, close to tears. "Tell me how I can find you. Tell me how I can help the Princess, as you promised."

His mother gave him a sad, weary smile. "The answer to your two requests is the same. Are you certain you wish to come to me? You cannot find me, without also finding *him*."

Will shivered and touched the base of his neck, where Amaranth had scalped him.

"Yes, Mama. I know."

Her eyes softened. "My brave one. I'm sorry for all that you've suffered, because of me." She squeezed her lips together in a paper-thin line. "I can help you. But what you ask for comes with the greatest price."

He shook his head once, releasing his wheat-blonde locks, so that the strands fell wild and untamed about his face. "Mama," he exclaimed. "Don't you know me at all? I am willing to pay *any* price."

Fiona examined him with loving discernment. "I remember how you nearly drowned for the Princess, just to bring her a tiny flower."

"*Yes*, Mama. Do you think I've changed? When it comes to loyalty, does a son of Owain ever change?" He was startled by his own intensity. A few minutes into finding his mother, and he was already arguing with her.

She laughed, as if his answer brought her the greatest possible pleasure. "Fierce with the fierce, that's the fiery Chisholm in you." Chisholm. His mother's maiden name, and the Scottish clan from which she came.

"I love her, Mama," he insisted. "She doesn't deserve to die. Not now. Not *this* way." His heart grew so full, the words wouldn't come.

She deserves to live a hundred years, he thought. *As princess and then queen of the most enchanting kingdom in the Otherworld. She deserves children upon children—her own, and all the peoples of Avalon. She deserves springtime and roses and fields of abundant grain, to make up for all her days spent in darkness.*

His mother's return gaze was compassionate and harsh at the same time. Will liked it. Fiona wouldn't lie to him. She would tell him the truth, whether he wanted to hear it or not.

"You want to save the Princess?" she asked. "Well. Let Amaranth take you, destroy you, in Philia's place. That is the only way."

Will flinched. The truth was ugly beyond a doubt.

"H-how, Mama?"

His mother placed her left hand over her heart. A shimmer of blue and gold caught Will's eye. Could it be...?

"The ring Enduri is divided into two parts," she explained. "I have one part, and you have its twin. I can use its Faerie magic to bring you to my place here in Amaranth's camp. When you find me, you will also find 'Ranth." She spoke his name with derision. "Tell him you volunteer to take Philia's place—to die in place of her, with Enduri as proof and witness of your oath before the Founders Seven. He will fight like a demon to take Enduri from you, but you mustn't give in. If you do, both you and Philia will perish."

"And if I don't give in to him?" Will asked. "What then?"

"Ah," His mother flicked her long red hair behind her shoulder. "Then you shall become that rare, rare thing. If you can accept all the humiliation and death Amaranth gives you, out of love for your Philia, then you will become a Green Blade. Enduri will take your sufferings—your *love*—and transform it into abundant life. You will win back Philia's life, and your own." Her eyes glistened with hope. "Enduri can save *two* lives."

Will sunk back on his heels, clutching the fountain wall for support. On the surface, what his mother had said sounded impossible. A delusional fantasy, making meaning where there was none. When a soldier died on the battlefield, he did not rise again, twice as strong to defeat his foes. When a watch warrior was captured by Avalon's enemies, she might be honored for her loyalty and courage, but not for magical, life-giving powers.

"Listen!" His mother insisted. She braided and unbraided a strand of her hair, chewed off one of her nails, then slid her fingers down the center of her palms.

Ways she's learned to cope, Will thought. *Little tricks she's learned to survive.*

"To save her, you must become a Green Blade, like me," Fiona continued. "It's…like a seed, my son, buried deep in this Isle's fertile soil. Bury it with affliction, water it with blood, sow it with a pure and selfless heart." She pressed her hands to her chest and spread her stark fingers like a flower. "And it will *rise.*"

Fiona reached forward. When she touched their point of connection, the edges of her hand glowed with soft emerald light. Will instinctively reached out in response, gasped when his fingers met hers in the flesh. Tough, cold fingers, with a constant low tremor. Not something he could have imagined—no, this was his mother's actual hand.

"Amaranth terrifies me, Mama," Will admitted. "I love Philia, but I am so sick of all his twisted games."

Her grey-green eyes narrowed with resolve. "Then beat him at his favorite game. Defy him with your constancy. Make him pay, Will. Show him you cannot be broken."

Will cried out, overwhelmed with a hundred powerful emotions. He wanted to save the Princess, yet his body wanted to live.

But Philia! Beautiful Philia. Full of gentleness and compassion even as her body wasted away with illness. Her bright eyes alight with a thousand radiant plans—for her life, her people, her kingdom. All those plans, about to be snuffed out like a candle at the wick.

He weighed his mother's proposition. He did not think himself strong enough for the task. He'd faced Amaranth once before, but the villain had not meant to kill him then. This time, Amaranth would torture Will until he gave in or died.

"I don't know if I can do this thing, Mama. But I mean to try." He clenched her hand. "Take me to him."

She nodded and wrapped her bony fingers tight around his wrist. Then she pulled Will in and through the starlit waters of the fountain.

Moments later, Will arrived in Fiona's dimly lit quarters, soaked through and gasping for air. He landed on his hands and knees, his fingers digging into a richly carpeted floor. Fiona knelt beside him and cast a soft towel over his shoulders, gently rubbing the excess water from his face and hair.

He let his mother do as she pleased. She had just told her beloved son that if he wanted to save Philia, he had to die. He could not imagine what this statement was doing to her motherly heart.

But when he raised his eyes, Fiona gazed at him with pride.

"My brave boy. Look what has become of you." She pressed one finger into his chest. "I see you. I see your lion's heart."

He embraced her stick-thin figure, breathed in her cinnamon scent. "I found you, Mama. At last, I found you." He could feel her collar bone jutting against his tear-stained cheek, and the raised ridges of her scars. "But I was supposed to come and save you. This isn't right. It isn't fair."

He wanted her to offer him an alternative solution. An escape, or a way out. But Fiona stayed silent, holding him close. She didn't waste her breath with empty promises.

All the same, he felt the warm pricks of her tears.

"Sometimes," Fiona whispered, "we cannot get what we want."

Will took in their surroundings. They stood within a spacious canvas tent. Luxurious, Avalian-weave carpets stretched across the floor, and soft, velvety cushions and couches lined the corners of the room. A bowl of imported oranges and pomchas, largely untouched, sat perched on a wooden table, beside a simple decanter of wine. The tent was illuminated with well-trimmed oil lamps, banishing every shadow. The lamps also made it impossible for an intruder like himself to find somewhere to hide.

Sapphire and violet fireflies buzzed in ornate glass lanterns from the ceiling.

Fiona followed his upward gaze. "I feel such pity for the poor creatures. I like to set them free whenever 'Ranth's not looking." A ghost of a smile touched her lips. "He *hates* that."

The sound of approaching footsteps passed loudly through the canvas walls.

Their eyes met in alarm.

Fiona laid a hand on Will's shoulder, then led him towards a hidden exit on the room's other side. "This door faces north," she whispered. "Take it and follow the tent's perimeter, until you reach a cluster of black and gold tents. The south-facing entrance is the gate to Amaranth's war council."

Will nodded.

"Once you reach the south entrance, hand yourself over to Amaranth's scouts. Let them wonder how you got so deeply into their camp." Her eyes glimmered with dark humor. "They'll assume you have powerful Faerie magic and take you straight to Amaranth for questioning."

"But I don't have any powers, Mama."

"Now you do." She took her half of the Enduri *modrwy* and slid it on top of the ring on Will's left hand. "I surrender this *modrwy* to William Madoc Owain, with my full consent and blessing. May the Founders Seven be my witness."

Will watched in amazement as the two rings merged, their

golden bands blending into one. The blue rose petals expanded and multiplied, while the emerald thorns doubled in both number and size. It was no longer just a pretty token, but a formidable magical object with weight to it.

"Enduri belongs to you now." Blue-toned lamplight glinted off Fiona's long lashes. "Go save your princess. Be a mighty thumb in Ranth's eye."

Enduri's presence filled him with fresh courage. Will envisioned what lay ahead of him: capture, torture, death. Then he imagined overcoming all these dangers, with Enduri's help.

I can do it. He clenched his left fist. *I was made to do this.*

His mother paused to drink in every inch of Will's features. He noted her grief, evident in her red-rimmed eyes, but also her hope.

"This will not be impossible for you, my son. Once you've offered your life in place of Philia, you needn't do another thing. Amaranth cannot force your hand. You will be…free."

Footsteps approached the tent. Fiona pushed Will out the hidden exit, hesitated, then kissed his forehead.

"May the Founders protect you," she prayed. "And may Enduri grant you every grace to *endure.*"

"May the Founders defend us both, Mama."

He slipped out and headed into the night.

22

Icebreaker

WILL HAD TAKEN no more than a dozen steps when a familiar voice called his name.

"Owain?"

He turned and surveyed the darkness behind him. He could just make out a tall shadowy figure, standing between two tents.

"Ewan." Will stared at his half-brother, who stepped out into the moonlight illuminating the enemy camp. To Will's surprise, Ewan looked far more curious than angry.

"Owain—how?"

"Mother helped me," Will explained.

"Is she trying to get you *killed*?"

Will couldn't meet his eyes. Before Amaranth had corrupted him, Ewan used to follow Will around Gwynedd Castle, asking him endless questions about fencing, watchmen, and horses. Was there anything left of that inquisitive little boy now?

"You need to get out of here, Will." Ewan's hand snapped around his sword hilt. "Take the north exit out of camp and don't look back."

Will didn't move. He evaluated Ewan's threatening posture.

"Are you going to hand me over to your father?"

His half-brother glared moodily and crossed his arms. "Damn it, Owain. Is that what you want?"

Will pictured himself pushing Ewan aside and sprinting for the north exit. He would survive this night, return to the Capital, find his father and...

"Philia," he whispered to himself, clenching Enduri in his fist. *For Philia, there are no other days.*

"Yes. I surrender." Will raised both hands above his head. "Take me now." He and Ewan used to play guard and prisoner all the time as children. But tonight, Will wasn't joking.

Ewan stared at him in disbelief. "You fool. Was your first encounter with Father not enough for you? Have you still not learned to keep your mouth shut and your lofty ideals far, *far* away from him?"

"I know what he's capable of," Will answered mildly. "I can picture exactly how the next few hours will go." He swallowed. "But any scenario where I can save Philia is better than going home to watch her die."

Ewan approached Will and disarmed him of his weapons. Well, at least the ones he could find.

"Knock me out cold and run for it, Owain," he muttered. "The man is the spawn of Satan himself. And he hates your guts."

Will shuddered. "Bind me up tight before I change my mind."

A light sparked in Ewan's eyes. "I'll be giving the orders from now on." Without warning, he sent an iron fist crashing into the side of Will's head.

Will pivoted, softening the blow, but Ewan punched him again, this time directly in the face. Will's vision tripled and blood gushed from his nose.

"Fight back!" Ewan ordered. "Or Father will be suspicious."

He answered Ewan with a jab-hook-uppercut combination that

sent his half-brother reeling. When Ewan tried to retaliate, Will's fist connected with his stomach.

"Better," his companion muttered, rubbing his abdomen. Ewan turned, kicked Will across the sternum, then shoved him to the ground with his iron-capped boot.

Will's body screamed at him to use his watchman's training, his years of fighting skills, his rapidly calculating brain to fight back and escape. He could do it. He could defeat Ewan in an instant, if he wanted to.

That's not your goal, Will. Let him take you.

"Listen, Owain." Ewan whispered in Will's ear. "Your capture has to look and feel real, or Father will see through the trick."

Ewan planted a knee in Will's back, then extended Will's arm out and back. Will squirmed, the unnatural position tormenting his past injured shoulder.

"Wh-what are you going to do?" Will asked.

"Brace yourself," Ewan breathed. "Time for Father's icebreaker."

There was a burst of dazzling red light, and then the "icebreaker" struck Will's upper arm with the force of twenty dragons.

Cra-ack!

When Will came to, Ewan was hauling him up to the main entrance of Amaranth's tent. Will's right arm hung limp, and his wrists were bound lopsidedly behind him. He couldn't feel his right arm at all, from his shoulder down to his fingertips.

What did Ewan do to me?

Four soldiers guarded the tent entrance, while a fifth dressed in nobleman's garb came striding up to Ewan. He was tall, with jaundiced skin and oiled black hair. When he saw the two brothers, his face twisted into a vicious leer.

"My lord Ewan, why is this boy still alive instead of lying dead in the woods?"

"He got through the first three levels of the scouts, Sir Denzel." Ewan shoved Will before the nobleman. Will just managed to keep his footing. "And this is no boy, sir. This is Lord Madoc's son."

Sir Denzel shrewdly examined Will's facial features and blue tunic. "Well, what do you want?"

Will swallowed the blood in his mouth, then dragged in a breath to clear his thoughts.

"I want to speak with Lord Amaranth."

"You speak like a northern princeling," Sir Denzel admitted. "And you look like one, too." He paced once around Will. "How did Owain get this deep into our camp?"

"I'm not certain, sir." Ewan smacked a fist into his palm. "I found him skulking outside the main tent and seized him there. Father will want to question him."

Sir Denzel grinned, revealing two rows of gold and silver teeth. His breath stank of smoke and dead things.

"Indeed." He seized Will by the right shoulder, at the point of his arm's numbness. "Did anyone come with you, boy?"

When Will remained silent, he squeezed his right arm and this time, Will felt it.

Top bone severed from lower.

An emptiness in between.

Will moaned and swayed on his feet. Bitter magical residue from Ewan's "icebreaker" dripped into his mouth.

"Tell me what you know, boy." Sir Denzel's voice was soft, but his grip on Will's arm was not. "Tell me, and I'll make it stop. I'll make it all stop."

Listen to him! Will's body screamed. *Listen, listen, listen…*

Will's cries sounded disjointed, as if someone was cutting his screams into jagged pieces.

"No—no one, sir," he finally managed. "A-alone." A word like a wail, sounding out over a sea of distress.

Sir Denzel squeezed harder and shook. Circles of blinding light popped behind Will's eyes. "I doubt that. Someone helped you."

"Here—" Will screamed, feeling Sir Denzel's fingers clasp around the jagged edges of his bones. "To see…Am'ranth," he squirmed, desperate to get the words out or die trying. "A—agh! Business matter…to…discuss."

Sir Denzel scrutinized Will with an expert, merciless gaze, then released him. Will sagged sideways into Ewan's firm hold.

Ewan supported him almost gently. Unlike Sir Denzel, he did not seem to have enjoyed Will's impromptu interrogation.

There's something like pity alive in his heart, then.

"Owain's body is weak," Sir Denzel assessed coldly. "But his mind is strong." He stepped forward and drew back the curtain to Amaranth's council chambers. "Tell my Lord Amaranth: be careful."

Ewan nodded. "Yes, sir." He pushed Will through the open curtain, muttering in time with Will's moans of distress. The pain in his obliterated arm expanded with each step.

"Hide Enduri from him," Ewan mumbled. "Until you make the oath."

Ewan, Will thought through the pain-cloud. *On my side…*

They continued forward. Will studied the ornate, deep red patterns on the carpeted floor. He heard men's voices in conversation upon entering, but the farther they traveled into the new chamber, the quieter the room became.

They've noticed me.

"My son and heir." Amaranth's silky voice cloyed at Will's ears. "Have you brought me a present?"

"Yes, Father." Ewan bowed deeply, then forced Will to his knees. His shattered arm sent Will's body into tremors. "Tell me what you think of him, my lord."

With a great effort, Will raised his head.

Lord Amaranth sat before him on a makeshift throne, dressed in fine black and gold robes. A long sword hung from his belt, and a glass of mead dangled from his fingertips. His white-blonde hair was neatly combed and pulled back from his forehead, and his presence exuded absolute command.

"Where did you find him?" Amaranth sipped his mead and eyed Will lazily over his glass.

"He was sneaking about the main tent, my lord. Alone and un-harmed." Ewan shoved Will in the back, forcing a cry out of his half-brother. "Well, unharmed until *I* found him. You can see he put up quite a fight."

Amaranth nodded, considering Will's bruised face and oddly broken arm.

"You used an icebreaker on him?"

"Yes, my lord." Ewan's tone was respectful and submissive. The perfect model of a son eager to please his father.

"Well done, Ewan. Well done indeed."

Amaranth placed his glass on a servant's tray. His smile was all menace; his blue eyes flat and impenetrable. "Come back for more, Owain?"

Will tried not to remember their last meeting outside Watch's Headquarters. He tried not to think of Amaranth's inhuman strength, his lust for cruelty, his barbed taunts or—

Stop. Remember Philia.

"Oh, look," Amaranth murmured, loud enough for the whole room to hear him. "He's injured. Poor thing." The generals laughed, as if this was a familiar game.

He rose from his throne and padded slowly across the carpeted floor.

"Poor Owain. Let me *fix* you." He seized Will's broken arm.

Agony. So great, Will nearly passed out.

"Hold him steady, Ewan," he ordered.

Will tried to remember why he had come here. It wasn't so Amaranth could torture and humiliate him, was it?

On his left, Ewan clutched Will's side with an iron grip. Ewan's fingers brushed Enduri, almost like a reminder.

Philia. Mama. I'm here for them.

Will's bonds snapped loose with one slice of Amaranth's knife. Another slash across his sleeve exposed Will's broken arm.

The room had fallen dead silent, as if every officer was holding his breath.

When Will searched their faces, desperate for a hint at what was coming, he read the deep-seated fear in their eyes. These men of combat, Amaranth's greatest warriors, gaped at Will and their commander with terror.

Whatever he's going to do, it's not about me, Will realized. *It's about keeping his men in line.*

"I've come to make—" he blurted out.

Amaranth's fist connected to his jaw.

Hot blood stung Will's cheek as Amaranth's rings gouged his skin. He bit his lip to keep from crying out.

Keep it together, Will. For Philia.

"You can beg for mercy all you like—later." Amaranth sounded impatient. "First, let's get you comfortable."

He ran his long, spidery fingers down the length of Will's arm. As he did so, the bones underneath Will's skin glowed blue.

Will recognized this magic; the watch medics had used this same procedure to determine where his wrist had been broken, after last year's Trials.

The breaks in his wrist had been bad, but at least they were natural. Ewan's icebreaker magic had severed the bones in Will's upper arm into two separate, jagged pieces. Yet all the damage lay hidden beneath his intact muscle and skin. No blood. No mess. Only pain.

Amaranth stroked the skin above his broken bones, then ran his thumbs in the empty space between.

Behind him, someone gasped. Maybe the servant girl holding the tray with Amaranth's drink. Will couldn't tell because Amaranth was speaking Faerie spells that made his arm glow blue, then gold, then—

A long, drawn-out scream. His own, certainly.

What is he doing to me?

Fear pelted through him, almost as debilitating as his physical distress. Amaranth was toying with him. Will had been thrust into his latest game, without knowing either the boundaries or the rules.

How do I beat him, Mama?

Amaranth bellowed more words in the Faerie tongue. Each word gutted Will's vision into nauseating swirls of light: visceral pink and acid green; chartreuse yellow and brilliant violet; moldy scarlet and rotted plum. His head pulsed a hammering resonance against his skull, an excruciating, nightmarish whirlwind of wrongness.

He cried out so the pressure would not destroy him.

More cruel words, and then Amaranth's magic blasted through him like a tidal wave.

Will had lived through one of those as a boy. One day in late summer, when he was catching frogs by the castle moat, he heard shouts and a loud rush of water from the beach. A killer wave, tall as the walls of Gwynedd Castle itself, came roaring across the sands and over the wheat fields, sweeping up everything and everyone in its sight. Will had woken tangled up in an old oak tree, a quarter mile from the castle, his clothes torn and seaweed dangling from his straw-blonde hair. It had taken his father Madoc and his men weeks to search through the wreckage for all the missing persons and livestock.

That was how it felt when Amaranth spoke the words of healing over Will's right arm, and wave after wave of pure, unadulterated Faerie magic restored the limb back to its original form.

Will must have continued resisting, because when his vision

cleared again, his throat felt raw and sore, and every part of his body ached, as if from a massive beating.

And his arm—it was better. Glistening with magical residue, but whole and strong.

When Will lifted his head, the first thing he saw was Ewan's face. His half-brother might have been a marble statue, for all the emotion he showed.

Until he met Will's gaze.

Those grey-green eyes. Their mother's. Their own.

Ewan's eyes held an apology, and something more.

Don't stop now, they pleaded. *I've got you.*

Then their humanity retreated once more behind Ewan's mask.

Will wished he could hide behind a mask right now. His right arm was whole, but every other part of him felt jangled up and broken. An icy-blue magical sheen oozed from his skin, his body's natural way of protecting itself from too much magical influence.

Because Will wasn't like Amaranth, or even Ewan. He was more than half-human, and too much Faerie magic could kill him.

And that monster Amaranth knew it. He knew it could have killed Will, but he healed him with magic anyway.

Good. He should have no problem with my proposal, then, Will thought wryly.

Ewan's gaze drifted away, but Will couldn't bear to look anywhere else.

Someone struck him sharply on the back. He felt the pressure, but it didn't hurt. Nothing could hurt after what Amaranth had just done.

"Breathe, boy."

Amaranth struck Will again. This time, the action opened Will's lungs, and he sucked in a wet, strangled breath. So shallow, he had to pump in air, five, six, seven times, before he felt any different. Before it felt like he was breathing.

"Come on, Owain. You want to live, don't you? You want to

see your mother's pretty face again?" He struck him a third time, close to his dragon wounds. "Then *breathe.*"

That last strike did the trick. Will's diaphragm spasmed, and he sputtered and coughed, spraying droplets of Faerie residue onto the carpeted floor. He retched icy-blue phlegm, shimmering with magic, coughing and gasping until his lungs were free again, and the horrible, manic sensation of the Faerie magic was purged from his body.

He couldn't hold up his own weight, or even his own head after that.

The generals murmured quietly among themselves.

"Pay up now," the first officer whispered. "I told you he'd be strong enough to take it. He's Madoc's son, not some low-born peasant boy."

"Not yet," said the second officer. "We haven't heard him speak. We might just be looking at a human shell."

That's me—a human shell.

He cried out, just to make sure he was still alive.

Ewan's arm was bracing him, but suddenly Will couldn't bear the touch of anything on his super-charged skin. He tore himself away and Ewan let him go.

He crawled away, then crumpled into a heap. Neither his arms nor legs were inclined to support him anymore. The generals and officers jeered.

"Can't take your medicine, boy?"

"Not much Fae-blood left in the Owain line, yes? A disgrace to his heritage."

"Yes, look at him. Madoc's produced a mongrel with that b—"

Fury gave Will all that he'd been lacking.

"Shut up! All of you!" Will forced his elbows to hold him, his head to rise. "Don't you dare speak one word against my mother."

Now that his blood was really flowing, his movements came easier.

"What now, boy?" said one general, the one who'd bet against

Will with his neighbor. He had pale, sallow skin and the meanest disposition Will had ever seen. *Sir Carnarvon.* Will remembered him from the Watch's briefings this winter. He could probably identify every officer in this room, given enough time.

"Have we said anything untrue, idiot prince?" Sir Carnarvon continued. "That your mother is Lord Amaranth's—"

"Mama is not a whore!" The declaration tore out of him, the words he'd longed to say for over a decade. "She loves Madoc, not your master. She surrendered herself to Amaranth, eleven years ago, to keep me and my father alive." He panted for more air, to curb his dizziness.

"Fiona is a thousand times more valiant than all of you combined." Will turned face-to-face with Amaranth. Since he was going to die a horrible death anyway, he might as well do it right. "She's not the whore, Lord Amaranth. *You* are."

Amaranth moved to strike him, but Will raised his left hand—the one bearing Enduri—to defend himself. The knife in Amaranth's hand, aimed at Will's throat, curved instead through empty air, cutting nothing but a few loose strands of Will's hair. Thin, golden locks drifted from his head like freshly shorn wheat.

The room fell silent.

Amaranth lowered his knife. He seemed more intrigued than angered by Will's defiance.

"My icebreaker didn't kill you, or make you lose your mind, like it's done to so many others. Those unworthy of being broken by me." Amaranth's words sent a chill down Will's spine. "Instead, you stand before me, a worthy opponent. Let us observe, then, your quality."

His long-fingered hand latched around Will's right arm as he dug one sharp, pointed fingernail into the center of Will's wrist. He entered at the exact point where Will had first broken his wrist, at the Trials. Where Master Corbin had smashed his arm against the walls of the Way. Where Hamish had forced Will to give up his protection over Philia.

The breaking of Will's wrist, then, was what had allowed Ewan to curse Philia.

How fitting, then, for Will to redeem the Princess with this very same wrist.

Amaranth pushed his fingernail deep into Will's skin. He murmured some words in the Fae language. Will shuddered as new magic was injected into his body. He squirmed, but otherwise stayed put.

You can't fail this test. He'll kill you, before you can speak the words to save her.

The Faerie dug deeper, touching a string of nerves Will hadn't known were there. But Amaranth knew. He drilled magic through the bones in Will's wrist, scraping out visible bits and pieces, the wound gushing blood, Will's nerves flooding him with—with—

I shouldn't be here

He glimpsed Ewan's face—a sickly green color. His half-brother couldn't stomach this, either.

Mama, why did I come?

Amaranth's nail—the magic—his wrist! Bony splinters, all the way down…

Why do I exist at all, in a world that allows this much…?

Will sobbed, his cheeks sticky with tears. "Why?" He dragged the word out.

Amaranth's magic continued until it had drilled clean through his wrist. He raised Will's hand like a trophy, letting blood and bone splinters rain on Will's face.

The world blackened for a moment, yet Will stayed on his feet. Maybe Enduri was helping him.

No. Enduri *must* be helping him. No man or Fae could have remained standing under such distress.

"Why have you come, Owain?" Amaranth demanded.

"I come to make an exchange," Will stammered, his voice brittle but clear. "I wish to exchange my life…for Princess Philia's." The pain overwhelmed him, but he kept going. Amaranth hadn't shut him up yet. "As…Ranger once did for…Bright-Eyes!"

Just saying their good names gave Will a childlike burst of hope. He held up his left hand and brandished the Enduri ring on his middle finger. "And I've brought the *modrwy* Enduri to make good on my oath." Will glared at Amaranth. "I have my mother's rose, and I'm never letting go of it."

Murmurs of surprise ran through the room. Clearly, no one had expected this. Some of the generals might not even have heard the tale of Ranger and Bright-Eyes.

But Amaranth knew it. Will could tell by the way his eyes glowed with fascination and just a hint of fear. He turned to a pair of guards by the entrance, then pointed a cold finger at Will.

"Take the ring from him."

The two guards rushed Will. He ducked the first guard, but the second trapped Will's left hand and laid his dirty fingers on Enduri.

At once, the guard yelped in pain and dropped his hold on both Enduri and Will. A burst of pure blue light shot out of the ring, throwing everyone in the room, including Lord Amaranth, to the floor. Only Will was left standing, stunned and breathless, with Enduri glowing brightly on his finger.

The power is real, Will thought with renewed hope. *Enduri, come to my aid!*

Amaranth rose, his voice undermined by sudden fear. He pointed at Ewan.

"You! Take the ring from him!"

Again, there was a burst of light. Again, everyone but Will found themselves thrown to the ground.

The generals began to whisper. Will heard them question the power he seemed to possess. Power strong enough to overwhelm even Lord Amaranth himself.

Amaranth paced one time across the carpet, pausing before Will.

"I wonder," he smiled sweetly, "what would happen if we just…
cut it off?"

Quick as lightning, he seized Will's left arm, then brought his
knife crashing down towards Will's hand. Will braced himself
against the coming blow.

But it never came. When Amaranth's knife touched his skin, the
whole blade, handle and all, melted into a flurry of blue rose petals.
The sweet odor of roses blossomed in the air. It was so unexpected
and beautiful that Will almost cried out.

Philia would have laughed to see it. She *would* laugh, because
Will was going to save her, and live to tell the tale. His mother had
promised him that Enduri could save *two* lives.

"The ring Enduri cannot be taken, even by Amaranth!" One of
the generals blurted out.

Amaranth issued a command, and a swift blade through the general's heart silenced both him and everyone in the tent.

"Nonsense," Amaranth snapped. "It simply cannot be taken by
force. The Owain boy must give it to me himself."

Will shook his head. "You'll have to kill me first."

Amaranth studied him for a moment. "Which is what you wanted
in the first place, yes?" He struck Will so hard, his vision spun. "Are
you still suicidal after all these years, little prince? Still throwing yourself down the castle stairs? Still crying for your Mama?" His eyes
sparked with hatred.

"Bring her in."

One of the lords, Sir Denzel, bowed and vanished into the tent's
smoky interior.

"Your death is worth more than some, but it is nothing in comparison with Princess Philia's," Amaranth jeered. He stepped away
from Will.

"Fiona, sweetheart. You have a visitor."

When Will raised his head, she was there. Still dressed in her tattered gown. Still battered. Still beautiful.

Fiona clutched at her chest. "You found me, Will."

She didn't make any sign that she had known he was here. Or that she was the one who had brought him to Amaranth's camp and urged him to make this sacrifice.

"Mama." Will stole one step towards her, but Amaranth struck him across the mouth. He dropped to his knees.

"Oh let him be, you monster." Fiona advanced and crouched beside Will, placing a tender hand on her son's cheek. "Look what he's done to you," she lamented.

Her tears landed on his mangled wrist, drops of clear water in an ocean of red. She raised her long lashes, revealing the heat, pity, and determination of her gaze.

"Don't let him win," she breathed. So quiet, Will wasn't sure if she'd spoken them, or he'd just imagined them. "Save your Philia."

"I will, Mama." Enduri burned on his finger, filling Will's heart with unquenchable hope. His wrist was a torment, his body broken, but at that moment Will felt he could save the whole world.

I have my mother and Enduri and Ewan by my side, he thought. *How can I fail in the presence of such love?*

Fiona smiled and embraced him. He retained her scent in his memory—spicy cinnamon and candle smoke.

"My Will." He heard her voice in his mind. *"Yes, it was for this purpose that I sent Enduri to you. May this be the test you shall not fail."*

Amaranth wrenched mother and son apart.

"I promised you, Fiona," he taunted, his spit flying in her face. "I promised that if Will came, I would break him. And you would watch."

Will recognized those words from his nightmare before the Trials.

When Amaranth pushed him, Will folded forward, his head suddenly too heavy for his body. He noticed that his right wrist was leaking far too much blood.

Then Ewan came beside him to wrap his wounded wrist with

cool gauze. "Father doesn't want you to die too soon," he explained. His tone was icy, but his eyes told a different story.

Will lay meekly on his side while Ewan fixed him.

"Tell me, Madoc's son," Amaranth asked, nudging Will in the gut. "How much do you love your Princess?"

Philia. A seventeen-year-old girl, doomed to die, both now and in eternity, haunted by a miserable crowd.

"She doesn't deserve to die like this—wasting away from your evil Curse."

"From what I have observed," Amaranth intimated, "you don't deserve to die this way, either. So why not save yourself?"

As he spoke, he pulled Will's head up by his hair, a slow, torturous movement that sent wave after wave of punishment through his body. He tried desperately to relieve the tremendous pressure, but with what? His energy and strength had already been devoured by the icebreaker and the Faerie-made hole in his wrist.

"Because," Will said faintly, "I love her. So go ahead, Amaranth. Do your worst."

"'Ranth," pleaded his mother. "'Ranth, *stop*."

High above him, Amaranth's expression shifted, equal parts angry, curious, and admiring. At last, he relaxed his grip on Will's hair.

"Very well. I accept your challenge." Amaranth gestured to Ewan and Sir Denzel, who secured Will from either side. They didn't bother binding him. Will was too weak to resist, and he'd made it clear he didn't want to run.

From now on, you go wherever the monster tells you.

"Come," Amaranth ordered. "Take him to the pasture yard."

23

Northern Lights

Madoc, Lord of Gwynedd, had attended to the King's military affairs through the late-night hours of the Princess' vigil. It was nearly morning when he returned to his palace apartments. He searched his quarters for his son, but neither the servants nor Will's friends seemed to know where he was.

He must have found a private place to grieve for the Princess, Madoc thought with sorrow. Will was experiencing a different sort of grief than losing his mother, but no less devastating.

Madoc sent out two of his servants to find Will, then settled in a chair by his bed. The night's events had exhausted him, and his body pulled him into a restless doze.

As he slept, Madoc had the most lovely dream. He saw Fiona, dressed in the emerald gown he had once commissioned especially for her. Her pale face glowed with happiness when she saw him. They ran and embraced, rich golden light streaking between them wherever their bodies touched.

"My man Madoc," she murmured, into the hollow of his shoulder that belonged to her alone.

"My fiery Fiona." As he held her tight, a deep peace fell over him. He never wanted to leave this sacred place, enclosed in his beloved's arms.

But Fiona pulled away. "Our son Will. He needs you, Madoc. More than he's ever needed anyone, in all his life."

Her grim expression filled him with fear. "What is it? What has happened to him, Fiona?"

She placed something soft and feathery in Madoc's hands: locks of hair, the color of autumn wheat. "Our son has given himself to Amaranth, to save the Princess' life."

Madoc's senses went dark for a moment.

"My son, my Will, gone to *Amaranth*?" he asked, in a voice that was not his own.

Fiona clasped his shoulders, keeping him steady. "He lies in the center of Amaranth's camp, close to the Rivershield. Ewan will show you," she said.

"My son. My Will. *Gone?*" He shook himself awake and lurched from his chair. The grey walls of his bedchamber tilted like a ship at sea.

Madoc drew in a breath, laced up his riding boots, and stumbled towards the door.

Far above Will's head, the full moon had been swallowed up by towering rain clouds. Great winds gusted up from the west: a storm front rolling in off Ascension Bay.

Ewan and Sir Denzel dragged Will into a grassy clearing outside the camp. Amaranth and his hand-picked mob of senior officers followed, carrying various disturbing instruments. Fiona came after this grotesque parade, her arms held tight by her guards. Her vibrant eyes remained fixed on her eldest son.

In the center of the dark meadow was a recently lumbered fence post, its wood discolored with blood.

They deposited Will by the post. He longed so badly to gaze at Ewan or his mother, to seek out some tiny modicum of comfort. Instead, he turned to Amaranth.

The Faerie studied him, his icy-blue eyes gleaming with pleasure. "No one has ever held out against me before, boy. Strong or weak, Fae or human, noble or not…they all bend to my will in the end." Chills rattled up and down Will's spine. "And you will do the same. I will break you."

Thunder rolled overhead, followed by lightning in the distance. Will felt a raindrop fall on his trembling arm.

Sir Denzel came up and ripped off what remained of Will's tunic and undershirt, leaving him shivering with cold. He leaned against the fencepost to keep from falling.

"What's your evaluation of the boy?" Amaranth asked Sir Denzel, coming up behind them.

Sir Denzel probed his fingers expertly across Will's naked back, pausing over the dragon wounds on Will's shoulder.

"He's been tortured before, my lord. He may endure more than you think." He tapped the dragon wounds on Will's right shoulder, prompting an involuntary gasp from Will. "This is a weak spot here. I'll have it taped off, so he doesn't die too quickly."

"Good," Amaranth said with anticipation. "Which instruments do you recommend?"

"A nail for his wrist, and mazine ropes. Lighter whips, to break his resolve without damaging him too swiftly."

The villain nodded. "Excellent. We shall give him a laddering, then."

A laddering? What's that? Will looked a question at Ewan, but his half-brother wouldn't meet his eye.

"Yes, my lord." Sir Denzel turned back and met Will's inquisitive gaze with a frown. "As always, my lord, exercise caution. He knows how to suffer, this one."

He paired this compliment with a brutal blow to Will's shoulder. Will groaned and crumpled to his knees. While he was still recovering, Sir Denzel wrapped thick layers of tape over the dragon wounds, paying attention to Will's reactions to decide the tape's placement. The process was so scientific, so *efficient*, Will deduced Sir Denzel had done this many times before.

"Who *are* you?" Will whispered, his teeth chattering.

Sir Denzel smiled. "They call me the Secretary of Torments." The Secretary unwound the gauze around Will's right wrist, then used it to secure both of his hands to the fencepost. "*I* am the reason Amaranth has broken every one of his victims. I examine their bodies, scrutinize their souls, and I *know* them."

"What do you know about me?" Will asked. He'd thought, wrongly, that his fear might subside as the night wore on.

The Secretary drew out a long, rusty nail from his cloak. "We're about to discover that," he laughed. "Aren't we, boy?"

Later, both Amaranth and Sir Denzel assured Will that he was a spectacular example of their *laddering* technique.

"Just look at those cascading horizontal scars," Sir Denzel gloated, as he cleaned his bloody whip. "Clear as starlight, from neck to waist." He turned to Amaranth. "We'll have to display his body afterwards, so your enemies can behold your masterpiece."

Amaranth smacked the Secretary across the face. "Silence! Owain will not be dying tonight. He'll be giving me that damned blue ring."

Will flinched at the sound of Amaranth's whip, shuddered as the stroke hit home. For the past hour, his tormentors had given him no relief. They were gentle enough to keep him conscious, and cruel enough to keep him in constant agony.

"Listen, Owain," Amaranth said. "You're bleeding both inside and outside now. Another few lashes in the right spot," he cracked his whip to demonstrate, "and it will all be over."

Will forced his torso upwards to steal another breath. He doubted he could draw too many more.

"Give up the ring, boy. Live to fight another day."

But that was it—his Philia had no other days. If Will gave in, she would die tonight.

Amaranth placed his hand over Enduri, jerked back as the ring glowed blue and hot. He roared with fury. "You dare defy me, even now?"

"Take me…instead of…Philia," Will panted.

"Bring his mother here," Amaranth shouted. "Have her talk some sense into him."

Will rested his head between ruined hands. Tears of hope ran down them. Tears for Philia.

Like a lens, they magnify the tiny bit left inside this body that's still me. Let the outside die.

"Will." His mother's voice. And when he lifted his eyes, a mother's face that would make the very stones weep. Fiona gazed at him as if each wound he'd received had also lodged itself in her maternal heart.

"Mama," he whispered. "You…should escape. Go to my father." He lifted his head higher for more air. "There's…a secret entrance. I could tell you."

Fiona shook her head. "No. I will not leave you." She reached out and touched his bloody fingers. Her hand grazed Enduri as she leaned in close.

"My son. My Will, if you ever loved me at all, don't give into

Amaranth. This…*crushing.* It is necessary, in order for you and Philia to *rise.*"

She caught the flow of blood from his wrists, held it in the curve of her hand. "Even now, the green blade can burst forth." Fiona breathed over his free libation. When she opened her fingers, dozens of tiny white percivals blossomed on her palm.

Their pure, wild scent penetrated Will's body and soul. Anything seemed possible again. Even a good and noble death.

"Come Will," Fiona whispered. "Let me show you how to *live.*" She stood beside him, looking like the incarnation of the Foundress Branwen herself, come to grace the Isle with the first green blades of spring.

Green blades.

"What is it, Mama?" Will's coughing sprinkled the white blooms with red. "What's a green blade?"

"I am." Fiona blinked. "You will be. Through the grace of Enduri."

He coughed harder, grimaced as the movement jostled the fasteners on his wrists. "Don't…understand…"

"You have taken the Curse for Philia, and the Curse's price is *death.*" Her compassionate gaze lanced his heart. "To become a green blade…you must accept it, Will. You must allow Amaranth to kill you."

I cannot I cannot too small weak useless I cannot

"Let him bury you, like a seed in Avalon's soil," Fiona continued, her words adamant. "And then–if she chooses it–Mother Avalon will cause you to rise–"

"Sweetheart," Amaranth interrupted. All the percivals vanished at the sound of his voice. "What do you think of Madoc's boy now?"

Fiona's cheeks flushed. "Be faithful, my son," she whispered.

She kissed the rose ring on his finger. It felt like a blessing.

Amaranth prowled closer, brandishing his whip. Before he could strike, Fiona twirled and planted herself between Will and Amaranth.

"Fie! A curse upon you, 'Ranth!" She planted her fists on her hips. "I was the one who brought him into the world. I placed his wee little body into Madoc's eager hands. I told him, 'Here is your child and heir: William Madoc Owain.'"

Will winced. *Don't provoke him, Mama.*

But Fiona marched through the mud and slapped Amaranth across the face. He snapped his hands around her wrists. She fought and struggled as Amaranth closed in.

"What's the matter, Sweetheart?" He kissed her neck. "Don't you know that I *always* keep my promises?"

"Leave… leave her alone…" Will gasped weakly.

Amaranth dragged Fiona away and placed her in the custody of his guards. He called for Ewan.

"Take her to my ship," Amaranth ordered. "I want her safely aboard before tomorrow's invasion."

Invasion? So soon?

"Yes, my lord." Ewan saluted. When Amaranth's gaze wandered to Fiona, he caught Will's eye and signaled to him in watchman's sign:

Don't let Father win.

Ewan was still on Will's side.

Madoc, Will signaled back with his ruined hand. *Tell him?*

His half-brother's eyes blazed with understanding. The slightest nod.

"No!" Fiona lunged towards Will, but Ewan and the guards grabbed her arms and led her away. "No! I must stay with my son!"

"Mama…" He watched her go, too weak to make any greater sign of protest. Saving Fiona had been his entire life, and now he would die without helping her. It was the last thing he had wanted.

"Northern Lights, sir." The guard's voice shook. "Here, in the spring rain."

"Silence!"

Will raised his head towards the sky.

Fantastic blue and green lights flickered across the stormy skies overhead. In his near-delirium, Will glimpsed the faces of those he loved, skittering just out of reach: practical, dry-humored Raven, who loved Will like a son; the good and noble King, who had faith in Will from the start; Dylan, ordering him not to die; loyal Madoc and valiant Fiona. Philia, dressed in turquoise, smiling, laughing, vibrantly alive. And the people of Avalon, increased a thousand-fold since the days of the Founders Seven. Since the days of Ranger and Bright-Eyes. The people needed their princess, just as Will needed her.

Will was too crushed to see these good things anymore.

But they were real.

"Any farther we go, and you will die." Amaranth's foul breath brushed Will's face. "You will die. And Philia, too."

Last chance to live, Will.

Last chance to fight another day.

But then, his mother's words: "*To become a green blade…you must accept it, Will. You must allow Amaranth to kill you.*"

"No, Amaranth." He had no voice left, so he whispered. "I don't know why we all suffer on this earth, or why people like you take pleasure in it. But here's my thumb in the eye. Tonight, at least, pain will have its purpose." He forced breath into his failing lungs. "I have Enduri. I'm never letting go of it. Not until I meet Philia again, in this world, or the next."

Amaranth stared at Will in disbelief. Then he spat on Will's face. "Kill him slowly, Sir Denzel."

"Yes, my lord."

Avalon, our mother, Will prayed, *accept me.*

The whips resumed, lash after bitter lash.

Break the Curse. Accept my life, in place of Philia's.

It was getting harder to breathe now. His lungs were filling up with fluid, and Will could no longer force his body upwards to take in more air.

A murmur of voices. The whips stopped.

Sir Denzel stepped forward, ripped the tape off of Will's right shoulder. His body jerked involuntarily, smashing his face against the fencepost. Sir Denzel laughed at Will's whimper of distress.

"You got what you wanted, Owain," the Secretary said. "What does death feel like?"

Tears ran down Will's cheeks. What if his life, his blood wasn't enough? What if he was dying for nothing?

Avalon, accept me. Please.

Sir Denzel lifted Will's head, then drew a knife across Will's throat.

As death claimed him, Will saw the lights again. Huge rainbow bursts, flashing across the sky. Northern Lights. In the middle of a rainstorm.

Impossible, he thought, and then his vision died.

24

Honor and Devotion

BEFORE MADOC HAD crossed the room, a thundering knock rattled his bedroom door. He hurried to answer it. The second knock nearly rattled the door off its hinges before Madoc could fling it open.

A servant he didn't recognize loomed in the doorway. He wore a heavy cloak over his Owain livery, and every square inch of him dripped with rainwater and mud.

Madoc's heart sank at the sight of him. "Who are you, young man? Why are you dressed in the colors of my house?"

In truth, Madoc cared little about the servant's clothes. He was hedging, reluctant to hear whatever this unwelcome visitor had come to say.

He reeks of death.

The servant raised an eyebrow. "Your son Will infiltrated Amaranth's camp tonight. Amaranth killed him for trying to save the Princess from her curse."

Madoc stumbled backwards, flung out his arms to keep from falling. He clutched the closest bedpost for support.

"How—how am I to believe you? What proof have you, that this is true?"

The servant closed the door behind him, then took a seat in Madoc's chair.

Madoc ignored the servant's insolence. He was more interested in what the stranger was drawing out from beneath his cloak.

Two throwing knives. The type used by warriors in the Watch. One longer hunting knife. And—

"No," Madoc moaned. "*No.*"

In the servant's hands was a beautifully crafted, spring green blade. Engraved on its wire-bound hilt was the Owain crest: two greyhounds pointing towards a tall ship. Only the year before, Madoc had commissioned a bladesmith to fit and carve its glass wind chimes to the exact measurements of his son. A princely gift for Will's eighteenth birthday.

"Llewgalon," he gasped. "If you have his sword, then…where is my son?"

The stranger sheathed *Llewgalon* and hid it beneath his cloak. "I told you, Papa. His body's lying in Amaranth's camp. I—I promised Will I would tell you." The servant's even features flickered with buried emotion. Sorrow? Remorse? Regret? "Damn him. Damn his foolish, loyal, *lionheart.*"

Llewgalon. Lionheart. Whatever this servant's intentions were for sharing the bitter news, Madoc perceived the seed of truth in them. It made logical sense: having discovered a way to save the Princess, Will would go immediately to Amaranth to accomplish it. It fit his son's character like a well-chimed blade.

Madoc glanced at the servant with fresh eyes. "You're Ewan, aren't you?" He observed the hints of red beneath the mud in Ewan's locks, and the glittery sheen of his grey-green eyes. Tearless, but unhappy. "Fiona said that you would come. She said you could take me to Will. Can you?"

Ewan nodded. "I can. I will. But you must swear to tell no one who I am. Or-or you'll never see your son again." His voice broke as he said it, removing all the potency from his threat.

"Ewan," Madoc said softly. There was still a trace, then, of the four-year-old boy that Madoc had once raised as his own. Amaranth had buried that child, but he hadn't killed him. "I won't tell anyone who you are...if you bring me to Will."

Ewan accepted this. "We'll have to leave the city walls," he cautioned.

Madoc wondered briefly how Ewan had gotten into Cair Tintagel, when all the Capital walls were guarded with such vigilance. Perhaps he used his faerie gift of shapeshifting to break into the city? However he'd entered, Ewan was unlikely to divulge the information to him.

Stop stalling, Madoc. Will needs you. Haste, haste, haste!

"I know an exit from the city," Madoc said, as he strapped on his leather jerkin and arm guards. His chain mail and Owain tunic went over the jerkin. He grabbed his own sword and cloak and strode towards the door. "We'll take the King's courier horses for the ride."

They raced through the palace, passing by the royal apartments on their way to the King's stables.

"Madoc."

He came to an abrupt halt and whirled to find himself face to face with the King. Madoc saw his own grief intensely mirrored in his friend's features. He didn't ask Bran about the Princess. They all knew she was hours from death.

"Will's gone to Amaranth," he blurted out instead. "He's handed himself over to save Philia."

"Oh Madoc." The King's eyes connected with his own. He glanced at Ewan in his muddy servant's garb, but didn't question his presence. "Are you leaving the city to find him?"

"I cannot leave him there, Bran," Madoc answered with vehemence. "Dead or alive, I cannot abandon him."

His King and best friend gazed at him with compassion, then turned to peer out the hallway window. "What does Will know that I do not?" he whispered, his voice soft and desperate. "What hope spurred him on to such a hopeless mission?"

"He was wearing his mother's ring."

Madoc and Bran both turned to Ewan, mutually surprised by his outburst.

"He believes it has the power to save Philia." Ewan continued, his eyes lowered and voice small. "Lady Fiona told him so."

"Enduri." Madoc stroked his golden beard. "The blue *modrwy*. Could it indeed do such a thing?"

The King's expression lightened, ever so slightly. "Let us go to him and find out for ourselves."

"You will join me then, my friend?"

"Yes. I will come." Bran laid a hand over the jeweled hilt of his sword. "We have failed to protect our children in life." His turquoise eyes blazed with grim fervor. "Let us go now to salvage what is left of their deaths."

Madoc nodded. He and Bran sprinted to the stables, Ewan close behind them.

Once they arrived at the stables, Bran selected a few choice members of his royal guard and four watchmen to accompany them on their desperate venture. The small company mounted the King's swiftest horses and galloped down the city levels. The rain had slowed to a drizzle, and a faint, greenish glow emanated from the northern sky.

"What is it, Master Owain?" asked the youngest watchman, a farmer's son from Gwynedd province. He pointed at the shifting green lights. "It cannot be dawn."

Madoc shifted on his grey stallion. "Not sure, Francis." He had no curiosity for heavenly phenomena at present. All he wanted was his son in his arms.

The five city levels seemed unendurably long, but at last they made it to the watchmen's exit, on the capital's northwest side. Courtney, the watchwoman on duty, ushered the King's company into the secret complex surrounding the hidden exit.

"Lady Courtney," the King called, "what news on Amaranth's army?"

She saluted. "Favorable news, Your Majesty. Two of our watchmen scouts just reported that the heavy rains washed away Amaranth's tents on the south side of the city. Their supplies were damaged or swept away, and they appear to have lost many of their horses as well."

"How much of Amaranth's camp was affected?" the King queried.

"About a third of his army, Your Majesty."

Madoc was startled by this unexpected windfall. *A third of Amaranth's armies, damaged and compromised?*

"The Founders have remembered us, after all," the King said, glancing at Madoc.

"What of the north side?" Madoc asked. Amaranth's main camp lay in that direction.

"Flooding was not severe there, my lord," she reported. "But Amaranth's troops have shifted their camps further east, away from the rising waters by the city."

"Is the land still passable?" Madoc pressed. "Could a rider on horseback cross from this exit to the northern camp?"

Courtney blinked at Madoc in surprise. "I don't know, my lord. But I imagine it might still be possible for a rider on horseback."

"Then we shall attempt it." The King kneed his horse forward. "Keep watch for our return."

The rocky terrain outside the exit was slick and slippery, making their progress slow. Madoc spotted a few waterlogged enemy tents, tangled amid other flotsam and jetsam, but no soldiers.

Courtney spoke true. Amaranth's troops have migrated further east.

On and on they rode in the pre-dawn rain, the meadows soggy but not impassable, the lighting muted but bright enough for Ewan to lead them, piece by piece, to Amaranth's camp.

Meanwhile, the green glow from the north had heightened. Luminous emerald and ruby colors now swirled in the rain, flashing across the clouds in dusty curtains of light.

The King urged his horse to ride beside Madoc. "Northern Lights, my friend," he said, just loud enough to be heard over the rumble of the hooves. "My heart takes courage at the sight."

When they reached the Wood, Ewan circled along the forest perimeter twice before finding the correct entrance point. They dismounted upon entering, and the King sent the watchmen ahead of them to pinpoint Amaranth's scouts.

Ewan drew his horse close to Madoc's. "I will have to leave you soon, before Father wonders at my absence." He hesitated, then pressed *Llewgalon* into Madoc's hands. "Take it. Father doesn't know that I have it. You…can return it to Will." Anger and guilt sparked in his grey-green eyes. His mother's eyes.

Madoc nodded. "Thank you." For a moment, he was tempted to ask Ewan to stay with the King's company, rather than return to his abominable father.

"I have to return," Ewan muttered, as if to himself. "I must protect my mother."

Madoc silently accepted this arrangement. He wouldn't break his word to Ewan by revealing his identity to Bran. And he wouldn't ask Ewan to stay. He had come here to rescue his son, not escalate a war.

"How is Fiona? Is she close?"

"She's furious, but she's safe. Amaranth saved all his rage for your son." Ewan spat off the side of his steed.

"My son…" Madoc repeated. He hunched over his grey stallion and bowed his head.

A moment later, Ewan slid off his horse and slunk into the Wood just as the watchmen scouts returned.

The first watchman reported to the King. "There is a clearing in the Wood, a short distance ahead, Your Majesty." He nudged his head towards the northeast. "Amaranth is there, with a dozen of his officers. We've subdued the scouts. If we attack now, we may have the element of surprise."

The King nodded curtly.

"I recommend entering the clearing by foot," the watchman continued. "It's difficult terrain for the horses, and the storm's turned the meadow into a mud pit."

Bran considered this new information. "Agreed. We will enter by foot." He turned to a pair of his guards. "Stay here with our mounts, and stand ready for our return. We will need to make a swift retreat."

Madoc dismounted his horse and grabbed the watchman's cloak. "Was my son there, good watchman?"

"He's there," the watchman confirmed, in a tone that gave away nothing. Madoc wished he could read the expression on his hooded face.

He clasped the warrior's arm. "Take me to him."

"As you wish, my lord."

The King signaled for the rest of his men to dismount and follow them. The watchman led Madoc and the King to a grassy clearing in the beech and maple wood. Most of the grass was flattened by recent flooding, and a pool of mud gathered in the clearing's center.

Amaranth's officers stood with their backs to them, their attention absorbed by whatever was located in the mud pit.

Will. His son Will was in the center.

Madoc's head swam dizzily. For a moment, his perception of the scene changed, like one of the Faerie visions his father David had been famous for. Instead of the mud pit, Madoc saw a garden overflowing with tiny, five-pointed flowers. Stark, pure, brilliant. They draped over his son's sleeping figure and ensnared Amaranth's officers with emerald green vines.

But then the vision faded with a nauseating lurch, jerking Madoc back into ugly, physical reality.

Amaranth's violence had left Will almost unrecognizable. His son lay in a crumpled, bloodied heap, fastened to a fencepost slick with blood.

An exceptionally tall officer with slick black hair crouched beside Will to examine him. A moment later, he rose.

"He's dead, my lord." The officer's words were addressed to Lord Amaranth, who stood some fifteen yards away, on the clearing's eastern side. Torchlight gleamed off Amaranth's flaxen hair.

"No," Madoc gasped, surging forward.

The King held him back. "Wait, Madoc. For our men."

But Madoc just wanted his son in his arms, and to make the officer take back his words.

He's dead, my lord.

"Bring me the ring, Sir Denzel," Amaranth ordered. "Then you may display your 'masterpiece' during tomorrow's invasion."

Sir Denzel hesitated. "I dare not touch the ring, my lord."

Amaranth snarled and released his long glass blade. "Do not try my patience! Bring Enduri to me, Sir Denzel, or I'll cut off your head."

The officer obediently sloshed knee-deep through the mud pool. He laid his hand over Will's lifeless fingers.

At the same moment, Madoc freed himself from the King's grasp and charged into the meadow.

"You will not touch him again!" Madoc roared, drawing *Llewgalon* from its sheath. The green blade chimed like birdsong in his practiced hands.

Several officers turned towards Madoc.

"Back away, old man!" the first one sneered, blocking his way.

With the strength of a man far younger, Madoc cut down the officer and left him lying in the mud. He sprinted towards his son's lifeless figure.

It was not Amaranth's men, but Faerie magic, that stopped him.

When Sir Denzel tried to remove the ring, Enduri came to life. The blue *modrwy* shone like a star on Will's hand, burning with an incredible sapphire radiance. Its rays passed first into Sir Denzel, launching him up and across the clearing. Next, its blue rays streaked up and down the fencepost, incinerating the fasteners on Will's wrists and releasing him from the pole.

Madoc cried out in dismay as Will's body descended into the bloody waters, burying him completely in mud.

"Will!" Madoc longed to rush closer, but Enduri's magnificent light and heat kept him at bay.

When the Enduri *modrwy* sank into the mud pool, the ground shook beneath Madoc's feet. He stumbled sideways and bumped into the King, who had come up beside him. Together, they held each other upright.

"What's happening?" Madoc shouted.

The King shook his head. "I don't know. But it's something *good*."

That's when they saw the ancient dragon emerging from the mud-pool.

The Navahogg's massive jaws rose out of the mud first, her teeth rising out of the earth like ivory stakes. She smashed the fencepost in two with her spiked head, then lifted Will's body into her mouth. Rust-colored mud dripped from her jaws as she seemed to swallow him whole.

Madoc sobbed with grief and brandished *Llewgalon* at the dragon. "Let my son go, you cruel serpent!"

The dragon paid him no mind. Her golden eyes narrowed into

crescents, and she purred with deep satisfaction, as if his beloved son was the most tantalizing treat she'd ever consumed.

Madoc took a steadying breath, then marched towards the Navahogg.

"Owain!" the King cried. "What are you doing?"

"I'm going to get my son back," Madoc answered stoutly. He would climb right down into the creature's belly, if he had to.

Across the meadow, some distance from the dragon, Amaranth laughed. "You will never get him back, Owain," he sneered. "The boy is dead, buried, and swallowed. You will never see his face again."

His words stabbed like knives through Madoc's heart.

Madoc gazed up, up, up at the dragon, her head and torso the size of a castle battlement. How could he fight such a creature? And if he did choose to fight, what would be gained?

"Oh great Navahogg!" Amaranth proclaimed. "Descend once more into the earth. Tomorrow is the time for feasting on Avalian blood. Tomorrow, I shall satisfy your hunger, once and for all."

The King stepped forward to stand beside his friend.

"You should leave, Bran," Madoc muttered, rousing himself from his despair. "Before Amaranth tells the dragon to eat us, too."

The King kept his position. "Amaranth didn't summon the dragon here. She came on her own initiative."

Madoc gave his friend a sideways glance. "How could you possibly know that?"

"Because," the King smiled, "the dragon just told me."

The tiniest flame of hope ignited in Madoc's heart. It was nothing more than a flicker, but light was light.

"What else is she saying?" he asked.

The King grew very still, as if he was listening to far off music. "She apologizes for the destruction she caused in Gwynedd, when she was controlled by Amaranth. And...she wishes to make her atonement, with a gift."

The dragon tilted her head, examining Madoc and the King with one coin-shaped eye. Smoke curled out of her nostrils as she lowered her head and made a strange gurgling sound in the back of her throat. A moment later, she dropped Will's mud-covered body at Madoc's feet. Enduri blazed on Will's left hand, with greater radiance than ever.

The dragon licked the mud and blood off Will's face and torso, then breathed on him. Everywhere she breathed, viridescent blades of grass with tiny white flowers poked out of the earth. They carpeted Will's body and spilled out into the meadow, a veritable river of blooms. Their delicate scent soothed Madoc's anguished spirit.

He didn't know how or why the flowers had appeared. But the King was right: they meant something *good*.

25

Avalon Our Mother

AFTER WILL DIED, he felt nothing. If he still possessed a body, it had ceased to torment him. The starry void of Death had numbed all sensations.

Straight ahead, a glimmer of green light appeared. It looked like the Northern Lights Will had just left behind.

As Will watched, the green lights shifted and brightened. A distinctly feminine voice called to him from the darkness:

"I was Cursed with Philia's blood; you set me free.
I was hungry; your body has satisfied me.
I required sacrifice; you died for your lover, and for ME."

As the voice finished speaking, an image appeared in Will's mind. He saw a tall, auburn-haired woman, robed in green and gold, scattering seeds upon freshly tilled soil. Wherever she cast her seeds, tender green blades sprung up about her feet. When Will dared to meet her gaze, the woman gave him a shy smile.

Let Amaranth bury you, like a seed, Mama had said, and Will had been buried. The only question now was whether or not he would rise.

"Who are you, who has required my death?" Will asked the woman.

She laughed, the sound rich and fragrant as fresh-tilled soil.

"Oh child, you know me. Ever since the moment
You first set foot on this earth.
I am Branwen's champion, the ancient dragon.
The Enchantress of the Enchanted Isle.
I am Avalon, your mother."

The auburn-haired woman disappeared, replaced by the dragon. She lounged beside Will as if she had been there the entire time. Her massive black body encircled him, and her golden eyes studied him curiously.

"You?" Will repeated in disbelief. "Mother Avalon is a *dragon*?"

"*The* Dragon," she hissed. "I have no rival. Jade summoned me last Novembre using the Princess' blood, and that blood gave me the Curse." Her eyes reddened and turned into slits. "It also made me Amaranth's slave…until you died, and broke the Curse."

Will soaked in this new information, before focusing on the three words that mattered most. "Broke the Curse? Did I save Philia, then?"

The Dragon chose not to answer. "You have died a hero's death, oh mite," she said. "You may go up to Founder's Home, and eternal rest, if you so choose."

She growled in irritation, then rubbed her snout against a section of her hexagonal scales. Will watched in amazement as a little child clambered out of the first scale, as if from a portal.

"Yes, yes," the Dragon purred. "Come out now, little ones."

More and more children emerged from the Dragon's scales—until Philia's entire miserable crowd gathered before Will. The children's faces were clean and bright, and they wore Branwen's colors, spring green and gold.

The last child released was Tamlyn, Philia's little girl. She climbed out of a flame-colored scale located above the Dragon's glowing heart.

"Will!" Tamlyn nearly flattened him with her embrace. "We've been trapped inside the Dragon all this time!" She promptly explained. "But when you died, you freed *all* of us children from the Curse!"

She hugged him again, her warm body grounding him more and more into this strange place. They weren't in Avalon, or in Founder's Home, but somewhere *in-between*.

Tamlyn grabbed his left hand, which made him realize he *did* have a hand—and an entire body along with it. Enduri twinkled on his middle finger, casting blue sparkles across Tamlyn's face.

"How…did I free you, Tamlyn?" Will asked, bewildered.

The little girl turned towards the Dragon, who yawned. The children squealed and scampered away from her fearsome jaws.

"Sixty lashes on your back, boy," she said. "A lash endured for each child."

"Sixty…lashes." Will repeated with a shudder. His body could not feel the wounds, but his mind remembered. He remembered everything, and wished he did not.

The Dragon cocked one great golden eye on Will. "You do not have to suffer anymore, child. Do you wish to go up to Founder's Home, to rest from all your sorrows?"

Will shook his head. "No. Please send the children Home instead." He swallowed, remembering his mother's instructions. "I wish to return to Avalon and become a Green Blade, for the sake of Philia and my people."

The Dragon didn't try to dissuade him. "Good. I've not had such a vibrant Green Blade in many a decade. You will do great things for Avalon—but you will suffer for it."

Will shrugged wryly. "I suppose suffering is what I do best."

The Dragon smoked him with an incendiary gaze. "You're also quite good at sticking swords into poor, innocent dragons."

Without waiting for Will's response, the Dragon sighed, her breath like the gale off the Western Sea. Relentless. Hypnotic. Pulsing with power.

"May the seed burst forth, and the Green Blade rise," the Dragon intoned.

Her breath thawed Will's numb body, returning sensation to his limbs. Will felt once again the myriad wounds of his sacrifice, in full, unadulterated intensity.

He screamed and collapsed beside the Dragon. His back, wrists, and arms. The cut across his throat, which had killed him. Pain in every part of his body, worse than anything.

The Dragon raised her head and came to Will's side. Will wondered if she would eat him.

Instead, the Dragon licked him. Her saliva tingled and burned, but a few seconds later, his pain lessened.

Will moaned with relief. "Th-thank you," he mumbled weakly.

Then he caught a glimpse of his wounded body in the Dragon's glassy scales. He moaned in dismay.

"Don't send me back to Avalon, looking like this," he blurted out. Will couldn't bear for Philia to see him in this state. "Why not send me back healed?"

Her serpent-eyes pierced him. "You would have me remove the proofs of your love?"

Will lowered his gaze.

"No, no," the Dragon hissed. "Rather, the vines that grow amid rock and stones develop the hardiest roots. They grow and thrive. My new Green Blade must be *strong*."

"How can I be strong," Will countered, "if my body's a broken mess?"

"You humans," the Dragon huffed. "So eager, so impatient, to steal wisdom from my claws!" Her body quivered, sending a beautiful ripple of movement across her jet-black scales. "You must learn how to be strong and broken at the same time, through *experience*. It takes months, years, decades, even, to learn this path. I cannot simply *tell* you."

Now the Dragon was sounding an awful lot like Raven during watchman's training.

"I don't understand," Will said, after a long pause. "But I do have to go home. Philia will need me."

The Dragon nodded. "When you return, call for Philia," she ordered. "You need her to return fully to the Otherworld, and she needs *you* to be healed. Then you may use Enduri to heal her."

The Dragon lifted Will onto her back, then slithered forward. "Come now. I must away to bite off Amaranth's nasty head."

Hmm. Still not a very nice dragon, Will mused. But who was he to judge? She was Avalon, his mother—and Avalon was a wild, unpredictable place.

Back in the meadow, Madoc heard the murmurs of Amaranth's men.

"Why does the dragon not obey you, my lord?" one of his officers cried.

"Her tether with me is broken," Amaranth answered, fear in his voice. "The boy's sacrifice freed her from my influence."

The officers filled the night with their curses. "Then what shall we do?"

The dragon ended their discussion. She lifted her body high, drew in a monstrous breath, and roared. Her howl of rage flattened the meadow and toppled a line of tannin pines on the forest's edge.

Everyone in the clearing fell to the ground. Madoc clapped his hands over his ears to block the deafening sound.

"RETREAT!" Amaranth screamed in terror. "To the ships!"

Amaranth and his officers tried to escape, but thick, thorny vines shot out of the earth and wrapped around their legs.

Meanwhile, the Navahogg shed her jet-black scales, revealing a smooth white dragon-skin underneath. She snapped her pure-white jaws and devoured three of Amaranth's men in one gulp.

The eastern horizon took on a rosy hue. Dawn was coming.

The dragon was coming, too. She who had terrorized Gwynedd and its people, now turned all her destructive power on Amaranth, her former master.

Amaranth slashed himself free from the vines with his sword, then sprinted east, towards his ships. The Navahogg snapped at his heels.

"Watch warriors!" the King called. "Follow the dragon's path. Send me a report when you discover the fate of Amaranth and his army."

"Yes, Your Majesty," the first warrior said.

"See how Mother Avalon has cared for us! She has turned our enemies against each other," said another.

With the dragon and Amaranth gone, Madoc's attention returned completely to his son. He fell to his knees and brushed the percival blooms from his son's body, revealing the full extent of Will's wounds.

My son. What have they done to my boy?

Madoc observed the red gash across Will's throat, which must have caused his death. The ugly, near horizontal scars across his torso, from Amaranth's whips. The inflamed scars ringing his left wrist and, perhaps worst of all, his son's right wrist, which looked like a creature had gnawed a hole straight through it.

By the Founders and all the powers of Avalon, Madoc lamented, *how could they be so cruel?*

"Bran? Can you help me?" Madoc's voice broke. "I—I cannot."

"Yes, Madoc. I'm here." The King joined Madoc in the muddy

flower garden. He removed his royal cloak, draped it over Madoc's outstretched arms, then laid Will gently in his father's arms.

Will's expression was marked with terrible pain, but now he seemed to rest peacefully.

Madoc sobbed and kissed his son's face and torn hands. Something sharp pricked him when he grasped Will's left hand. It was a tiny thorn from the rose ring around Will's finger.

"Enduri," Madoc whispered, remembering the *modrwy*'s clear blue light.

With sudden hope, Madoc brought his head to Will's chest, listening for a heartbeat, a lung drawing breath, any sign of life.

Slow seconds passed by in silence.

Thump-thump. There! A fragile heartbeat inside Will's chest. *Thump-thump*, it went again. It was irregular and slow, but the heartbeat was there.

"He's alive," Madoc cried out, hardly daring to keep hoping.

Bran gazed at Madoc in astonishment. "How can this be?"

Madoc shook his head. "He *was* dead, when we entered this meadow. He was dead when Enduri freed his hands and buried him in the mud. He was most certainly dead when the dragon swallowed him." He placed his ear once more over Will's heart. *Thump-thump*! "But he's *not* dead now."

"The Dragon's gift," the King whispered. "She has given you back your son."

Madoc locked gazes with his friend. "His heart is beating, but he needs the healers' care."

The King's shoulders drooped with sorrow and exhaustion. "Philia…"

"Your Majesty." The head of the King's guard stepped forward and knelt before the King. "It's not safe for you to stay here. We must ride home to the Capital, and share our news." He helped the King rise to his feet and escorted him to the horses.

With Will wrapped securely in his arms, Madoc rose to his feet and trudged after them. The King's men helped Madoc to mount his horse and then place Will before him in the saddle. Madoc could still hear the *thump-thump* of his son's heartbeat as the company headed back towards the city.

The return journey was slower, because Madoc was afraid to jolt Will too much in his delicate state. And yet, no one stopped them on their way back to the Capital. Chased by the dragon, Amaranth's army had fled to their ships. Across the river valley, Madoc could see a few of those ships unfurling their sails and heading east, towards Valeria.

Still, the King's watch warriors were careful to cover their trail on the way back to the secret entrance, in case any of Amaranth's spies should try and follow them.

A shout rang out as they rode into the Watch's complex. Morning light streamed in from high glass windows—a cold, blue, sleepy glow. Two watchmen offered to take Will from his arms, but Madoc refused them.

"He's my son," he said steadily. "I will carry him."

The King heard him, and their eyes met over the swirl of warriors and medics. The two friends gazed at each other in silence.

"You saved him, Madoc. Amaranth cannot hurt him anymore."

Madoc nodded gruffly in thanks. "Go and attend to your people, Bran," he said. "They need your leadership."

The King turned and began delivering orders to his royal guard and watchmen.

"We saw Amaranth's ships retreating to Valeria," he told his warriors. "We must ensure they continue sailing east, away from our people. Lady Courtney, send the Watch's best archers to defend the southern riverbanks, to deter Amaranth from turning back towards the Capital. Master Paul, send out messengers to the eastern town and villages along the River. We must warn them of Amaranth's return journey to Valeria."

As the King continued issuing orders, Madoc let his royal voice fade into the background. Will needed him *now*.

The watchmen murmured in dismay as Madoc rode between them. Will lay limply in his arms, his broken body partially concealed by the King's cloak.

"Who is it?"

"Didn't you hear Lord Owain? It's Sir William."

"By the Founders, no! Not one of our own."

"What did they do to him? Those *monsters*…"

Madoc was halfway down the room when Raven came racing through a side door. The Watch master's usual tidy hair was blown awry, and he panted for breath as if he'd run all the way down from the palace.

"What's the—" His whole body stiffened in horror when he saw Madoc.

"Will went to Amaranth," Madoc's voice cracked. "He sacrificed himself to save Philia." He told Raven what he had seen in the Wood: Sir Denzel, Enduri, and the Dragon. The percivals covering the meadow, and the fragile heartbeat in his son's wounded chest.

"He's alive?" Raven asked. He gazed down at Will's grievous wounds. "By the Founders, Madoc. We must pray he's beyond all feeling."

For the first time, Will's head stirred a little in Madoc's arms. He mouthed a single word.

"Philia," Madoc and Raven said, at the same time.

If possible, Raven's expression grew even more grim. "Let's bring him to the healers. He will need both of us now, more than ever."

Raven borrowed one of the Watch's horses, and then he and

Madoc rode through the Capital's first level. Madoc spared a moment to recall where Raven had come from—the Princess's vigil.

"How fares the Princess, Raven?" Madoc asked. He glanced down at his son, who was beginning to shake and sweat with fever. Fever was good; it meant his body was trying to live.

Raven concentrated on maneuvering through the streets, ignoring the curious stares of the pedestrians as they rode by. "She's still alive. When I last saw her, she was sleeping."

Madoc felt his grief for Will mix with grief for the sweet princess. But then the blue rose of Enduri glittered on his son's red hand.

Oh Enduri, do what you were created to do. Bring our children back to us.

26

Remember When It Rained

THE FORECAST IN all of Philia's dreams was rain. At first, the pain of the Curse overpowered everything else, and she could only dimly hear the thunder of rain on the palace roof. But then the pain began to lift, and the sound of the rain grew louder and louder.

Philia.

Her dream-eyes viewed Will, drenched in rain and painted with blood. Amaranth hovered over him like a menacing shadow.

Philia, Will whispered. *Come for me.*

She could not come. The Curse had paralyzed her. Every one of her shallow breaths was numbered.

I need you.

Her blind eyes sprung open.

I'm coming, my love, she answered him in her heart.

Philia's stiff limbs bent and lifted her out of her deathbed. She was not cured. She was not better. A moment ago, moving had been impossible. Soon it would become impossible again.

But nothing is impossible for a woman in love.

Her icy feet eased onto the cool marble floor, and a damp breeze fluttered the edges of her nightgown.

"Philia?" She heard a real voice now, the tender speech of her mother.

"Dear Mum. I love you." Better to say it now, with her every breath numbered.

"Philia, how are you…? This is impossible. You—you were near death."

Still near death. Philia stepped away from the bed. *This is just a delay.*

"Mum, be my eyes. Will needs me, and I must go to him."

"Will?" Her mother repeated in bewilderment.

"Yes. Amaranth killed him, but he isn't dead." Philia wasn't sure how she knew that. "Will's here in the palace somewhere. Mum, be my eyes. *Please.*"

Her mother was silent. Philia couldn't bear it. She had to go to Will now, or it would be too late.

"Mum, you have always believed in so many things that seemed impossible, but ended up being true." Philia blinked back tears. "Please, believe me tonight."

Rain and footsteps rumbled through the palace room. Her mother brushed her cheek and then drew Philia deeply and securely into her arms.

"Now I really have gone mad," Vivien murmured into her daughter's ear. Her hand locked over Philia's as she led her out of the royal apartment.

Nobody disturbed the two women's search for Will. It was as if Philia and her mother had become invisible to the outside world, just as the outside world had become invisible to Philia.

"This way, Mum." Philia pointed to her right.

"In the infirmary?"

Is this the infirmary? Well, of course.

"Yes."

The rain had stopped falling. Her mother led her into a breezy chamber that smelled of herbs and *inglewort*, an Avalian antiseptic. They walked a few more paces until her mother came to an abrupt stop.

"What is it? Do you see him?" Philia asked eagerly. She hoped so; her time was running short. The Curse would take her soon.

Her mother's hand trembled in her own. "I do," she choked out, grief tearing into her words, "and I am glad that you cannot."

"What can you mean?" Philia broke free from her mother's grasp, stumbled forward in her Cursed darkness. She knocked over a chair and banged her shins on the bedside.

"Will," she called, reaching out both hands. "Will, where are you?"

He didn't answer with words, but she could hear someone's ragged breaths and quiet moans. Beneath the stench of blood and sweat and antiseptic, Philia thought she could just catch the aroma of sea salt and pine.

The Curse bit into every inch of her skin with fierce, unyielding agony. She staggered along the bedside and fell to her knees. When she reached out once more, she found his hand on the bed. It was wet, sticky, and burning with fever. His wrist was covered in layers of gauze.

"It's okay, Will," she said, clinging tightly to his bloody fingers. Something sharp and metallic, like a spiked ring, was wrapped around his middle finger. Philia wondered why the healers hadn't removed it from his hand. "Your Philia is here. We—we can die together now."

She clawed the sheets, seeking to push herself onto the bed beside him. He needed to know she was there, *with* him.

"Here, Philia." Her mother helped her onto the bed, and laid Philia's cursed left hand over Will's heart. She could feel his fading heartbeat, as well as the brutal gashes in her beloved's skin.

Unfamiliar voices buzzed overhead, warning of infection and contamination.

"Let them be," her mother ordered, like the true queen she was. "Your medicines cannot help either of them now."

Philia laid her head on Will's shoulder. "Here I am, Will," she whispered to him. Her tears slipped down onto his fevered chest. "It is the end. But I am with you." She wrinkled her eyes shut. She couldn't see anything with them, anyways. "Even if I die, I will always be with you. Here, in Avalon."

Will stirred and rested his head against Philia's.

She smiled. He had heard her.

Now I can die in peace. She buried her face into his shoulder, where she could weep her last tears without an audience. Will's warmth and short breaths lulled her into one final sleep.

Phantoms of Amaranth and his men haunted Will's dreams. They beat and mocked and scourged him to death, over and over again. He had no means of escape. When he opened his eyes, the pain of his grievous wounds overpowered him, driving him back into his wretched world of nightmares. Again and again, the icebreaker, the whips. Again and again, his mother dragged to the ships.

Again and again, until Philia came for him. His father Madoc had carried him into the infirmary, an airy hall hung with pure white curtains and cream-colored beds. Philia came and placed her hand over his heart, then rested her soft head on his wounded shoulder.

He was dying until she touched him.

With the last of his strength, Will placed his left hand over

Philia's. Enduri warmed on his finger, sending out clear blue waves of iridescent light. Will urged that light to flow into Philia.

Avalon, our mother, accept my prayer, Will pleaded. *Take all that I have endured, and use it to save Philia.*

As he prayed, Will's tormented reality parted to either side, like a curtain. He saw the Dragon, no longer black-scaled and hideous, but white as the fresh-fallen snow. She looked at him with compassion and a certain fondness.

Well done, you mite, she hummed. *I accept your prayer.*

A glorious warmth stole over Will's body, softening his pains. At last, he could rest. The same warmth passed also into Philia, pressed close beside him.

As his vision faded, Will saw one last wonderful thing: Tamlyn and the children, laughing and singing. Their little bodies glowed bright as they ascended upwards towards Founder's Home.

Say good-bye to the Princess for me, Tamlyn called, waving at Will. Her smile left dimples in both her cheeks.

I will, he promised. *We will never forget you, Tamlyn.*

She laughed and skipped her way up into the heavens.

Philia opened her eyes and found her Curse was gone. Gone. Her vision had returned and the pain was only a fading memory. She lifted herself up from beneath soft, fresh-scented sheets and stretched out both her hands. The Curse's mark on her left palm had faded almost to nothing. The pain was gone so completely, Philia felt a little unsettled. She'd been sick for so long, she'd forgotten how it felt to be well.

She pushed the covers away from her bed. The infirmary was empty, except for the muted glow of cloudy daylight through the tall glass windows. How long had she been asleep?

Philia's bare feet found purchase on the floor. She stumbled to the nearest window, and she saw…she *saw*…

"Will," she breathed, pressing her fingers against the glass. Rivulets of rain dripped down the panels. There he stood, his clothing slightly damp, in the infirmary courtyard.

"Philia," he mouthed to her through the glass.

"I'm *seeing* you, Will," she told him incredulously, blinking away sudden tears.

His face lit up with the most beautiful smile.

She slid open the window just in time to catch his next few words.

"You're seeing me," he agreed, grey-green eyes sparkling. How she had longed to see those ocean eyes again!

"There was a night, Philia, not so long ago," he said, now pressing his fingers up on the other side of the glass, so that they almost touched hers. "Do you remember that night? Do you remember when it rained?"

"I'll remember if you tell me." Philia opened her lips into a hopeful smile. "Last night I dreamed of the Northern Lights. They lit up the sky in rainbow colors. Pinks, purples, greens, and blues."

Will nodded. His wheat hair fell loose about his shoulders, curling a little in the wet weather. "Stay where you are a moment."

He placed his hand along the courtyard wall and limped out of sight. A minute or two later, he reappeared in an alcove to Philia's right. She came to him and seized his hands as they both sat down on the edge of her bed.

"Philia, I have the most awful and wonderful thing to tell you," Will said. "When you laid your burden down, I took your burden up. It happened three weeks ago, on a cold and rainy night."

"You always said you would save me, and now you've gone and done it!" Philia exclaimed. Then she paused, realizing that he'd said it was awful as well as wonderful. "But how did you take my Curse away?"

"That's the awful part." He had difficulty meeting her eyes. "I went to Amaranth to make the exchange."

Philia's smile fell, and her heart began to pound. "Oh Will, you didn't. What happened?"

"I'll show you." He squeezed her hands, his life and energy pouring into her at his touch. Just sitting in the presence of this *new* Will was intoxicating. "But first, I want you to know that I had help. My mother helped me, and Ewan. And…Mother Avalon. I was not alone. Do you understand?"

She shook her head. "How can I, unless you show me?"

Will unbuttoned his shirt. For each button he pulled off, Philia shed fresh tears. When all the buttons were undone, he pulled his shirt off and twisted around so she could see his back.

She choked at the sight of his scars. Ugly scars, like red brush strokes on canvas, signifying only agony. His left wrist ringed with vivid violet scars. And his right wrist, with an irregular white hole running straight through it.

"No, Will." She dug her fingernails into her palms to keep them from shaking. "I'm not worthy of this."

Will carefully slipped his shirt back over his wounds. Then he glided his strong fingers into hers, nudging her nose with his slightly larger one.

"It's a gift, Philia," he said softly, pulling back. His fresh breath made her skin tingle. "A gift of my love."

She listened to him, trying to understand. Will told her how when he put Enduri on his finger, his mother appeared in a courtyard garden.

"Mama told me that in order to break the Curse, I had to offer myself to Amaranth in your place," he explained. "She said that Enduri could save *two* lives."

Philia flinched. "H-how could your mother say that to you? How could she tell you to die?"

Will clasped her hands, as if sensing her distress. "She wasn't simply asking me to die, Philia." His voice was soft but confident. "Mama was teaching me how to become like her: a Green Blade. A person who accepts suffering and death for the sake of others, and turns it into tremendous healing and life."

"But…how?" Philia asked. "How do you become a Green Blade?"

He lowered his gaze. "I had to die, Philia. I had to let Amaranth kill and bury me, like a seed in Avalon's soil." He gently released his hands from Philia's, then cupped them together into a ball. Enduri sparkled on his left hand. "I had to ask Avalon, our mother, to accept my sacrifice, on your behalf. And then," he met her eyes, smiling, "Mother Avalon chose to let me rise again. Like the first green blades of spring."

He opened his hands. Green. Green blades of grass, sprouting out of the palms of his hands. Tiny white flowers flowing from his fingers. Bluebells dancing up his sleeves.

"I died, Philia." His words and their meaning reverberated through the infirmary. "And Avalon, our mother, who makes all things grow, brought me back to life again. To bless and heal our kingdom. To heal *you*." Tears came to his eyes, and where they landed on the bed, little crocuses sprouted from the mattress. "I live to see you again, my dearest Philia."

Philia shook her head with amazement. She pushed aside the bluebells to view the gash in Will's wrist. Through his white shirt, she could glimpse the outline of his scars.

"Your wounds," she whispered, choking on her words. "Are they…still causing you pain?"

His expression grew serious. He took a long time to answer her.

"Sometimes," he admitted. "They are healing, and the pain is better than it was." His sudden stillness frightened her. "But yes, they still hurt me. My body is healing, but my mind…remembers everything."

The joy and suffering on his face were so entwined, Philia could not tangle the two apart. Together, they formed one entity–her beloved Will, victorious and broken at the same time.

"Philia?" Will tried to meet her eyes. "Are you angry with me?"

"Angry? No. *Yes*." Philia lifted his mutilated wrist and kissed it, then cradled it close to her heart. "It's just… how could you let them do this to you? It's awful enough that Amaranth tortured and killed you. But that it should be for *my* sake…"

She sighed. It was terrifying to be loved so profoundly. But also…wonderful. She could trust Will with anything now.

"Once I knew there was something I could do for you," Will said, his eyes wet, "I had to go out and accomplish it. Any fate, any torment was far better than watching you die."

He told her many more things, about his mother, and Ewan, and the twisted customs of Amaranth's camp. Despite every trial and danger, he said, Enduri's power gave him the strength to endure to the bitter end.

Will revealed yet more marvelous things: his death at Sir Denzel's hands. The Dragon, once Cursed, who was actually Mother Avalon. Amaranth fleeing to the ships. Tamlyn and the children, freed by his sixty lashes, rising up to Founder's Home.

Will had told her stories before, but never a tale as glorious and unexpected as this one.

"Do you understand, Philia?" he asked when he was finished. "Do you believe me?"

She cupped his anxious face in both hands. "Enduri's power *is* real, Will." She scooped up the bluebells growing on his sleeves. "And you are most certainly a Green Blade." She laughed, a little with joy, and a little with sorrow. "Look! We're both alive and together again, aren't we? Ready to take the next step on our journey, *together*."

He smiled at her, and she thought it must be the happiest moment of her life.

"My beautiful Philia."

He leaned forward to kiss her. When his lips touched hers, Philia forgot all about evil curses, and thought only of how much she loved him.

No, she decided. This *is the happiest moment of my life.*

END OF THE GREEN BLADE

ACKNOWLEDGMENTS

Throughout the time I was writing *The Green Blade*, I was also struggling with a serious chronic illness, with often debilitating symptoms. I could not have written this book without the support I received from my family members, friends, and health providers. For the team of wonderful, compassionate people who took care of me, so that I could take care of my family and write this book, THANK YOU!

Special thanks go to my brother-in-law Jack, who urged me to keep seeking the best care for my illness; my sisters April and Teresa, who supported and listened to me when I was in emotional distress; and my brother, who read *Avalon Lost* and gave me regular updates on his progress, much to this author's delight! Thanks also to my parents and little sister, for their love and support during this time.

Thank you most of all to my pastor, Father Andrew, who gave me timely counsel when my illness became life-threatening, and who gave me the spiritual graces to survive it. I owe my life to Father's discernment, knowledge, and practical compassion.

Thank you to my two editors: Katelin Cummins, who helped me structure this story into a compelling narrative; and Mary Rakow, who provided invaluable insights and edits.

Thank you so very much to Dominic de Souza, who supported me throughout the entire creative process. He coached me in world-building and plotting; recorded my daily word counts to keep me accountable; read my finished manuscript; and helped me reconstruct the novel's last chapters into a worthy, satisfying ending. All hail Dominic, founding father of *The Green Blade!*

Thanks also to the very best beta readers in all the land—Zephyr, Grace, Julia, Emilie, Zelie, and Celeben. You made this book stronger and better, and I will forever treasure your feedback, emojis, and comments, both witty and sincere. You are awesome!

Thanks to my local critique group, the Creative Writers Workshop, who took my story seriously and offered me hundreds of helpful edits and suggestions. Thanks also to my rowdy Stories: LIVE! group on Legend Fiction, who amped up this story's worldbuilding. Even on my worst days, you never failed to make me laugh.

Thank you to Benita Thompson for the beautiful cover design, interior formatting, and endless patience with my bookish perfectionism.

Thank you to my ARC readers, for helping me spread the word about this book, and for believing in me and this story. Thank you to my Cloistered Heart sisters; my Sisters in Christ; and my women's Bible study group, for your faithful prayers.

A very special thank you to my husband James, my "writing manager", who took care of so many things to give me the time and space to write this book. Thank you to my three children, who fill my days with joy and messiness and life. Thank you to my mother-in-law, who often watched one or more of our children so that I could write and connect with other authors.

Last of all, thank you to my past, present, and future readers:
May this story plant a seed of light and hope in your heart.

May it encourage you to keep fighting, despite all of life's challenges and heartbreaks.

May it teach you how to "stay alive" like Philia, and to love without measure, like Will.

And if the book somehow teaches you angelic archery skills like Dylan…well, let's just consider that an extra bonus. ☺

All glory, laud and honor be to Jesus Christ, my Lord and King – for out of love for Him, and His beautiful, sorrowful Face, I wrote this story. He wants so much to be known and loved—may His beauty and love shine forth from these pages, and incite all who read them to turn to Him, and take pity.

Other Avalon Titles

by Mary Rose Kreger

Avalon Lost

Book 1 of the
Secrets of Avalon Trilogy

✶ ✶ ✶ ✶ ✶

"A wonderful and exciting
adventure"

"A must-read tale of epic
perseverance, chivalry, and love"

"[A] mix of fantastical and
modern-day settings"

"I can't wait for the sequel!"

Available in eBook, paperback
and audiobook at **Amazon.com**

Fiona's Choice

A Prequel Short Story to Avalon
Lost *and* The Green Blade

Experience the tragedy of Flaxen
Grove through Fiona's eyes in this
poignant fantasy romance!

Coming soon to
Amazon Kindle
Spring 2026

Available on
maryrosekreger.substack.com

Mary Rose Kreger lives in the metro Detroit area with her family, where she crafts fantasy books for teens, mentors Legend Fiction writers, and teaches her children how to fence with (foam!) swords. You can read free Avalon stories and receive author updates by subscribing to Mary's Substack account, Heart and Sword.

maryrosekreger.com
maryrosekreger.substack.com

Thank you so much for reading this book! If you enjoyed this story, please spread the word. You can **leave a review on Amazon***, Goodreads, Google, etc., so that other readers can discover a book they might really enjoy. Your support makes a tremendous difference!*